# All I Want for Christmas

## BAILEY BLACK

# Dedication

*To anyone who's ever looked at their life, whispered "Nope,"
and fled to a tropical town only to accidentally develop feelings.
It's fine. We call that character growth.*

# A GIFT ♡ FOR YOU

Thank you so much for purchasing my paperback!

If you're like me, you probably like to read in the dark, which can be difficult if you don't have a light or you have a partner who is a grumpfish and doesn't like the light. I get around this problem with ebooks and as a thank you for your support, I'd like to offer you a FREE ebook download on my website.

Head over to my website www.baileyblackbooks.com, or scan the QR code and find the Ebook titled **Mason and Tinsel**. This is the Special Edition Ebook version of this novel.

Use the code **HoHoHo** at checkout and your ebook will be emailed to you through bookfunnel.

Download Your Ebook

# Chapter One

TINSEL

"What do you mean my villa was double-booked?" I stare at the woman behind the front desk and try my best to keep my voice calm.

She shifts her weight from left to right, ever so slightly, and her reindeer earrings jingle from the movement. She's round and rosy-cheeked, maybe in her mid-forties, and her thick black curls are pulled back into a red holiday scrunchie. She's dressed like an elf, minus the fake ears, with red tights, a green velvet tunic trimmed in gold, and a candy-cane-striped belt cinched tightly around her middle. I know it's the middle of December, but this woman looks like she popped out of the North Pole itself.

The real estate office, that I was forced to find when I never received a door code to the villa I booked, smells like peppermint and copier ink, and looks like it hasn't been remodeled since shoulder pads were in style. But someone has tried to make it festive by adding a plastic poinsettia beside the trash can and a string of blinking multicolored lights along the counter's edge.

"There seems to have been a glitch in the system." Brenda, whose name tag is just as *delightful* as she is, frantically taps at her ipad. "And the other guests have already checked in, but don't worry, Dear, I'm sure we have...something." She trails off as her smile falters.

My stomach churns at the expression on Brenda's face, because I know that look. It's the same one my mother gives Father when something has gone awry in the toy shop. The panicked, *how do I tell him the bad news,* look that she seems to wear daily once December first arrives. The very same look she's probably making right now as she tells him, Santa's head elf, that the future Mrs. Claus has run away two weeks before Christmas.

The unmistakable look on Brenda's face mixed with every stress-filled moment I've run away from hits too hard, and I'm unintentionally grumpy when I practically growl, "What?"

"Oh, nothing for you to worry about." She folds the tablet's cover over, hiding the screen and hugs the device to her chest—another bad sign. "Just give me thirty minutes and I'll have you squared away. Why don't you have some cocoa while you wait?"

"Cocoa? Are you insane? It's, like, ninety degrees out," I snap. I almost feel bad for how I'm talking to her, but if this woman knew that I stole Christmas Magic to shimmer across the world to be *here*, she might understand why I'm a little high-strung.

Brenda's smile tightens. "You are absolutely right. Which is why our slush machine makes *frozen* cocoa." She gestures toward a festively decorated drink station. "There are candy canes, straws, and mini snowflake marshmallows on the counter. The fridge underneath has whipped cream, and we even have cocoa powder, too, if you want to make your cup pretty and tasty. Help yourself to whatever you'd like. I'll be right back."

Brenda disappears into the back office and closes the door. I watch through the frosted glass as she frantically dials someone, waving her hands in the air like the fate of the world depends on this phone call.

I drag my suitcases to the side of the room and wander over to the cocoa bar. I've had enough hot chocolate to last me two lifetimes. I could probably survive another hundred years without another cup. But peppermint and candy canes? That's a different story. There's something comforting about them, something steady and sweet. I grab a peppermint stick out of the cup and remove the plastic wrapping. I suck on it, letting the crisp candy soothe my nerves, and stare out the window at what Winter Key calls *downtown*.

It's a single street with Edison bulbs strung from rooftop to rooftop, making a canopy of lights stretching the span of storefronts...this one included. Across the street there is *Last Call*, a bar that looks to double as a cafe during the day. How do I know? The Chalkboard sign out front has the day's special, green eggs and ham with hash potatoes, and the night's special, Grinch beer. Which both, in my opinion, sound horrible.

Beside *Last Call* is *Hopkin's Pharmacy*, and a boutique called *Mermaid Tales*. This side of the strip is even more uneventful. I think I saw a trinket shop, a vacant shop, and a mini-market on my way in. That's it.

From what I can tell, the rest of the town is only a few streets wide and mostly homes. It's secluded. Quiet. And most importantly, thousands of miles away from snow. Exactly what I need to detox and figure out what I'm going to do about my Santa Claus problem. In a perfect world, I would have found a place that was anti-Christmas, but this is where the Christmas Magic in my ring took me.

So... Here I am.

Brenda whips the office door open and strides into the room like a woman who's just had the best orgasm of her life—glistening with sweat, a little flushed, and grinning from ear to ear. "Problem solved, and it didn't even take a Christmas Miracle."

If we need a Christmas Miracle to find me a place to sleep, Winter Key might be in worse shape than it looks. "You found me a villa?"

"Not exactly," she says, running her hands over the front of her tunic. "But I did secure you a room in a very private...er... bungalow."

"A room? I don't think so." I twist the ring on my thumb and look at how much gold is left glistening in the swirly engraving.

I used a little more than a quarter of the dust shimmering across the world to be here. I only have enough Magic left for one trip home and a few, small emergencies... maybe.

It crosses my mind to try to shimmer somewhere else, but Magic has a will of its own. I wished to escape the North Pole and this is where it took me. I would have preferred a beachside hotel with a pool and sexy cabana man, but the Magic popped me in front of a bait shop. A closed bait shop, I might add. The only perk was that it had a bulletin board on the side wall with business cards, one of which was for *Heartwarming Realty* and information about their Villa rentals.

"I think you'll love it," Brenda insists. She sets her tablet on the desk and opens a desk drawer for her keys and purse. "It's right on the water, so you'll have a dock to sunbathe on, and here's the best part: it's completely free. We feel awful about the mix-up, and all we want to do is make it right. Mason, the guy who owns the bungalow, is such a sweetheart. He normally never rents out his spare room, but he's making an exception for you."

"You said it's free?" I ask, lifting an eyebrow. Free is good. I only have a thousand dollars to last me until I go home. The more I can stretch it, the longer I can delay the inevitable—ruining my life or ruining Christmas for the whole world.

No pressure. Right?

Brenda nods enthusiastically, and her ignorant glee grates on my nerves. It's not her fault she reminds me of half the elves in the North Pole, or that she looks like she's auditioning to play one of Santa's helpers at the mall. She's just excited for Christmas as she should be. While I lost my Christmas spirit a long time ago.

I blow my long white bangs out of my face and sigh. "Fine. I guess I'll give it a shot. Tell me where it is and I'll check it out."

Brenda gasps and her hand rushes to her chest. "Oh, no! Absolutely not, my dear. I'll take you."

I hold my smile, though I think my right eye might have

twitched. "Really, you don't have to do that. I'm sure I can manage on my own."

"I insist." Brenda loops around the counter and grabs my suitcases. "It's the least I can do. Besides, Mason's place is a little off the beaten path, if you know what I mean."

I don't. This whole town feels off the beaten path to me, but I get the feeling that arguing with her will be more frustrating than it's worth. The sooner we get to Mason's house, the sooner I can decompress and try to forget Brenda and everything Christmas-related. So, I follow her out the back door to a little red Honda Civic that has...drumroll please...antlers sticking out the windows and a big red nose on the hood.

Rudolph would be embarrassed if he could see this likeness of himself.

Brenda lifts my red and green suitcases into her trunk and chuckles softly. I try to ignore whatever merry little thought is running through her mind, but as soon as she's settled in the driver's seat, she says, "I love how your luggage matches your hair. Is the white blonde natural?"

I click my seatbelt in place, refusing to look at her. "Unfortunately."

So are my red and green ends, but explaining how my hair grows like this would likely put me in an insane asylum. People love to fantasize about Magic. They want to read about it and watch renditions of what the world has to offer on their screens, but when real Magic stares them in the face, people can't believe what they see. It's partly why Santa's sleigh has never been seen flying through the sky. Too many non-believers would ruin the wonder of it all.

"Well," She looks over her shoulder as she backs out of her space. "You look ready for Christmas!"

This time, I glare at her. I don't want to talk about Christmas, be it in relation to me, my family, or the actual holiday. Hopefully, she'll catch the hint. "I'm not."

Brenda hesitates a second longer than necessary at the stop

sign and blinks at me, surprised. "Oh, golly. Christmas is my favorite holiday. I just...." She pauses. "I can't imagine..." She bites her bottom lip. "Um, I noticed you're checking out on the twenty-third. Are you planning to spend the holidays with your family?"

"Not if I can help it."

MASON

My phone rings and I accidentally hit my finger with a hammer. I mutter, *fuck,* under my breath as my earbud cheerfully chimes, "Call from Brenda. Do you want to answer it?"

"Sure," I say, sucking on my thumb, though it does nothing to ease the throbbing. Blood has already pooled under the nail, turning it a shade of purple so dark it's almost black.

"Oh, thank God you answered!" Brenda is frantic and sounds like she's minutes away from a full-blown freakout... which isn't good for anybody. She can be a bit neurotic. Pair that with the fact that she has no sense of personal boundaries and tends to create more chaos when she's trying to solve a problem than the actual problem itself, I'd say answering this call might have just saved Winter Key from a Christmas catastrophe.

"Good morning, Brenda. How can I help you?"

People have a tendency to come to me when things go wrong. I don't really know why. It started with a simple request to carry Mrs. Oliver's groceries a little over a year ago and has spiraled into me becoming the town's *Mr. Fix-It Man* ever since, which makes zero sense to me. There are plenty of other, more qualified, residents in Winter Key, but for some reason, I was the one unofficially elected. And in a town this small, there's no running from whatever title you've been given... good or bad.

"We have a problem," she says.

*Of course you do.* I stare at the closed sign hanging over the bait shop's front door. Not closed for today or even closed for the week. Closed for forever. And I was the one who had to make the decision of what to do with the shop not even a year after Dad passed.

His dying wish was to see me turn it around and make the shop something worth being proud of again. I promised him I'd do whatever it took, but Candace and I could only afford to keep one of the family businesses going. As much as I loved this place, her bar, *Last Call,* actually turns a profit. Whereas *Hook, Line &* *Sinker* bled me dry.

Slowly.

Painfully.

One unsold bait bucket at a time.

"Well, you know how we started renting out the villas over on Orange?" she asks, though I don't think I need to respond.

Everyone knows the villas on Orange Ave are Winter Key's attempt to garner tourism. Our little town is so small, barely a mile wide, that it's forgotten off most maps. We're either folded into Islamorada or mislabeled as part of Duck Key. Nobody outside of the locals really knows we exist.

Actually, that's a lie. *Hoeper Industries* is *very* aware of Winter Key and their eyes on us has made everyone jumpy.

The idea of some big corporation coming in and buying out those of us who can barely keep our heads above water has left a sour taste in everyone's mouths. It's why our mayor started renting out the villas in the first place, but her plan isn't working because we don't have anything to offer.

Outside of my now closed bait shop and *Last Call,* Winter Key only has a few small businesses that have been around since the dawn of time, though even they aren't doing so well. We've also got one gas station, one grocery store, that's really just an oversized Farmer's Market, and one Dollar Spot. That's it. Our biggest selling point is our price. Anyone willing to drive the fifteen minutes into Islamorada can get a two-bedroom villa for pennies on the dollar comparatively.

"Is there something you need me to fix, Brenda?"

"Everything's working beautifully. At least as far as I know it is." She hesitates, then mumbles, "I should probably check on Villa Two's air conditioning."

I run my hand down my face and sigh. Today is too heavy to deal with her chaotic thoughts and I still need to work my shift at *Last Call* tonight. "If there's nothing you need me to fix, then what is it?"

"We are booked solid," she says, but there's a blanket of dread covering her words.

"That's great," I try to sound enthusiastic, but it falls flat.

Without *Hook, Line & Sinker*, I feel like a boat without an anchor—drifting, spinning, waiting to crash—and it's all my fault. I used the bait shop and the house as collateral to cover Dad's hospital bills. I didn't pay enough attention to the store, which led to the loss of our customer base. I ruined everything Dad built because I couldn't manage the doctor's appointment, the bills, or the business.

And now, I've done the one thing this town will never forgive me for.

"Not really, but somehow Villa Three got double-booked, and the first tenant has already checked in," Brenda says, her panic pulling me from my spiraling thoughts. "Now this girl is here looking like Christmas on legs, and I have nowhere to put her."

"So, what would you like me to do?"

"I don't know!" Brenda half-laughs, half-panics. "I don't know what to do."

"Send her to Islamorada. I'm sure there's an open hotel or two she could check into." I walk around the side of my building and untack all of the business cards from the display board.

"If I send her away, she could leave us a bad review," Brenda practically hyperventilates into the phone. "People might stop coming, and we only just started getting guests. If we can get twenty five-star reviews before summer, we might stand a chance of booking solid for the mini-season."

Right, and that's the goal. Put us on the map so that people will come and stay with us. A bad review about someone who couldn't even get into the room they booked would be problematic.

"Tell me about the girl."

"She's pretty."

"Not what I mean, Brenda." I stare at the thirteen business cards on the bulletin board out back, half of which are so sun-faded I can barely read the inked words. I don't know what to do with them. Throwing them out is the logical choice, but these are the breadcrumbs of what's left of a dead legacy. One I let die. "Is she traveling alone? Does she have a family? Does she have pets or other people expected to stay with her? How long is she staying?"

Brenda shuffles through papers on the other end. "As far as I know, it's just her. She's checking out on Christmas Eve, so I doubt anyone will be coming down to stay with her, but I can ask. I don't see any pets, unless she has one hiding in her suitcase, which would be scary, and did I mention she's cute with no ring on her finger?"

"Two weeks," I mutter more to myself than to Brenda. Two weeks of smiling and pretending that this isn't the worst Christmas of my life. Candace says it'll get easier, that the first holiday without a loved one is always the worst, but that's what she said about summer and Thanksgiving. And things don't seem to be getting any easier.

An idea forms while I'm internally dreading Winter Key's annual Holiday Countdown kickoff on Friday, and the fact that my brain went *there* is a little shocking. I barely have time to mull it over before Brenda rattles on.

"Yes, it's the longest reservation we've had to date, and I can't even honor it! All three villas are full. Their reservations are short, but they practically overlap. I could move the woman for a day, maybe, but that might aggravate her more than anything. Getting settled only to have to pack up twenty-four hours later... I would be mad if I were her. I'd never come back, and I'd leave a horrible review about how this was the worst place I ever ever visited. Oh, God, Mason," she practically cries into the phone. "What are we gonna do?"

*We. Always a we.* I unzip the pocket of my board shorts and slip the cards in. I may have ruined Dad's legacy, but maybe I can save this girl's vacation. Besides, if she's who I think she is... I want to be the first to get to know her. "See if she's open to renting a room."

"Renting a room?" Brenda echoes.

"Yes, she can stay in my guest room. Let her know that it's available at no charge and that I'm rarely there, so she'll have most of the house to herself." Not a lie. Between helping Candace with *Last Call,* Winter Key's Christmas Countdown festivities, and the general chaos I usually get roped into, I won't be home much. The girl and I might cross paths a handful of times, but it should be fairly easy to avoid each other...if that's what she wants.

"Oh, Mason, that's awfully kind of you. Are you sure you don't mind?"

I mind. I've barely been able to walk into the guest room since Dad died. Candace and Camryn had to come pack his things up for me because it hurt too much to look at it all, but Brenda doesn't need to know that. All she needs to know is that I have a safe, quiet space for her tenant to reside in.

"I'm sure. Give me about twenty minutes so I can pick up a few things, and then you can let her in. I'll put a key under the mat."

"Mason, dear, how do you plan to introduce yourself? This is a sticky situation. It has to be done tactfully," Brenda warns.

"I'll come by later and handle that. Just make her feel welcome. Let her know that my home is her home. If she's hungry, she can help herself to whatever is in the house. Tell her to think of this like a bed and breakfast, only food is available all day." I actually don't know how much food is in the house, but I'll take care of that, too.

"Okay." And then she excitedly adds, "I owe you one."

*That you do, Brenda.* I hang up the phone. *That you do.*

## Chapter Three

TINSEL

This *bungalow* is not what I expected.

When I heard the word bungalow, I pictured something tropical and beachy with a thatch roof, flamingo lawn ornaments and a driftwood welcome sign. You know, the usual seaside charm meets classic *rent my house* vibes.

But this? This is a small, nothing-to-look-at house. There's more dirt than grass lining the driveway and oaks instead of palms. The one-car carport is half the size of the actual house, and the roof is flat shingles. From the outside, it's far from cozy and welcoming, but it's a free room. The least I can do is try it for a night. If my stay is horrible, I'll pack my things, Christmas Magic be damned, and find a cheap Motel for the rest of my trip.

Brenda unlocks the front door and pushes it open, revealing an open floor plan drenched in natural light, cool tile floors, and panoramic windows showcasing the canal like it's a private exhibit. A wooden dock stretches into the water, bobbing gently in time with a small boat that's tied off at the end.

Between the dock out back, the mounted swordfish above the couch, and the shark jaws on the walls, I'd say this guy likes to fish. Nautical nuances aside, there are almost no homey touches. There are exactly zero personal photos. No clutter. No framed sunsets or inspirational quotes. And, thankfully, no Christmas decorations.

Not a single stocking. No garland. Not even a rogue Santa mug in the kitchen sink, and I couldn't be more grateful.

Brenda smiles, catching the way I scan the walls, likely assuming my glee is from falling in love with the home and not from the first easy breath I've taken all year. "Crazy, right? Most houses in Winter Key are already dripping in lights, but not Mason's. He doesn't decorate until the ten-day countdown starts, and even then, his sister usually has to bribe him to bother."

"Mason?" I ask, barely listening. Something about this place feels warm and welcoming despite the lack of homey touches.

Brenda waves vaguely toward the back of the house. "He's the fella renting you the room. A little history on the home, this is a family property. Mason's granddad bought this place back in the seventies, passed it to Mason's dad, and now it's his. He works down at the bait shop, runs all the town events, and helps his sister, Candace, with her bar *Last Call*. He's usually up at the crack of dawn and bustling about doing a little of this and a little of that until the bar closes at one a.m. I doubt you'll see much of him."

I nod, still quietly taking it all in, half-hoping to catch a glimpse of this elusive landlord in a dusty frame somewhere, but there's nothing. No trace of the man who lives here at all.

"Anyway," Brenda says, walking toward a side door. "This room is yours. There's the bedroom, a private bath, and a million-dollar view. Oh, and Mason said to make yourself at home. His casa is su casa. The food, the couch, and maybe even some late-night cuddles are yours if you want them. I'd kill to cuddle with that man." She mutters that last part so quietly I almost miss it. I don't, but I choose to ignore her odd comment.

I follow Brenda into what's to be my room, dragging my suitcases behind me. The bedroom is bigger than I expect, with the same ocean-brushed light pouring in from the windows. There's a queen bed with crisp white linens, a TV mounted in the corner, and a small desk that overlooks the canal. It's surprisingly peaceful. If this cohabitation situation turns out to be awkward, I think I'll be comfortable hiding in here, watching movies, and maybe even sunbathing on the dock when I'm alone. The North Pole has sun, but it's ridiculously cold every damn day. I'm usually bundled up in at least three layers, and no one would be caught dead in a bathing suit trying to catch a tan up there.

Brenda pats the doorframe like it's a puppy she wants to take home, and then smiles softly. "Mason is a good guy, even if none of us girls have managed to lock him down."

I raise a brow. "Good to know."

*Great. I'm living with a single heartthrob. Perfect.*

Brenda just laughs, squeezes my shoulder, and then breezes out like her job here is done. And I guess it is. She's delivered me to my *bungalow*. Now it's my job to make the most of my time.

I head straight for the kitchen and open the fridge. You can tell a lot about a man based on what's in his fridge, which, for this guy, isn't much. There's a pint of overripe strawberries that gives the fridge a sour yet sweet smell, a gallon of milk, a carton of orange juice, and a take-out container with a half-eaten steak left in it. The freezer is the opposite and stocked with Ziplock baggies filled with fish fillets. Given the boat out back, I'm guessing he probably caught what's in here, which only adds to Brenda's claim that Mason is rarely home.

I check the pantry next and smile when I see it's filled with spices and junk food. I grab a bag of Cheetos and make my way to the couch to start my binge-cation. I want to do absolutely nothing this week but soak up the sun and watch everything and anything *not* Christmas themed. In fact, I think I might start with Halloween and Horror movies. Nothing says anti-Christmas like murder.

I find the TV remote and flip through the streaming options. Though I barely make it through the first ten movies, my phone buzzes. I sigh before I even look. There is only one person who would know to call me on a phone I'm not supposed to have.

Technology is for humans, and Santa says we are above the confines of society. Unless we have explicit permission to build something, like the streaming projector in the Town Square, all human *trinkets* are considered contraband.

### *Workshop Office*

I debate letting the call go to voicemail, but decide against it. After all, this is Mom's emergency phone and I may have stolen it before swiping a handful of Christmas Magic this morning. Both acts will probably land me on the naughty list this year, but I don't care.

Technically, this phone should only be used if Santa's sleigh breaks down due to Christmas Magic Mayhem, so he has a way to reach us. Basically, emergencies that Magic can't solve. While my desperate need to flee the North Pole might not count as an emergency in Santa's eyes, it is in mine. So, maybe, my stealing the phone isn't stealing. Maybe it's only borrowing because the reason is kind of, sort of justified.

"Tinsel Marie Evergreen! You stole the emergency phone and turned off your location!" Mom whisper-yells.

"Yes." *Because I don't want to be found.*

"You know we can't locate you, even with Christmas Magic. You're not like the humans, sweetheart. You're an elf. And not just any elf, you're the Grand Elf's daughter! You're expected to be better than this."

"I know. But I just... I can't do it this year. It's too much. Christmas is too much." The expectations of getting engaged to the next Santa Claus is too much, but how do I explain that to the woman who's responsible for arranging our engagement back when I was six?

My whole life I've known my purpose. Bake the best cookies. Have a perfectly flawless pageant smile. Mitigate elf drama. And marry Chris Kringle before he turns thirty. My parents would have preferred us to get married the day I turned twenty-one, but

Chris knew I wasn't ready. He knows I'm still not ready and he's never pushed me. He's also never kissed me, but that's a different story. Unfortunately, he turns twenty-nine in February and if there's no sanctioned Mr. and Mrs. Claus by his thirtieth birthday, Chris loses the right to inherit Christmas.

Santa has never not been married in time, so for all we know, nothing will happen. The familial Magic *could* still be passed down and everything *could* be fine, but no one at the North Pole wants to risk ruining Christmas for billions of people, which is why his engagement is arranged during childhood. The goal is for the two love birds to grow up side by side and for their friendship to easily slide into a relationship.

The only problem with this theory is that Chris is hot, and the girls back home had no problem chasing him, even though they knew that they had no chance of staying with him. His interests strayed more than a handful of times when we were teenagers, and he never once made the effort to move our friendship from platonic to more. Eventually, after watching him break half of both his and then my graduating class's hearts, Chris realized he needed to stop screwing around and step into his role. But just because he's done being a playboy doesn't mean I'm ready to be a wife.

"Tinsel," Mom says gently. "You and Chris are supposed to ride off into the night together on Christmas Eve. This year marks the official start of your engagement. If you don't show up, you'll let everyone down. Worse, Chris could lose his Magic."

"He won't," I say, jaw clenched. "He doesn't have to be married until after next Christmas. Which means *technically*, Mrs. Claus doesn't need to be in place until then. He'll be fine."

"I don't understand. You *love* Christmas. You've been looking forward to riding in the sleigh since you were little, and it's finally time. Why are you letting cold feet ruin this holiday?"

Tears sting the backs of my eyes. I press the heel of my hand against them, then look up at the ceiling. I don't know how to make Mom understand that I don't want this life anymore. I don't want to be trapped in the North Pole for the rest of my life. I don't want my freedom to be chained to someone else. Most importantly, I don't want to fail at the job I was basically born into and let the whole world down.

For once in my life, the fates must be on my side because someone knocks on the front door, giving me an out of this conversation. "I can't talk about this right now. Someone's here. I gotta go."

Before Mom can argue or even ask where *here* is, I hang up. I storm to the door, whip it open—partially out of panic, partially out of the hope that it's just Brenda again—and come face to face with a man that can only be described as trouble.

He's tall. Grinning. Tan in a *yeah-I-live-on-the-water way*, with sun-kissed cheeks and two dimples deep enough to fall into. His bright blue eyes sparkle like he knows *exactly* what kind of chaos he's about to cause. And he's wearing swim trunks.

Holiday swim trunks covered in candy canes and Christmas sharks.

*Seriously?*

"You must be Tinsel," he says, holding out his hand like we're about to do business instead of engaging in a full-blown personality clash. He is everything I want to avoid wrapped up in one very pretty but ultimately troublesome package.

"Not interested," I mutter, and move to shut the door, but his foot slides into the frame before I can close it.

The man cautiously pushes the door open again as he says, "Whoa, hey. I'm not here to bother you. I *live* here."

I narrow my eyes on the guy who can't be older than thirty-five—a solid ten years younger than Brenda. Unless she's got an age gap fantasy, I doubt this is Mason. "Sure you do. Move before I make you."

The guy steps back and raises both hands like he's surrendering. This time, I slam the door before he can talk his way in again, turn the deadbolt, and shake my head. That man must think I'm an idiot. No one in their right mind would knock on *their own* front door.

My phone buzzes again in my pocket. **Workshop Office** flashes on the screen once more, but this time I heed my own advice and ignore the call. So far, day one of my vacation has been anything but relaxing. My villa was overbooked. A creep tried to weasel his way into the house. My mom wants to know why I skipped town. And now...

The man knocks on the door again. I grip my phone in my hand and take a deep breath. This can't be happening. The warning video we watched in the fifth grade about humans being inadvertently wicked and wanting to steal Elf Magic can't be true. There would be so many more people on the naughty list. Still, the memory strikes a nerve of fear and I look around for something to protect myself with. There is a very pretty, likely sharp, set of knives sitting in a block on the counter. I bet that would scare the creep away. I bet he'd think twice about bothering a sweet, twenty-seven-year-old traveling by herself if he knew I could take care of myself. I bet...

The deadbolt turns, pulling me from my crazed train of thoughts, and that infuriating, stupidly attractive head pokes back in. "Told you I live here."

Well, I feel stupid.

And a little relieved. I cross my arms and take a step back as the man comes inside. "That's still debatable. You could be a nosey neighbor with a key trying to creep on the new tenant."

He laughs and the sound is... well, it's infectious. Paired with that grin of his, I find it hard to hold my grimace. Hard but not impossible.

He runs a hand through his dark blonde hair, a move that looks like a nervous tick more than the desire to tame his unruly locks, and then rubs the back of his neck. "Nope. Not a neighbor, but I'm curious. Why don't I live here?"

"You knocked. No one knocks on their own door."

The man, who *might* be Mason, laughs again and then leans

to grab something from the stoop. I prepare myself for... well, I don't know what I'm preparing for, but my muscles are tense, my stance is defensive, and even though my arms are crossed, my fists are balled. You know. Just in case.

"I thought knocking might be less alarming than just walking in." He turns back to me, carrying two large, brown paper bags, and I feel a little ridiculous. "You don't know me, I don't know you. I figured barging in might not make the best first impression. I'm Mason."

That actually makes sense and it's annoyingly considerate. *Damn. Cute and kind.* "Fine. Thanks... I guess."

I watch Mason work his way around the kitchen as he unpacks his groceries. It's enchanting to watch him. I don't know why, but my eyes are drawn to his arms, his chest, and that smile. I get it now, why Brenda and probably every other woman wants to take a bite out of Mason. He's magnetic.

And I plan to avoid him at all costs.

"Don't worry. I won't be here long. I just needed to drop these off, grab a quick shower, then I'm headed down to *Last Call*. I know hanging out with your roommate isn't what you signed up for, but do you want to join me?"

"Excuse me?" I squeal, my cheeks flushing red.

Mason closes the fridge and those blue eyes cut straight through me. They are as clear as the winter sky. There's a small crease of confusion between his brows, and it's the second cutest thing I've seen all day. The first being him. "What? What did I do?"

"You asked me to take a shower with you. That's what you did!"

Mason is quiet for a moment and then he laughs. Laughs!

"Oh, shit. No. I meant, do you want to come to *Last Call*? It's the family bar that dubs as a cafe during the day. We could grab a late lunch if you want. I wasn't planning on hosting anyone this week, so I don't have much ready for you. Sorry about that."

Oh. Well, I feel *really* stupid now. "It's fine. I found some cheese puffs."

"Cheese puffs aren't lunch."

"Says the man with almost no food in his fridge."

Mason shrugs. "Cooking for one feels pointless."

Something about the way he says that lingers, and I almost ask what he means, but instead I shake my head. Whatever Mason has going on isn't any of my business and even though it goes against every instinct that's been forced into me, I leave it alone.

I'm not here to solve someone else's problems.

I'm not spreading Christmas cheer or doing whatever else Elves do in the mortal world.

I am relaxing. I am detoxing. And I am undoubtedly avoiding this possibly troubled, painfully handsome man. "Thanks, but no thanks."

For the briefest second, something flickers in his eyes—sadness, maybe? Or disappointment?—but it's gone before I can decipher if I imagined it or not.

"Suit yourself. If you change your mind, you know where to find me." He folds the paper bags, leaves them on the counter, then heads to his room.

I linger at the kitchen island, cheeks still warm. Mason is a walking reminder of everything I swore I came here to escape—Christmas, easy charm, and a smile too pretty to be safe. Those eyes could swallow me whole, even though they probably don't see me that way. Not that I care.

I'm not interested in Mason.

Wouldn't be.

And I'm absolutely not kicking myself for turning down what wasn't even an invitation to shower with him.

Because that would be reckless.

And ridiculous.

And exactly the kind of trouble I should avoid.

# Chapter Four

## MASON

It's been a long night, but an even longer day. I left the house feeling excited for the first time in months. Tinsel is cute and feisty, and for a while thinking about her was enough to chase my demons away. But as the night went on, I couldn't escape the feeling that everyone knows what I've done. No one has said anything yet, but it's just a matter of time until the whispers start. Though it's what happens after everyone finds out that worries me most.

I know I'll be the town's pariah, but what will happen to Candace? Will people stop coming to *Last Call* because of me? Will she have to take out loans to stay afloat, but eventually face foreclosure, too? Have I accidentally ruined her business just like I ruined Dad's?

I try not to overthink all of the *what-ifs* as I carry a tray of clean tumblers from the kitchen to the bar, but it's hard. Two of our three regulars are already here, sipping on beer and bourbon, their eyes lingering on me, then darting away as soon as our gazes meet. They know. They have to, and are silently judging me. Waiting to cast their stone, though not wanting to be the first to throw.

I'm mid-stack, refilling the glasses behind the counter, when I hear the creak of the kitchen door and my sister's voice cutting through the silence. "Mason! Tell me Riley was joking when he said you rented out your spare room?"

Her words barely land. My head is still stuck in the same dark loop, but then, like a crack of sunlight through a boarded-up window, Tinsel slips into my thoughts.

It's ridiculous, really. I barely know her, and yet somehow she manages to quiet the noise in my head, even if just for a breath. A small, reluctant smile tugs at my lips. There's something about her. Something I can't explain. And for a fleeting second, it feels almost good to not understand.

"Nope. Brenda was in a bind, so I helped her out," I say, keeping my eyes on the bar. I don't need to look up to know Candace is wearing that smirk. The one she always has when she's trying to stir the pot. Though in a town as small as ours, the pot is usually coffee cup-sized, and it doesn't take long for everyone to know each other's business. Which is exactly what I'm afraid of.

"That's *all* I get?" Candace steps closer, arms crossed, and her head tilts with faux innocence. "Mason, you won't even let your friends crash on the couch when they're drunk. You'd rather drive everyone home at midnight just so your precious *peace and quiet* stays untouched. And now suddenly you've got a *roommate*? And a *girl*, no less?"

It was actually Dad's peace and quiet I was worried about, but tomato-tomahtoh. Old habits die hard. I shrug. "What was I supposed to do? Let her sleep in the sand? I was just extending some Winter Key Christmas kindness."

Candace arches her eyebrows, clearly not buying it. "Right. And this has *nothing* to do with the fact that our newest short-term resident is supposedly the hottest thing on two legs?"

Something twists in my stomach hard enough to make me pause. I don't know why the thought of someone else knowing how beautiful Tinsel is aggravates me. But demoting her to "hot" feels cheap, and whoever dubbed Tinsel that needs to have their eyes checked. "Who'd you hear that from?"

"Why? Are you jealous?" Candace grins, but she's wrong. I'm not jealous. I'm just being... protective. Yeah. That's it. I'm protecting Tinsel from all the slimy, single guys who only want to stick their dicks into the newest girl in town.

"Nope. Just curious."

"Brenda said it. So did Hannah. Oh, and Jason. And Kevin. And Tamara. And pretty much everyone who saw her wandering around town today."

My shoulders tense, just slightly. I hadn't realized how much the idea of people noticing Tinsel would bother me. She's just a stranger. A temporary one. Still, the thought of someone flirting with her, or worse, sparks a rage inside me I haven't wrestled with since high school.

I'm quiet for a beat too long and Candace's eyes light up when the realization that I might have a crush on my new roommate hits. "*Oh my god.* You've seen her, too." I finally look up, and sure enough, she's biting her bottom lip, eyes sparkling with mischief. "Mason... you saw her first, didn't you?"

"Maybe," I mutter, carrying the empty tray of glasses to the back and grabbing a new rack.

Does it make me a creep to admit that I saw a beautiful woman lingering outside the bait shop this morning? That if I were in a better place mentally, I would have introduced myself and welcomed her to Winter Key? Or that when Brenda called to tell me about the double booking, that I was quietly hoping it was *her* who needed the room and that fate was giving me a second chance to make a good impression?

Candace gasps like she's just solved the mystery of who decapitated Rooster (the town's ceramic mascot) last year, and her hand flies to her chest. "That's why you rented the room out!"

"Leave it alone, Candace." I set the rack down on the counter harder than I mean to.

"You like her!"

I run my hand through my hair and sigh. Candace isn't going to let this go. Not until I admit *something*. "Tinsel is just a girl who needs a place to stay. The fact that she's pretty is a bonus."

Tinsel's spicy side is fun too, but I keep that bit to myself. The look she gave me when I walked into the house, the *I'm going to murder you if you take one step closer* expression that was about as convincing as calling a rabbit vicious, was downright sexy. And her mind slipping into the gutter at my invitation to join me tonight was fucking sexy. I would have welcomed her in a heartbeat. So, yeah, I like the girl, but I also understand there are boundaries.

She's my tenant.

I am her landlord.

These are lines that can't be crossed.

"Oh, I know that look." Candace's eyebrows jump.

"I don't have a look." I probably have a look, but I'm not about to admit to my sister she's right. I'd never hear the end of it.

She sputters a disbelieving laugh. "Right. And I'm Mrs. Claus."

"You could be this year," I shoot back. "I hear the apron is up for grabs, and your cookies have come a long way since Easter."

Candace rolls her eyes. "You're deflecting."

I turn back to the bar, grab a rag, and wipe down the counter. "You'll meet Tinsel eventually. There's not a whole lot to do around here. She's bound to wander into the bar sooner or later."

"No, no. I don't think I want to wait." Candace slips behind the counter and scans the bottles like she's planning a heist. "I think I'm going to introduce myself and make a new friend."

"Candace," I warn. "You have *plenty* of friends. Leave this one alone."

"And *you're* being prickly, which makes me want to meet Tinsel even more." She disappears into the back and returns with an oversized purse slung over her shoulder. I eye the bulging sides warily as she loads it up with supplies: a bottle of peppermint schnapps, a jar of maraschino cherries, a can of whipped cream, as well as a few other things from behind the bar.

"Seriously?" I ask.

"I'm bringing *gifts*, Mason. You want me to make a good impression, don't you?" Her hand hovers over a bag of kettle chips. After a quick moment of hesitation, she tosses them in, too.

I level her with a glare as I finish unloading the last glass from the rack. "You're crossing lines."

Candace just grins, all mischief and zero shame, and shrugs like barging into my business is as ordinary as breathing. "And you are acting suspiciously like a man who doesn't want me to meet the girl living under his roof."

"No, I'm acting like a man who's trying to give his tenant the peace he promised."

"Peace is overrated," she fires back with a careless wave of her hand.

"I'm serious, Candace. If you want me to bartend tonight, you'll leave her be."

My sister slings the bag over her shoulder like a purse fairy godmother. "Sweet baby brother, I ran this place without you for two years before you became my partner. I can manage one night, especially if it means I get to meet your future bride."

"You've had too much frozen cocoa," I run my hand over my face. My sister has lost it. Absolutely lost it. "All that sugar has gone straight to your head."

She hesitates in the doorway, ignoring my insult, then looks back at me. "I've got a feeling about this one, Mase. Things with this girl could be great."

"Or a complete disaster."

"Maybe." She shrugs, then pushes the door open. "But either way? It's gonna be *fun*."

## Chapter Five

TINSEL

The sun sinks beneath the horizon, turning the sky into soft streaks of orange and red. It's hard not to notice the shift into twilight through the big windows. I could close the curtains, but this was always my favorite time of day back home. It is the only time when my world is more than just red, white, green, and, of course, blue. I love looking at the oranges, the pinks, and the purples. I love how each day the change into night is different. I love how, even though I know what to expect, each night there is always a level of unknown.

I don't know when I realized my life would forever be the same, but when I did, it was like a weight had fallen on me. Once Chris and I are married, I'll be expected to oversee everything. I'll be making the lists so he can check them twice. I'll be in charge of the bakery, the clothing store, and every workshop station in the warehouse. I'll need to make sure Chris's clothes are pressed and his cocoa is hot. My life will shift from belonging to me to fragmented pieces that everyone else holds in their hands.

I've watched the current Mrs. Claus stress over everything, trying to solve everyone else's problems, while putting her own needs aside. Even worse, Nick, this generation's Santa, is so busy, he barely notices how burnt out his wife is. They have a working relationship, not a marriage, even behind closed doors.

I don't want a life like that. I want excitement and adventure. I want a man who looks at me like his equal, not his employee. I want love, and affection, and the doe-eyed yearning that comes with falling in love.

I want a relationship that feels like I'm having all of my firsts again, only with the stability to be my last.

My friends don't understand. They say I should be happy, that being the next Mrs. Claus is an honor. Hell, some have flat out said they were jealous of my future. They envy the responsibility, the Magic, and the muscular body that hides under the Santa suit.

But I envy their freedom.

They have the choice to stay in the North Pole, assimilate into the working crew in a field of their choice, or go out into the world to learn about the latest and greatest fads. Those elves, the ones who get to experience life, are the ones I envy most. They aren't trapped in the ribbon-wrapped box built for them.

This freedom, the ten days and Christmas Magic I've stolen, are all I will get. I know I have to go back to the North Pole by Christmas Eve to don my red velvet dress and be at Chris's side. But for now, I want to experience life, even if all I'm doing is watching movies, binge eating, and napping. I want my day to be unscripted and I want to choose what I do.

And today, I choose to lie on the couch with a half-eaten bag of cheese puffs while watching people be murdered.

Halfway through the third movie of the day, someone knocks on the door right as the character on screen falls to the ground. I wait, half-hoping whoever it is will move on, and watch the blonde girl be stabbed by a man in a Ghostface mask. I wasn't sure how I'd feel about the series, and truthfully, I wasn't a fan of movie number three or four's trailer, so I skipped them, but number five has my attention. I'm almost disappointed to break my binge streak, but the person knocks again.

Considering there's no jingle of keys or turn of the deadbolt, whoever is out there clearly expects me to let them in. I find the remote to pause the movie and begrudgingly walk to the front of the house. *So much for peace and quiet, Brenda.*

When I open the door, I'm greeted by a woman with glossy dark curls, bright eyes, and a smile that's *way* too cheerful for someone knocking on a stranger's door so close to nine PM.

"I'm not interested in whatever you're selling," I say, automatically.

Her eyebrows knit together in the most adorable expression of mock hurt, like if a golden retriever could pout. For half a second, she reminds me of Snowball, my dog back home and the first pain of regret flares in my chest. I miss her, but she'll be okay. Mom will feed and walk her. She loves Snowball almost as much as I do.

"Oh, totally fair," the woman says, nodding. "I hate door-to-door salespeople, but don't worry, Winter Key doesn't really *do* that. Too many nosy neighbors. It'd be social suicide." Her grin stretches nearly ear to ear as she pulls a bottle from a holiday tote bag covered in glittery snowflakes and candy canes. "That said... How do you feel about candy cane cocktails?"

I love the idea, but who is this woman? And why is she here?

"I'm Candace," she says, practically reading my mind. "Mason said you were staying with him for the pre-holiday season and I figured you might need a friend."

Ah, Mason. Somehow, I'm not surprised this is his fault and yet, even though I want to push the woman away, something about her sucks me in. Maybe it's the elf side of me. I've always had a sense for those who are naughty and those who are nice. Or maybe I just want to try a candy cane cocktail, but I don't immediately shut the door.

Still, I cross my arms and create a pseudo wall between us. "That's really sweet. But I don't usually let strangers into places I'm temporarily living."

Candace doesn't flinch. "I get that, but Mason is my little

brother. So, this is basically my second home. I'm just dropping in to say hi and maybe bribe you with alcohol. It didn't sound like you had any family coming down with you and holidays could be lonely sometimes."

"You don't seem like the type of girl that knows what it's like to be lonely," I say, and her brown eyes widen. It takes me a second to realize what I could be implying, and I immediately apologize. "Oh, no, I don't mean it like that. It's just you're friendly and talkative. People like you don't usually have a problem finding people to hang out with."

She shrugs. "I'll forgive you for implying that I'm anything but wholesome if you let me come in and make you a drink."

"Well," I say, stepping aside reluctantly. "I guess one drink won't kill me, and I do like peppermint."

"Atta girl!" Candace beams, practically dancing through the door.

I look past her, out into the driveway, to see if there are any other surprise Winter Key guests waiting to join us. Thankfully, Mason's street is quiet. His neighbors are far down the block and the only things scurrying around outside are the squirrels. I close the door and in the minute it takes me to survey the street and turn around, Candace has set everything she needs out on the counter.

"And you're right," she says, turning to pull two glasses from the cabinet. "I don't have trouble making friends. My twin sister, Camryn, on the other hand, is a hermit. She says I have all the social skills, while she has the brains. She's a doctor. I'm a bartender."

So, Mason's the little brother. I almost ask how many other siblings he has, but I change my mind because I don't care. I don't care that he's hot or if he's single.

I don't care about Mason.

Period.

"Both are noble professions."

Candace snorts as she pours alcohol and ice into the blender.

"Nice try, but no. Camryn is literally saving lives while I'm earning tips by..." she pauses. "Well, let's just say some of my outfits earn more money than others." She glances at me, then groans and covers her face with her hands. "Oh, my *God*, that sounded terrible. I swear I'm not out here flashing people."

I laugh, falling into a comfort ease I never found back home with this woman. "I understand what you mean. No judgment."

Candace drizzles the inside of her cup with grenadine and then pours the contents of the blender in. By the time she's done, the glass looks like a candy cane and the one she hands me tastes like it, too. The cocktail is deliciously sweet, pepperminty without a hint of alcohol, and I've already decided that this drink is going to be my downfall.

"So," Candace says, casually, "is *Tinsel* your real name, or is it like a nickname because you're obsessed with Christmas?"

A jolt of terror runs through me. Does she know I'm an elf?

Can humans sense this sort of thing?

I always thought we looked enough alike. There are even some elves on assignment who have assimilated and had children with humans. Even though technically we're a different species, we're genetically compatible. Compatible enough that no one can tell those kids are half-elf. But I'm a full elf and Santa's head elf's daughter, no less. I was picked to be Chris's wife because I'm special, or so they say. Does that specialness make me stand out from everyone else?

I freeze mid-sip and look her in the eyes. "What makes you think I love Christmas?"

Candace gives me a slow once-over, then raises her eyebrows. "You're basically a walking holiday advertisement. The hair. The clothes. Just..." she waves her hand in a small circle that I think is supposed to embody everything that is *me*.

It's a fair assessment. My hair alone, platinum white with red and green highlights, is probably the most Christmasy thing about me. However, I did come straight from headquarters and even though I'm not in uniform, objectively, my dark red shorts and white shirt could pass for a holiday outfit.

"The red and green ends aren't by choice. They're kind of a family thing," I admit. "Every girl in our *family* gets them done. But the white? That's natural. My hair has always grown in this weird snow color."

It's always grown with the red and green, too. Colors the elves choose to add to their hair once they turn sixteen, but I don't even try to explain because I can't. My hair is an anomaly even Santa doesn't understand.

Candace plops a thick candy cane stick into her drink and then hands me one. "So, Christmas is, like... a family thing?"

"You have no idea," I mutter, setting down my drink. *Why is this so tasty? And how is half of mine gone already?* "It's basically their entire personality and not just during the season. My family literally lives and breathes the holiday all year long. It's not just my parents either, it's the whole town. They never take down the lights, the trees are permanent fixtures that were planted, I don't know how many generations ago, and collectively everyone's favorite color is red, which pairs perfectly with the year-round snow. It's why I ran away. I needed a change. I wanted to sweat in the sun, not shiver, and to... I don't know...experience something that wasn't pre-planned for once."

Candace gives me a sympathetic look. "I'm guessing your family isn't thrilled you're here instead of there, considering Christmas is a little more than a week away."

"Not thrilled is an understatement. They're old-school. They expect me to step into a part of the business that I'm not ready for. I don't even really want the job, but it's just expected that I'm going to accept it because this *promotion* has been in the works since I was a kid. Technically, I already accepted the job, but I was six when they offered it. How was I supposed to know that I'd spend the next twenty-one years preparing for a position I don't actually want?"

I groan and drop my head in my hands. All the weight I've

been carrying falls to a pit in my stomach. I've never actually said all of this out loud. I've hinted my reservations to my friends, but they didn't understand, so I stopped trying to explain.

I push my long bangs back and meet Candace's gaze. I don't know what I expect to see in her eyes. Disgust? Frustration? Disappointment? That's what everyone back home shows me. But all I see is empathy.

Candace reaches across the counter and squeezes my hand. She smiles and I return the gesture. Maybe it's the cocktail, but for the first time, it feels like someone's actually listening to me. Like I have my first real friend.

I pull away, using the excuse to slurp the rest of my drink, then shrug. "I guess that's the best way I can put everything without telling you exactly how morbidly fucked up my family is."

"You know…" She points to the blender, offering me another round, and I nod. "I'm a big reader and this is giving arranged marriage vibes. I don't actually know your situation, but those stories usually end up okay in the end. Could yours have an unexpected happily ever after?"

"Not likely," I say, as she adds whipped cream and a cherry to a new batch of yummy goodness.

"Well, we all have messed-up families, but yours does sound *extra*." She pauses, grinning. "Not that it's a competition."

"Thanks?" I say through a laugh, because if I don't laugh about my life, I'll cry.

Candace slurps the last of her drink through a candy-striped straw and slams her glass down like it's a dare. "If it makes you feel better, my mom once kissed my sister's boyfriend."

I choke. "I'm sorry, what?"

"Camryn and I had just turned twenty-one and our dad was long out of the picture. I should mention that Mason and I have different dads." She flicks her wrist, dismissing the tiny bit of family tea she dropped and jumps back into the story. "Anyway, Camryn brings this guy to the bar—*my* bar, where I work—

because they're getting serious. He comes in, says hi, all normal. And then my mom walks in and *immediately* starts flirting. I mean, 'what's your sign, do you like older women' flirting. And then out of *nowhere*, she kisses him. Camryn comes out from the bathroom and sees the whole thing. It was absolute chaos, but the craziest part of this whole story is that guy was almost our step-dad. He dumped Camryn, dated Mom for a year, and then proposed. Thankfully, she has commitment issues, so as soon as he popped the question, Mom dropped him."

I gape at Candace, trying to process while simultaneously *not* imagining a faceless dude hooking up with a mirror image of her, then hooking up with a faceless version of her mom, then holding a tray of Christmas cookies and smiling like he'd done no wrong.

Candace grins. "So, yeah. Holidays are *wild* in our house."

"Well," I say, holding up my glass, "My mom's never done *that*, so... you win."

"Damn right I do." She takes my empty cup and starts making another round of drinks.

"You're dangerous," I tell her when she slides a new, full cocktail my way. "These are addicting."

"They're just one of our holiday drink specials. You should come to *Last Call* tomorrow. My shift starts at nine."

I hesitate. "That's your bar?"

"Yup. It's *Hot Cocoa & Holiday Ink Night,* if you're into that sort of thing." She pulls up her pant leg and shows me a tattooed ankle bracelet with three charms. "Tyler comes to town once a quarter and does tiny festive tattoos for ten dollars. Snowflakes. Candy canes. Santa hats. That sort of thing. This will be his fourth time and I can't wait to add a new *charm* to the bracelet."

"That's cute."

"Thanks and if tattoos aren't your thing, we have a *decorate your own cocoa mug* station. It's the first unofficial event of our holiday countdown. Dora, our mayor, would have a fit if the tattoos were actually on the calendar. Oh! And the Tree Lighting festival is on Friday! You absolutely have to come to that."

"I don't know…" Holiday tattoos and a tree lighting sounds exactly like what I'm trying to run away from. Well, sort of. If the tattoos weren't Christmas-themed, I might consider getting one. I can practically see the fit Mom would throw at me for *ruining my perfect skin.*

"Oh, come on, Tinsel. You won't be alone. I'll be there, and I'll make you another one of these. On the house," Candace lifts the blender's lid, trying to tempt me with the peppermint goodness. "And I'll personally make sure you don't end up with a snowman tattoo on your ass."

That makes me laugh harder than I expect, and I let my guard down a little. "Fine. Maybe."

"That's the spirit!" Candace beams, and in that moment, I don't mind the Christmas conversation, the red and white, or even the way this woman barreled into my life uninvited.

Candace may be sunshine personified, but she's *real*. And against my better judgment, I like her.

*Chapter Six*

TINSEL

I'm curled up on the couch, half-watching another Halloween movie, my fifth today, when I hear the bathroom door open. Mason steps out, hair damp from his evening shower, water still clinging to the ends. He's in black board shorts and, of all things, a ridiculous button-down Santa shirt covered in little reindeer. It makes me smile before I can stop myself.

"Are you headed to *Last Call*?" I ask, tilting my head at him.

"Yep." He shrugs, casual. "Pretty much every night for the rest of my life. Why? Do you want to come with me?"

I hesitate, feeling a rush of nervousness, then nod. "If you don't mind... yeah. Candace invited me to tattoo night tonight and I'm going a little stir crazy."

Mason's mouth tips into an easy grin. One that probably means nothing but makes my heart race despite knowing better. "Awesome. Tyler's great and the whole experience is a blast. I need to head out in about five minutes. Think you can be ready?"

"Yeah." I push off the couch and run my hands down my jeans. "Just let me grab my purse real quick."

In my room, I take an extra minute to look at myself in the mirror. Santa has a strict dress code for the elves, including how our hair and makeup should be set, but I've never been one to care about how I look. Today, though, I hate my hair. It's frizzy and unruly no matter what I try to do with it. I settle on a side braid and add some red rouge to my lips. If I had earrings or a necklace, I'd probably put them on too, but all of my jewelry is back home. I didn't think I'd need it and using Magic to conjure accessories for an outing with a hot guy seems wasteful. With nothing left to tweak, I guess it's time to go.

Mason waits for me by the front door, then opens it and gestures for me to go first. He does the same when we reach his truck and doesn't go to his side of the vehicle until I'm buckled in and settled. The chivalry should feel old-fashioned, nothing more than a polite habit. Instead, I find myself staring out the window, refusing to look at him, because something as simple as opening a door should not make my pulse skip.

And yet, it does.

The truck comes to life with a *roar*, and then we're off. As Mason backs out of the driveway, he says, "The AC is broken. You might want to roll the window down."

"Oh." I look for the handle, then crank it a few times to move the glass. "Thanks."

"She's an old girl." He says as he taps the side of his dash, proudly. "But she's still got a lot of life left in her."

We drive with the windows down, listening to soft music spill from the speakers. I stick my hand out into the night, playing in the wind and enjoying the smell of salt and seaweed.

"So," Mason says after a beat, "where are you from?"

"A little snowy town up north you've probably never heard of," I answer, still looking out the window. I need to memorize each street and turn so I can make my way downtown again while I'm here without having to ask for help. Two lefts, and a right. Then up ahead is the glow of downtown's Edison lights. "It's so small most days it's left off the map."

"Kind of like us. Winter Key gets lumped in with the other Islands half the time, like we don't even exist."

I smile and look at him for the first time since getting in the truck. He meets my eyes, just for a second, and something flickers between us. A thread of understanding, fragile but real. Maybe.

"Yeah," I murmur, voice softer than I mean it to be. "That's exactly what my town's like."

The drive to *Last Call* doesn't take long, less than five minutes, and I don't know why, but I'm sad when Mason pulls into the parking lot. This is the first conversation I've had all day. The peace and quiet have been nice, but it's lonely, too. I'm almost never alone back home, and the change is a bit bewildering.

"Hang tight." Mason cuts the engine, steps out of the cab, and circles around to my side. He opens my door and then extends his hand to me.

I roll my eyes at his incessant chivalry, but *oh my reindee*r, I'm practically swooning. I know the gesture is nothing in the grand scheme of things, but Chris has never held a door for me. He's never helped me up or out of my seat, and I've never had this weird stomach twisty feeling around him. But when Mason's hand holds mine, I feel like I'm on the sleigh for the first time, about to shoot off into the night.

Mason's hand lingers against mine, our fingers tangled together as we walk across the street toward *Last Call*. But when he opens the door for me to go through first, he doesn't reclaim them. I try not to let it bother me. He probably didn't even realize our hands were still together, but it was nice. *Oh well.*

The bar is surprisingly busy, even though it's only seven. Families fill the room, kids and adults laughing side by side as they sip cocoa and color ceramic mugs with Sharpies. Even with the tattoo artist set up on the left side of the room, it doesn't feel like a bar, but more like a gathering spot. Like the big red barn at the North Pole, where everyone gets together on Friday nights, listens to music, and hangs out. It's our community bonding place. *Last Call* feels like that.

It feels like home.

"Tinsel!" Candace beams when she spots me. She hands off a tray of bright green drinks and pulls me into a hug. "Come on, I have so many people for you to meet."

Before I can reply, she takes my hand and drags me around the bar, rattling off introductions to everyone we pass before insisting, "You have to try our Sugar Cookie Martini. It's basically a dessert in a glass."

I laugh despite myself. I don't know if an alcoholic cookie is a good thing or a bad thing, but I'm curious. "How can I say no?"

She slips behind the bar and grabs bottle after bottle, tipping them upside down and mixing them all together in a shaker before pouring the drink over ice. I take a small, cautious drink and am pleasantly surprised. The cocktail is sweet with a slight kick, but it's so good.

I spend the next hour perched at the bar, meeting locals as they wander up to say hi, and polishing off three more rounds. By the time I start my fourth drink, I'm warm and fuzzy and can't seem to take my eyes off the blondie floating around the room. Every time our eyes catch, he tosses me a grin that makes my pulse skip in ways I don't want to think too hard about, but I can't drag my eyes away.

Someone yelps at the tattoo station and the Mason trance breaks. I whip my head to the left and watch the man work, fascinated by the steady hum of the machine and the way everyone crowds around to peek at the art. Until Mason's voice cuts in close to my ear. "You thinking about getting one?"

I startle, caught off guard by his closeness, and shake my head. "I don't think so. I've already got enough Christmas in my life, I don't need it tattooed on me."

He chuckles, stepping in closer, his arm brushing mine as he leans against the table. "Come on. It could be fun. I might even get one."

That makes me turn my gaze to him. "Really?"

Mason shrugs and the corner of his mouth twitches upward.

"Tattoos aren't usually my thing, but something about this season... I don't know. Maybe."

I glance down at the flash sheets spread throughout the bar. There are ten different options varying from the size of a dime to my fist. The small ones are colorful and intricate, while the bigger tattoos are beautiful, but simple. My eyes snag on a candy cane that's about the size of my finger, simple but neat, and before I can school my expression, I feel my mouth twitch. I guess if I had to pick one, I could live with my favorite candy inked on me.

"I'll get one, if you get one," he says suddenly.

My gaze darts back to that ridiculously pretty smile, a little surprised. "Oh? And what are you gonna get?"

The side of his pinky brushes against my arm when he says, "Don't care. Pick for me."

I tap a sketch of a fist-sized, white, fluffy puppy with a Santa hat, knowing there's no way Mason will go for it. I'll call his bluff and then tease him for being a wimp. The bonus will be that I don't have to get a tattoo and my *chickening out* will be all his fault. "That one."

"Perfect," he says without hesitation and his conviction catches me by surprise. From what I can tell, Mason doesn't have any ink on his skin, and he wants this to be his first?

"Are you sure?"

"Yep."

"Fine." I exhale, nerves fluttering low in my belly. "Then you get to pick mine. What am I getting?"

"It's a surprise." Before I can second-guess myself, Mason reaches down and takes my hand, gently tugging me toward the tattoo station. "Come on."

My pulse kicks up as we weave through the crowd, and when we reach the table, I realize there's no line. Just the artist, Tyler, waiting with his arms crossed, like he'd been expecting us.

"Me first," Mason says as he drops into the chair. He shows Tyler his soon-to-be tattoo, and the fluffy dog doesn't even faze the guy. Maybe he's used to men getting adorably cute tattoos. Or maybe he's just seen enough antics not to care that the tattoo doesn't match the body.

I hover at Mason's side, trying to act casual while he fills out some paperwork and swipes his credit card, but my heart races a mile a minute. I'm nervous, half hoping Mason will back out at the last minute, and low-key freaking out because I think he's going to go through with this.

"Fill this out," Tyler says, handing me a paper and pen. "Pretty boy has already paid for your ink."

"What?" I look up at Mason and he shrugs, like it's no big deal. "I mean, thank you."

"Call it a welcome to Winter Key present."

"I need you on the bed," Tyler says, as I scribble as much information as I can on the paper.

Name. *Easy enough.*

Address. *I'll just copy what Mason wrote. Technically, I'm living with him, so it counts. Right?*

Driver's License number and expiration date. *Oh.* I don't have one of those. I look at Mason's paper again, noting how it's just a letter with a bunch of numbers after it. I copy half of his, then change the numbers at the end. Hopefully, by the time Tyler realizes the ID is a fake, I'll be long gone.

"I'll need both of you to give Candace your driver's licenses before the night's over so I can add a copy of them to your file," Tyler says, while opening sterile packaging, as if reading my mind.

I force a smile, feeling nervous for a whole new reason, and nod. "Sure, thing."

Mason slides from the chair to the bed and lays face down on the table so Tyler can prep his leg, shaving the hair on the back of his calf and disinfecting it. He glances up at me, and a small wrinkle has settled between his brows.

"Don't worry about me, Snowflake," he says teasingly. "I'll be okay."

"I'm not." I roll my eyes and fold my arms to hide how tightly I'm clutching my purse. It's not Mason I'm worried about. It's the needle, the pain, and the possibility of Tyler realizing I don't have a driver's license because I'm not from this realm. "I'm just shocked you agreed to get a fluffy puppy."

"Santa hat and all." Mason grins, and the simple curve of his mouth eases the tightness in my chest.

The buzz of the gun starts and the sound is sharp and steady. I wince in sympathy as the needle glides over his skin, but Mason barely flinches. His expression is calm, almost smug, as if he knows I'm watching every move. When Tyler wipes the fresh ink for the last time and starts wrapping it, Mason casually sits up like permanently marring his skin is nothing.

"Boom!" He stands and flexes his calf where the tattoo sits. "How's that for the most badass tattoo you've ever seen?"

The fluffy puppy looks entirely out of place against Mason's broad frame—ridiculous, really—but somehow that only makes it sexier. He tips his chin toward me, then points at the chair. "Your turn."

I take a deep breath. I'm nervous, but a deal is a deal. Mason got a mirror image of Snowball on him. I can't back out. "Okay. What am I getting?"

"Can't tell you. It's a surprise," Mason says, and my jaw practically drops. He chuckles, likely sensing the panic growing inside me. He drapes his arm over my shoulder and escorts me the ten steps to the tattoo table. "You're just going to have to trust me."

"Trust you? I just met you." I glance up at him, but this time that easy grin doesn't settle my nerves. The edges of my vision are blurry and my head is spinning. I think I might pass out. I can't do this. Can I?

"Relax, Snowflake." Mason squeezes me tight and rubs his hand over my arm. "You'll be fine. I promise, but there's no shame in changing your mind. You don't have to do this if you don't want to."

I do actually, because a deal is a deal, and as scared as I am, I'm no quitter. "I'm fine. Let's do this."

"Where do you want it?" Tyler asks, trying to hurry us along.

"On my ankle." I point to the soft spot of skin near the bone. Whatever it is, I should be able to hide it easily behind my boots when I go home.

"You should probably lie down for this one." Tyler motions for me to get on the table. "Ankles hurt and I don't want you passing out."

"Great." I lay on my side and he cleans and preps the spot. What felt like it took hours for Mason takes minutes for me. Before I know it, the gun is buzzing and there's a gloved hand on my leg.

"Ready?" Tyler asks.

"Yup," I squeak, but I'm not because the moment the needle touches my skin, I flinch. The needle stops, and even though no one says anything to me, I mutter, "Sorry."

Mason swings a chair around and drops it in front of me, straddling it backward. One arm drapes casually across the backrest while the other extends toward me, steady and open.

"Here," he says, palm up, like it's the simplest thing in the world. "Squeeze as hard as you want and try not to think about the tattoo."

I take his hand, grip it tight, and close my eyes. My leg feels like it's on fire. The needle hums with each pass across my skin, though I don't feel the vibration, just a burning heat. "Right. Because that's so easy."

"You're doing great, Snowflake. You've got this. Just a little longer," Mason says, voice softer, trying to distract me.

My first instinct is to argue that I really don't got this, but his words stop me cold. A shiver slips down my spine because compliments aren't exactly common where I come from. I can count on one hand the number I've ever been given, and encouragement? Even rarer.

I could drown in those words—in the way they make me feel seen—and never bother coming up for air.

It reminds me of the first time a boy called me pretty, how I melted for him, how easily he coaxed my firsts from me with flattery I was desperate to believe. Looking back, I was naïve. Stupid. But Mason doesn't want anything from me. He's just being nice. Supportive. And fuck… Why does that turn me on?

I lock eyes with Mason, trying to figure out why I feel so hot and gooey when the needle drags across my skin again. I grimace. *Oh, my reindeer, this hurts!*

"Tell me," Mason says, the sound of his voice grounding me when all I feel is pain and confusion. "Why'd you pick that puppy?"

"Huh? Oh… um… it looks like my dog, Snowball," I admit, swallowing against the sting. "When I saw it, I couldn't resist."

"That's cute." Mason chuckles. "And unoriginal, considering you said you're surrounded by snow year-round."

I open my eyes and narrow them on him. I never told him that. I told Candace about my snowy hometown, but not Mason. Which means they've been talking about me. I should be angry, but I'm more irritated at the judgmental smirk on his face. "Says the man who calls me Snowflake."

Mason laughs again, but he doesn't look away. He holds my stare, forcing gravity into his words when he says, "It suits you. You're beautiful to look at, fair, and a little icy, but so much fun to have around."

Well, damn. I kind of like the comparison. Heat flares low in my body, sharp and uninvited, and I catch myself biting the corner of my lip, trying to wrestle it back under control. I can't deny that I'm attracted to Mason, but giving in to that attraction is not going to happen. Technically, I'm still engaged, though if I take Chris's track record into consideration, our monogamy won't start until we officially say *I do*. But even if the whole Mr. and Mrs. Claus bit wasn't an issue, he's my landlord and my roommate.

Say I make a move and kiss Mason, and it's horrible… how am I supposed to look him in the eye every day for the next nine days? Or worse. What if he's a *really* good kisser? What if I can't stop thinking about those lips and how good the rest of his body could be?

Nope. I really can't go there.

Mason's blue eyes drop to my mouth, and the urge to grab him by the shirt and pull his lips to mine is almost strong enough to make me forget where we are and that a needle is burying ink in my skin.

Almost.

"Although, if I'm being honest, I can't even imagine being in a place where it snows. I'd die," He says, and his words hit me like a splash of cold water. "It feels so good here, just walking around in shorts and a T-shirt."

I stare at him, momentarily shocked, because he said *living* not *being*...right? Surely I heard him wrong. He's seen snow. Everyone has seen snow at least once in their lives. Haven't they? "Wait, are you saying you've never seen snow?"

"Nope."

My jaw drops. How is that possible? Has he never left Florida?

I never left the North Pole before this week, but that's because I couldn't find a way out. No one but Santa knows where the Christmas Magic is kept. It would still be a mystery to me if Chris hadn't been trying so hard last week. But he showed me, fucked up the delicate balance we've maintained the last fifteen years, and gave me the opening I needed to escape.

Before I can reply, Tyler's gun stops buzzing. He leans back, sets his needle on the tray, and looks at my ankle appreciatively. "All done."

"See, I knew you could do this," Mason says as he helps me sit up, steadying me with a hand at my elbow, and having him hold me, even innocently, feels too natural.

I roll my eyes, trying to seem unaffected by everything that is Mason, and glance down at my new ink. My breath catches when I see the most perfect red and white candy cane. The same candy cane that caught my eye. I didn't think Mason noticed, but I guess he did.

"It's adorable," I whisper, unable to stop the smile spreading across my face.

When I look up, my gaze collides with Mason's. Tension builds between us and I can tell there's something he wants to say, but before he can, Candace saunters over and ruins the moment.

"Oh, my God, Tinsel! I love your tattoo!" She bends down and looks at it more closely, then nods approvingly when she stands again. "It suits you."

"Thanks. Mason picked it out for me."

Her eyebrows jump, and I'm not sure I like the smirk she gives us. It's like she knows I have a crush on her brother, which is crazy because I only just realized it. "What's your plan for the rest of the night? My shift officially starts soon, but—"

I shake my head, and all of the excitement falls off her face. "I think I'm gonna head back to the house and watch another movie."

Candace scrunches her nose, clearly not approving of my plan. "Halloween horror flicks again?"

"Probably." Mason teases. "She's been binging them since she got here."

"How do you know that?" I whip my head toward him, feeling a slight tingle of nervousness. Is Mason stalking me? Does he have cameras in his house watching me and uncovering my deepest, darkest secrets?

He shrugs and swipes a chip out of the bag Candace is holding. "I see them in my recently watched section when I log into my account. My *For-You* has gotten a little murdery, too."

"Oh." Heat rises in my cheeks. Right. That makes sense. "Sorry. I didn't realize I was messing up your algorithm."

"Nah. It's fine. It probably needed a shake-up anyway." He reaches for another chip, but Candace twists so he can't get one. He flicks her off, in what I'm assuming is playful, sibling banter, and she sticks her tongue out at him.

"Hey, Tinsel?" She asks, tilting the bag of chips toward me. I shake my head, and she continues, "How exactly are you getting home tonight?"

I shrug. "I don't know. I figured I'd walk."

"Absolutely not." Her voice cuts sharp. She points at Mason. "You're driving her."

He opens his mouth, probably to protest, but she silences him with a look. "You are not letting our precious new friend walk home in the dark. Besides, I don't need you anymore tonight, so have fun, kids." With a flick of her wrist, she waves us off and disappears back behind the bar.

# Chapter Seven

## TINSEL

Mason glances at me from across the kitchen, his gaze steadily following me as I grab a bottle of water and cross into the living room. "Tired?"

"Not really," I say, shaking my head as I get comfortable on the couch. I should probably go to my room, close the door, and keep the walls between us up. But I don't. I curl into the corner of the couch instead, half-hoping Mason will call it a night and go watch TV in his room, half-terrified he'll leave me and do just that.

I catch a ghost of a smile playing across his lips and then a flicker of hesitation. I grab the remote and try not to watch him pop a bag of popcorn into the microwave, but it's impossible not to notice his presence. My body hums whenever he's near. It's crazy, really, and unexplainable, but the only time that weird, tingly, shaking feeling goes away is when he touches me. Even the simplest brush of his hand against mine stills the anxiousness inside me.

The bag finishes popping and he shakes the kernels into a large bowl. "How's your ankle?"

"I feel it." I give a little shrug, and we both smile at the understatement. It doesn't hurt per se, but it has a steady throb that won't let me forget it's there.

Mason rounds the couch a few minutes later with the bowl of popcorn in his hand and sits next to me. "What are we gonna watch tonight?"

"We?" I arch my eyebrows, though that aching tingly feeling ramps up from a low hum to a full-on buzz. "You're lucky you brought a snack or I'd be banishing you to your room."

He tosses a popcorn kernel at me and as much as I don't want to, I laugh. I like him and the more time we spend together, the harder it is to deny it and I think he likes me, too. Which would be great if I were looking for someone to spend my vacation with, but I can't afford to get tangled up in a guy right now, no matter how sweet or unfairly attractive he is. Feelings complicate everything. And my life is already messy enough without adding Mason to the pile.

He shifts on the couch and his leg touches mine. It's casual. His knee barely leaning against mine means nothing. But all the chatter inside me finally quiets and suddenly all I can hear is him. "Are we sticking with Halloween and horror?"

I nod. "Yeah, it feels like the most anti-Christmas option."

"You and your hatred of Christmas." Mason grins. "May I?"

"Oh, sure." I hand him the remote and our fingers brush against each other. Just a flicker of contact, but it sends my thoughts spinning in a whole new direction. Is he doing this on purpose? Innocently touching me, knowing it drives me crazy?

Chris used to do that—poke and prod, always pushing until my cheeks burned, then grin like the Cheshire cat when I snapped. I hated him for it. Hated the way he thrived on making me small compared to him and his untouchable Santa persona.

But Mason isn't trying to embarrass me or get a rise. He's just here, close, steady in a way that feels dangerous because I like it. I bite my lip, forcing myself to breathe. I'm overthinking this. I have to be.

Mason scrolls through the options and stops on an animated

cover with a skeleton, a ghost dog, and a cool but odd-looking mountain, and I'm trying to figure out how a cartoon can be scary. "Have you seen this one?"

I squint at the screen, realizing he's serious. "Considering I'm not twelve, no, I haven't."

"It's a classic," Mason says, almost excitedly, and his eagerness has me biting back a smile. "It's not the least bit scary, but one of my favorite Halloween movies."

"Is it now?"

"Yeah," Mason says, and this time there's no denying what I'm seeing. Pure Christmas joy. The kind of stuff we're told only happens on Christmas day when children around the world open their wished-for gifts. It's fascinating. I've never seen it in real life and I didn't even know adults could still experience the feeling. But here Mason is, practically glowing while talking about a movie. "Fair warning, though, it's a little Christmasy, but only because Jack, the skeleton dude, tries to steal the holiday. He's the Pumpkin King and knows nothing about gift-giving. He actually gives one kid a severed head. It's kind of funny."

"Sounds like this movie might be an actual nightmare." I tease, wanting to hear him tell me more.

"Oh, and I feel like I should warn you," he adds, casually draping his arm across the back of the couch, just behind my shoulders. "It's a musical."

"So, no blood, no gore. Just music? Why do I get the feeling you're a big softy?" I tilt my head toward him, teasing, only to realize just how close we are. Close enough that if I leaned in, even an inch, I could erase the space between us and kiss him.

"Let me guess, you're the kind of girl who goes for the bad boys." Mason's gaze drops to my lips and without realizing it, I lick them.

The silence between us is charged with possibility. All I'd need is to move toward him, just a little, and I think he'd kiss me. My heart races, and I almost do it, but instead, I reach for the popcorn, shoving a handful into my mouth like it can drown out the need.

I can't kiss Mason. Can't let myself tumble into those bottomless blue eyes. And I really, really can't afford to catch feelings for a man who seems too good to be real. "Technically, I was never allowed to date. So, there wasn't really a 'go for anybody.'"

Mason rears back a little, his eyebrows pushing together into a concerned yet curious line. "Seriously? You've never had a boyfriend?"

I shake my head.

He shifts, closing the space between us again, and asks, "Never been kissed?"

His gaze drops to my mouth again, lingering there long enough to drown any doubt about what he wants. I want it to, I don't think I've wanted to kiss anyone as much as I want to taste his lips. But if I'm already this attracted to Mason, simply because of his infectious smile, kind personality, and good looks, I'll be ruined if he's a good kisser. Addicted, wanting more of a man I should never have.

"I never said that. I've been kissed."

"Is that all you've done?"

The question lingers between us, heavy, and I shift, sliding an extra inch or two away to break the spell. Tucking one leg beneath me, I force a casual tone I don't feel. "Are we watching this movie or what?"

Mason's gaze lingers, but after a tense moment, he starts the film. The movie is cute, whimsical, really, though somewhere between the songs and the swirling animation, my eyelids grow heavy. I don't know when, but I drift off, and when I wake, the sun peeks through the curtains, and my head is in Mason's lap. He's asleep too, cheek resting against his fist, snoring softly.

I try to sit up, careful not to wake him, but he's stirring before I'm fully upright. "Good Morning."

"Morning." I yawn and stretch my back. It's stiff and angry from being stuck in that position. I make a mental note that if we do another sleepover, it needs to be in a bed... not that we would. Because we won't. It's just good information to know. "Sorry. I didn't realize I fell asleep."

"It's okay. You dozed off and, in your half-asleep state, laid in my lap." He gives a faint smile. "I didn't want to risk waking you, so... here we are."

*Oh, my reindeer, this is embarrassing. I hope I didn't drool or talk in my sleep!* "Again, I'm sorry."

"I didn't mind." He stands, stretching, and his shirt rides up just slightly. The man has abs and that deep V by his hips. *Reindeer, help me.* "Do you drink coffee?"

I shake my head and look away because this man is intoxicating. I'm going to need to have a real come-to-Christmas conversation with my needy lady-bits if we're going to cohabitate with Mason. I can not, will not, sleep with my landlord. It's not happening. Nope. Nope. And...nope.

"Just cocoa, peppermint tea, and water. I guess alcohol now, too, which might explain why I passed out so early."

Mason pops a coffee pod into the machine and lines up his glass. "Don't feel bad. Candace's drinks sneak up on everyone. She doesn't like her alcohol to *taste* like alcohol. She wants sweet treats with a surprise punch."

"Well, she definitely accomplished that."

Mason pulls a bowl of fresh-cut fruit out of the fridge and sets it on the counter. He picks up a piece of pineapple, then asks, "What do you have planned today?"

"Same thing, different day. Hang out, maybe watch TV. Might try to get some sun so I don't look so snowy. What about you?"

"I might go fishing for an hour or two. I used to head out on the boat before sunrise, but since the bait shop closed, my mornings have been... off." He tosses a whole strawberry into his mouth, then rummages through one of the kitchen drawers. He finds a pen and a notepad, then writes his number down and slides the pad of paper across the counter to me. "Here. If you have any questions or need anything, call me."

"Thanks."

"I've gotta run into town later and grab supplies for the tree lighting tonight. So, if there's something you want stocked in the kitchen or if you need something for your bathroom, just let me know. *Hopkin's Pharmacy* has most of the basics, but anything beyond single-ply toilet paper and two-in-one shampoo, we've got to go into Islamorada for."

"Candace mentioned the tree lighting. Is that a big deal around here?"

"Yeah, it's our official Christmas kickoff event. Every night up until the twenty-fifth, the town hosts different activities for the community."

"That sounds fun," I say, though *exhausting* feels more accurate.

"It's something." He shrugs, and for the first time since I met Mason, there's a little sadness in his eyes. "This is just one of the many things on my never-ending list that the town asks me to do. But I have the time now and I don't mind. Plus, you know how it goes...scratch my back, I'll scratch yours. This town is basically one big family. We're all here for each other when we need it."

"My hometown's kind of like that, too. Mostly functional, but you know how families can be." I can't get into the details of how the wood shop elves hate the metal workers. Or that the elves North of the barn are basically rivals to those South and crossing into each other's turf causes a miniature gang war, but that's neither here nor there.

"So... will I see you tonight at the lighting?"

I'd rather not. I am *really* trying to detox from Christmas, but I'm being invited. When was the last time I was invited somewhere versus expected to be there? Outside of tattoo night... I really can't remember. "Yeah. Sure."

Mason twists the pen between his fingers. A beat of silence hangs between us, growing thicker until he says, "Do you, maybe, wanna ride with me? I'll be down there setting up around one, but I can swing back, grab a shower, and pick you up before the event."

It's not a date. Just two people who live together, going to the same place in the same truck. If he were asking me on a date, I'd have to say no. But since it's not a date... "That would be nice. Thank you."

"Cool." He grins, and just like that, the worry shadowing his face lifts. " See you around."

"See you," I echo.

I realize, in all of my planning, and despite throwing nearly a million things into my suitcase, I didn't pack a bathing suit. In all fairness, it wasn't top of mind at the time. I've never had much need for one back home. Sure, Chris has a hot tub, and almost every elf in our graduating class has dipped their toes in it a time or two, but I was never brave enough to strip down to my bra and panties and join the fun. I wasn't exactly invited to *that* part of the night either, so... there's that.

I stare at the ground and look at the clothes I've thrown everywhere: six pairs of jeans, three dresses, one skirt, eight shirts, two pairs of shorts, shoes for almost every occasion, but no bathing suit. My other suitcase has my pillow and blanket because I didn't trust the Airbnb's pillow to be as comfortable as the one I'm used to. The two times I've traveled to the other side of the Pole, stayed in one of the guest cottages, and not brought my own, I slept like shit. As for the blanket, it's more of a comfort than a necessity.

"Great. Just *freaking* great," I mutter.

I'm so mad at myself, I could scream. I even had one of the sewing elves, Cherry, make me a sexy two-piece bathing suit specifically for this trip. She thought I was crazy, but when I told her it was for a beach vacation, she assumed it was for my honeymoon and was more than willing to help. Seeing as she thought it was for Chris, she called it our little secret and made it to my exact size. And now it's sitting at home, useless.

The sun catches on the stolen Magic in my ring, and an idea crosses my mind. I look at the gold swirls again, mentally measuring how much dust I'll need to get home versus what I have left. I think I have enough Magic for a few small bits of mischief... or Christmas Miracles as Santa likes to call them. In all fairness, I could use a mini-miracle right now. Maybe the Magic will do just that for me. Make some *magic* happen.

"I need a bathing suit," I whisper, twisting the ring. I close my eyes and picture my bikini, hoping the Magic brings mine to me or creates something similar. Maybe it'll put it on me. Maybe it'll put it on the bed. I don't really know. I just know I need a bathing suit and I need it now.

I close my eyes and focus on the wish, because that's all Christmas Magic is... wishes granted. Kids wishing for dolls, or toys, or video games. People wishing for Santa Claus to bring some joy and believing in the ability of their wishes to come true. I wish for my black bikini, and I believe that the Magic will bring it to me. I count to ten, even though Magic doesn't usually take that long. Warm tingles coil around me. They vibrate the air, like a music note resonating, and then just as quickly as the sensation started, it's gone.

I open my eyes to look at my reflection and frown. "This is not a bikini," I say to the Magic, even though it clearly can't hear me.

The ring has conjured a black puffer snowsuit, combat boots, gloves, and a wool-lined hat included. Cute, but completely impractical for the Florida Keys.

Thankfully, my red top and floral skirt survived the spell. I unzip and drop the extra layers to the floor, and shake my head at the glitter fading from the ring. "Well, that was a waste."

I grab my purse and decide to walk the six blocks into town.

I'm pretty sure I remember the route Mason took last night. Besides, if I get lost, I can just call and have him rescue me.

Walking down the street, I can't help but notice how Winter Key is a sleepy little town, but kind of charming. It has a small homey feel, like everyone's parents and grandparents might've grown up together. And there's a generational coziness that seeps into the moss hanging from the trees and the gravel roads. It's easy to feel comfortable here.

I follow the path, listening to birds chirp while the sun warms my skin. I'm not sure why the Christmas Magic chose to send me here, but so far I'm glad it did. I love feeling the sun on my skin, and I love how, even though the holiday is right around the corner, its residents aren't throwing Christmas in my face. Although as I make my way closer to downtown, I notice decorations have started popping up in store windows. Oh well. I guess that was bound to happen eventually.

I duck into *Mermaid Tales*, the boutique that caught my eye a few days ago, first. It's cute, filled with jewelry, dresses, and holiday knick-knacks, but no swimsuits. I step back outside and scan the stores. Based on their shop names, I don't think any of the stores will have what I'm looking for. *What am I gonna do?*

I chew on my bottom lip and figure that, since I'm already here, to pop into *Last Call*. If Candace is working, I can say hi. If she's not...well, no harm no foul. The smell of bacon and eggs hits me the second I open the door, and even though I wasn't hungry a few minutes ago, my stomach grumbles. The bar is quiet, and the contrast from last night to this morning is a little jarring.

"Sorry, we're done serving breakfast," Candace calls from the back. She appears a moment later, wiping her hands on a rag.

"That's okay. I'm not much of a breakfast eater," I say. "I was actually looking for a bathing suit, but the boutique didn't have any."

"Hey, you." Candace greets me with a grin and tosses the rag on the bar top. "Yeah, the locals usually drive into the bigger Keys or we order whatever we need online. The Boutique's more for tourists."

I arch my eyebrows, surprised that's who *Mermaid Tales* is catering to. "Tourists?"

"Well, our future tourists. Renting the villas and trying to attract outsiders is a fairly new notion. It was a town commission that was proposed about two years ago, but really only went into effect in the last month or so. We're hoping to garner some traction before lobster season next year."

"Oh." Lobster season. I'm not sure what that is, but I've seen pictures of lobsters. They're kind of scary. I nod, my mind running away from me, imagining giant red critters crawling out of the ocean like zombies in the night, attacking people.

I shudder as Candace says, "Yeah, there's not really much going on in Winter Key, but we're doing what we can to try to keep the jobs local and people from having to move out. We don't want to be bought up by a developer and turned into some copycat, generic, cookie-cutter resort."

"Developers would probably pay a lot for this land," I murmur, still semi haunted by the thought of zombie lobsters... *Maybe I've watched too many scary movies this week.*

"They definitely would," she says. "We've all had offers, but this is our home. There aren't many places like this left in the Keys, and we want to keep it the same as it's been for the last... I don't even know how many years. Two generations?"

"I'm sure they'd leave some of the houses and preserve the small town feel." But before I can even finish, Candace gives me a look that tells me she doubts it, which I don't understand. Winter Key's appeal is its untouched look. Why would a developer come in and change what's probably its biggest selling point? "You did say the town was struggling. Maybe some change will be what you guys need to get on your feet again."

"Maybe, but we're fighting it tooth and nail. Home doesn't feel like home when someone else comes in and redecorates." Candace huffs out a breath and crosses her arms. "Anyway, if you need a swimsuit, the Reef Club's your best bet. I can take you tomorrow, or you could call Mason. He'd happily help."

Something inside me flutters when she mentions his name. Something I need to rein in and take control of. I've had crushes. I even had a crush on Chris once, though I quickly realized that liking someone and being engaged to them are two different things. I looked at him and turned into a stupid, giddy girl. He looked at me and saw a stupid, giddy girl. Not a woman in the making. Not his future bride. Just another fan in the crowd that followed. Needless to say, my infatuation didn't last long.

"Isn't he working?"

Candace smirks and something in the way she looks at me makes that fluttery feeling kick into overdrive. It's like she knows I have a thing for her brother, but she can't know. Because I don't. I just like having someone to hang out with. Mason, so far, has been cool. That's all. We're friends. Nope, not even that. Room-mates. Just roommates. *Who am I trying to convince here?*

"Working's a stretch for what that man does. I send him on errands to keep him out of my hair. Trust me, he'd drop every-thing to help a pretty girl out. Specifically, you."

"I think you give your brother too much credit."

Candace laughs and walks behind the bar. "And I think you don't give him enough. He's curious about you."

"Why?"

"Do you want a water?" she asks. I nod and she grabs a glass to fill with ice. "You're new. You're pretty. You're kind of mysteri-ous. What man wouldn't want to know more?"

"Plenty, back home," I mutter.

"They're idiots." She hands me the glass and plops a straw into it. "Anyway, I've gotta get back to prepping for the lunchtime rush and the tree lighting tonight." She takes a step, then hesitates and stares at me for a beat. "You know, with your background, we could use your Christmas expertise. Our lighting ceremony is *okay,* but you might have some tips that could take us over the top. Like we could really get some eyes on us this year and get some traction."

I don't really want to help. I want to keep my distance from Christmas, but Candace has been nothing but kind. How can I say no? "What time do you need me?"

"Now would be great. We light the tree at seven, but people start showing up around five for the potluck. The sooner we have it done, the better." Her phone buzzes, and she glances at the screen with a smile. "Speak of the cheeky devil." She holds up her finger to me and answers the phone on speaker. "Mason, I was just talking about you. When are you going to the Reef Club next?"

"I'm good. I don't need his help," I whisper. "Promise."

"Fine," Candace groans. "Never mind. Just grab the lights and get back here. We needed to start an hour ago." She hangs up and shakes her head playfully. "That man, I swear..."

# Chapter Eight

## MASON

We've been using the same ten-foot Christmas tree for the last five years, and looking at it now... well, it's seen better days. The Florida sun has bleached its once-deep green into a dull grayish hue, and I swear more needles are on the ground than on the branches. I'm hoping the lights and decorations will hide the flaws, but honestly? I'm not optimistic.

I grab a strand of white lights and crouch at the base of the tree, tucking them between branches. Some spots end up clumped to try and fill the gaps, others sparse where the needles are thicker, but I figure it'll even out once everything's plugged in. If not... Well, it is what it is.

"You're doing it wrong," Tinsel says from behind me.

Her voice pulls a smile across my face before I even turn around. This girl... For someone who claims she wants time to herself, she's managed to cross paths with me every single day she's been here. Not that I mind. She pretends to be tough, to scowl and grumble her way through things, but I've seen glimpses of the softness underneath. She might deny it, but her heart is big, and when she lit up over the Christmas tattoos last night, I knew I wasn't imagining it.

"There's a wrong way to string lights on a Christmas tree?" I straighten, brushing plastic pine needles off my hands as I face her.

Tinsel is in red again, but not holiday red, though, as her skirt is patterned with flowers. Not exactly festive, but then again, I wouldn't expect candy-cane stripes and glitter from her.

"Of course there's a wrong way," she says matter-of-factly. "You have to start at the top."

"And why is that?" I challenge, folding my arms across my chest. I'm pushing her, trying to discover what makes her bloom, like when I told her she was beautiful. Her breath caught, and those emerald green eyes widened with surprise. But this, poking at her, makes her defensive, is the exact opposite of what I'm trying to do.

"Because then the lights cascade down the branches. Otherwise, you draw attention away from the topper. That's supposed to be the star of the show, literally. And if you've got too many lights clumped up top, it all gets lost." She lifts her chin a little, warming up to her lecture. "Also, your ornament-to-light ratio has to be balanced. Too many lights and the ornaments don't stand out. Too many ornaments and everything looks like a cluttered, chaotic mess. There's actually a mathematical equation to it."

"Sounds like you know what you're doing," I say, and the compliment has her fighting a smile. This is how I'll win Tinsel over. Not with big speeches or flashy moves, but with truth. With reminding her how remarkable she already is. Maybe then she'll let me stay close, let me keep being part of her world. God, I need her to. Because when she's near, the weight I carry doesn't press quite as hard. The air feels lighter and for the first time in a long time, so do I.

"Let's just say Christmas decorating was ingrained in me from birth," she replies. "May I help?"

"Sure." I hand her the tangled strand of white lights.

Tinsel walks around the tree, slowly surveying all that needs to be done, then says, "I'm going to need four chairs evenly placed around the tree so I can move in a circle. This tree is what... ten feet tall?"

"Eight, but you were close."

"Hmmm." She looks at the tangled mess of lights in the totes I pulled from *Last Call*'s attic and the three boxes of new strands I grabbed from the Walmart in Islamorada. "Do all of those work?"

"Maybe. I'm not sure. I figured I'd test them when I needed them."

She dumps the first tote over, creating a tumbleweed of green wire and tiny bulbs, and begins untangling the strands.

"Do you need help?" I crouch down and reach for a strand.

Tinsel pops my hand with a, "Nuh-uh. I've got this. Go find my chairs."

"Yes, ma'am." I give Tinsel a two-finger salute, which earns me an eye roll, but I see her peeking at me as I make my way to the sidewalk and don't even try to hide my smile as I walk down Main Street.

For once, no one's looking my way. Or maybe I just don't care if they are. My mind isn't circling the same dark questions—what they know, what they whisper. Right now, I'm just a guy, floating on cloud nine because of a pretty girl.

I haven't felt like this since I came back to Winter Key. Care-free. Unburdened. Almost... happy. Just a man enjoying the day for exactly what it is.

Halfway down the block, I slow to a stop in front of *Mermaid Tale's* window display. Their window is decked out with frosted garland, seashell ornaments strung like beads, and a driftwood tree wrapped in twinkle lights. It's whimsical, over the top, and exactly the kind of thing that should make tourists stop in their tracks.

I catch myself smiling at it, and the strangest thought hits me. Maybe I should ask Tinsel if she wants to decorate the house. God knows I haven't touched a box of lights since Dad died. The idea feels foreign, dangerous even, but as I stand there with Christmas

Magic glinting back at me through the glass, it doesn't seem quite so bad. Not if it's with her.

Shaking my head, I pull myself away and push into Heartwarming Realty. The overhead bell jingles as I step inside. "Hey, Brenda."

She looks up from the book she's reading and greets me with her usual warm smile. "Mason. What can I do for you?"

"Can I borrow some folding chairs? Tinsel's helping to decorate the tree for tonight." I hitch my thumb over my shoulder, so she understands I'm talking about *our* tree. Not just any 'ol tree at *Last Call* or somewhere else. "And she wants chairs instead of a ladder to walk on."

"Of course." Brenda's smile shifts into something sly, and I already know where this is going before she even asks the question. "How are things going with you two?"

"We keep to ourselves but cohabitate just fine. It's been nice having her around... Helps fill the silence."

Brenda nods like she understands, but I don't think she does. I haven't lived with anyone since Dad died because I don't want to, but there are days when I miss having someone to talk to. With Dad, it wasn't just about taking care of him, it was about not coming home to an empty house.

I've never been able to fill the void he left because roommates suck and the few girls I brought back after a date somehow got the idea in their heads that they could stay. They set expectations for a relationship when I was only looking for a hookup, and I felt like an ass when I had to break their hearts.

"She seems awfully sweet," Brenda drawls, her Florida accent thickening with amusement.

"She's lovely," I admit, trying to keep my tone neutral, but she sees right through me. The thought of being so transparent is terrifying. If it's this obvious that I like Tinsel, am I unintentionally projecting to everyone what I've done?

The thought guts me. Panic slices through, hot and violent. My chest seizes, my vision speckles with dark spots, and suddenly the air in the tiny real estate office feels thick and sour. Too hot. Too close. Too much.

I force myself to stand still, to keep my face blank, like nothing's wrong, like I'm not on the verge of unraveling. One wrong breath and I'll give it all away. So, I fight to keep it buried, even as every nerve in my body screams for escape.

"Maybe I'll get to know her better at the lighting ceremony tonight."

"Maybe," I echo, trying to be encouraging, but my voice comes out thin and brittle. Her brows pinch, and she studies me for a beat longer than usual. Not suspicious. Just... concerned. Like she can sense I'm off but can't name why.

I don't blame Brenda. Sometimes even I'm afraid to be alone with myself. If she ever saw through the walls, realized I'm not the wonderful Mr. Fix-It everyone thinks I am, she might run for the hills.

"Right. Well, you know where the chairs are," she says, her tone a little too brisk as she heads back toward her office. "I need to check on my crockpot. Those meatballs won't cook themselves."

I let out a quiet chuckle, though it feels hollow. Of course the crockpot will cook them without her. That's the point. But the way she rushed off... it gnaws at me. Did she notice something? Did I slip? God, what if it was written all over my face—how close I was to losing it? My chest tightens again, my mind racing through every worst-case scenario until the walls feel like they're closing in.

And then I spot Tinsel.

She's fussing with that tree like it's the most important thing in the world and the sight of her is like sunlight breaking through fog, chasing back the shadows for just a moment. My breathing evens and the panic loosens its grip. I feel steadier. Not fixed, but steadier.

As I carry the chairs back to her, I notice the tree again. Somehow it looks different now. The color is richer and the needles are fuller. It looks as if it's been brought back to life again just by being near her.

"The tree looks amazing," I say, staring at it in disbelief. "What did you do to it?"

"Nothing much. Just fluffed the branches. You didn't do it right the first time." Tinsel crouches at the bottom and gently shapes the lowest row.

"They were fluffed," I protest, still trying to figure out how she took this tree from on the brink of being tossed into the trash to full and vibrant. It's like the years of use and sun damage just vanished. Like somehow she brought out its best self the same way she brings out the better side of me, without even trying.

"Not properly." Tinsel smirks, brushing off her skirt as she stands. She sets her hands on her hips and appraises her hard work. The smallest smile tugs at her lips before it tilts into something sly as she glances my way. "You just don't have the magic touch like I do." Her gaze flicks to my waist. "I see you got what I asked for."

I rest the folding chairs on the ground to give my arms a quick break, anticipating that she's going to have a specific way she wants me to send these chairs up, considering there was a right and a wrong way to decorate the Christmas tree. "How do you want them?"

Tinsel shrugs and then reaches for the box of new lights. "Just circle the chairs around the tree so I can walk around it."

I lay all four chairs on the ground, then open first on the side of the tree nearest me. "Do you want me to help with the lights or anything?"

Tinsel tosses the box on the ground and steps on the first chair, as I open the second. She finds the end of the strand, then stands on her tiptoes and begins tucking the white lights between the branches. "Nope. Just give me space to do my thing."

"And what exactly is your thing?"

She pauses, fingers stilling on the strand of lights, and lifts her gaze to meet mine. A flicker of mischief, and something softer, lights her eyes as she says, "I make Christmas something worth looking forward to."

Her words settle in my chest heavier than I expect. Because she does.

Damn it, she really does.

## *Chapter Nine*

TINSEL

I may have used some Christmas Magic, but my defense in Winter Key's tree was horrible looking. *Horrible* doesn't even cover it. The branches were so bare it looked one strong gust away from becoming the Charlie Brown Christmas tree. Okay, maybe that's an exaggeration, but I couldn't let the town's centerpiece look like *that*.

And besides, it was just a little Magic. I still have enough to get home and some for a bit of emergency Mischief if I need it. I wasn't even sure the ring would listen to me or if the Magic would work after my bathing suit failure this morning, but I had to try. I'm so glad I did.

Seeing the awe on Mason's face when he laid eyes on what's basically a new tree made me feel so good. I get it now, why Santa and the elves do what they do all year long. It's for this feeling. The pride of knowing that I caused a spark of joy. In watching the Magic of Christmas ignite right before my eyes. It almost made the next two hours of sweating in ninety-degree heat while wrapping a tree in lights and perfectly placing nearly six dozen ornaments worth it.

Almost.

Once the tree was set and glowing, Mason and I went back to

his place to change for the evening, and this is where my mind seems to be stuck on replay. I can't focus on the lights or the music. Or even the people coming up to me to compliment the tree.

All I've done the last hour is watch Mason and think about how he looked shirtless, his hair still damp from his shower, when he opened his bedroom door. The sight of him half-naked was so jarring, my stomach flipped, and I almost forgot why I knocked on his door in the first place.

*"Can you help me? My zipper is stuck?"*

*I turn around to show him and he steps closer without a word, his hand brushing the small of my back as he finds the zipper of my shirt. His knuckles graze my skin as he effortlessly tugs the metal piece I've been struggling with. His breath is warm at the crown of my head, steady but heavier than it should be, and for one insane second, I think he might dip his head and kiss my shoulder.*

*I hold my breath, waiting. Hoping. But he steps back. The heat from his body disappears and a shiver rolls through me. When I turn to look at him, his gaze flicks to mine, unreadable, before he quietly says, "There you go."*

And then boom, the door closed.

Whatever moment we could have had was gone.

By the time I saw Mason again, he was dressed and ready, leaning against the kitchen counter, scrolling on his phone, like nothing had happened. He's still acting like nothing happened, smiling, laughing, and shamelessly flirting with everyone who stops to compliment him on how great the tree looks. It kills me, because I want him to come to *me* and flirt with *me* the same way he does with those other girls, even if it means nothing. But I've never chased a man. And I never will.

"Tinsel," a mom in her thirties says as she crosses the street to where I'm standing. "Mason says this tree is all you're doing. It's beautiful."

I smile, feeling that swell of pride again because the wonder in her daughter's eyes is everything. The girl, who can't be more than six, sucks on a candy cane and just stares up at the tree, like it stretches on forever. Like it holds the key to all her Christmas wishes. The wonder in her expression is addicting. If I could, I'd give everyone in Winter Key this feeling.

"It really was no trouble."

"Well, it's gorgeous," the mom says, touching my arm. "Did you try the lobster mac and cheese yet?"

I blink, pulled from my thoughts again, momentarily re-trau-matized by my earlier day-nightmare of Zombie lobsters. I put on my best pageant smile so as not to offend her and say, "No, not yet."

"It's a family specialty. I can't wait to hear what you think of it." She taps my arm with a smile that lingers a beat too long before heading off. "See you around, Tinsel."

"Bye, Merrilee," Mason says with a wave as he comes to stand at my side.

I'd like to say I didn't see him coming, but that's a lie. I haven't stopped watching Mason since we awkwardly arrived at the tree lighting together. He parked, opened my door, and helped me out, but then he scampered off. First to Candace's drink booth and then to pretty much every booth and table since. I'm not sure if he was avoiding me or just being a social butterfly, but now that I've caught his attention, I don't plan to let him go.

I loop my arm through his and slowly walk down the street, absentmindedly pretending to look at all the window displays now that he's with me. "Is Christmas always like this?"

"Kind of. Small towns look for any excuse to throw a party. It's why we have ten of them before Christmas, but everyone's right about one thing. The tree this year is next level. You did one hell of a job, Tinsel. I know people keep saying it, but I don't think our tree looked that good when we first bought it."

"What can I say? Christmas is my gift." I drop his arm and pretend to look at a storefront that caught my eye. It takes me a minute to realize we're standing in front of *Hopkin's Pharmacy*. They turned their big window into a giant gingerbread house, complete with frosted cardboard walls and a miniature lollipop garden at its base. The whole scene looks like a mash-up of Candyland and a snowy Christmas village, whimsical and over the top in the best way.

The band—four guys in their fifties who, if I had to guess, are just local dads moonlighting as rock stars—strikes up a lively version of *Jingle Bell Rock*. The music spills across the square, a little offbeat in places but infectious all the same. Kids dart between the crowd with candy canes, couples sway with steaming cups of cider in hand, and the whole town seems to hum with holiday cheer.

Mason turns toward me, hand extended, that infectiously addicting smile tugging at his mouth. "Dance with me?"

"Oh, no." I shake my head quickly. "I don't dance. Thanks, though."

"Come on." Mason wiggles his fingers in invitation. "A dance with me is kind of a big deal."

*I bet it is. I bet all the single girls can't wait for him to give them a speck of his time.* I clench my teeth and look away. I hate that I'm jealous. That I like Mason enough to be jealous. But most of all, I hate that he likes me too, and I can't do anything about us. "So, offer your hand to one of the other girls."

"I don't want to dance with them. I want to dance with you."

Damn him. Damn this need pooling between my legs. And double damn the way Mason's gaze darkens when he looks at me. I'm going to fall apart like an under-mixed cookie if he keeps looking at me like that. "Can we file this request under the *leave me alone/personal space* section of the unofficial contract we agreed on when I moved in?"

Mason tilts his head as he pretends to consider my request. "We could. But since you spent most of the day with me and my sister, I'd say that clause is moot. Which, let's be honest, we're both terrible at abiding by it anyway."

A laugh slips out of me before I can stop it. He's right. I can pretend that I want my space, and maybe sometimes I do, but when it comes down to it, I get lonely after a few hours and a little bored. And I like spending time with Mason. "We are, aren't we?"

"Come on, Tinsel." His voice drops to barely a whisper. "Don't break my heart."

The way he says it cuts through me like a blade, sharp and unexpected. I should keep my distance. I know I should. But instead, the word slips out before I can catch it. "Fine."

I place my hand in his and Mason spins me once, right where we are. A laugh that sounds more like a squeal escapes me, and he pulls me to his chest. He holds me there, one hand on my lower back, the other holding my hand to his chest, as we take swooping steps. In seconds, we're in the street, woven between families, dancing. His hands settle firmly on my hips in a PG-family friendly way as he sways us to the beat, but nothing about the way his body pressed against mine feels friendly.

Mason holds me close for the duration of a verse, then spins me again. He guides me into a series of simple steps I've never done before, but with him leading the way I keep up. The music eventually swells toward its end and Mason dips me low just as the last note fades.

But he doesn't pull me up.

Instead, his gaze catches mine and holds his face so close I can make out the flecks of gold in his eyes. My pulse thunders in my throat, the world narrowing to the warmth of his hand and the weight of his stare. His eyes drop to my mouth, and suddenly I can't breathe. Can't think. All I can do is ache with the question of what *would it feel like to finally kiss him?*

The thought burns, hot and reckless... right up until the sharp jingle of bells splits the night, shattering the moment like glass.

"Ho, ho, ho!" a booming voice calls.

*They found me.* Fear cuts through any warm feeling I may have had, drenching me in a blanket of cold sweat. I jerk upright so fast I lose my balance. If Mason hadn't been holding me, I'd be on the ground, crawling away.

"Hey. Are you okay?" he asks as I duck behind him, trying to find the source of the *ho, ho, ho* while simultaneously hiding from the man who bellowed it.

"Yup." I place my hands on his shoulders, trying to make him stand still so I can peek over them. "Who...uh...who do you have playing Santa?"

"I'm not sure. You'd have to ask Dora. Why?"

The bells grow louder as a horse-drawn carriage rounds the corner of Main. A path clears and kids excitedly wave to Santa as he makes his way to the tree. The man in the red suit does his job well, waving cheerfully and bellowing *ho, ho, ho* every few minutes. Despite the big belly, white hair, and rosy cheeks, our Magic suit cloaks its wearer with, I recognize the elf in disguise. It's Cable, my pseudo-finance's best friend. And the second his eyes land on me, lingering just a moment too long, I know he recognizes me too.

"I have to go," I blurt, panic clawing up my throat. *They've found me. I have to go.*

Mason turns to face me, but I can't see him. Everything around Cable blurs into a mess of color. I barely even hear Mason say, "What? We haven't even lit the tree yet."

"I know, I'm sorry. I just...I can't stay."

"Do you want me to give you a ride home?"

I shake my head, already backing away. I should have left the second I heard the first *ho, ho, ho,* but I half hoped Winter Key's Santa was someone's grandpa in costume. I didn't know they'd splurge for one of ours. If I had, I never would have come to the tree lighting. "No. Don't let me ruin this for you. Really. Stay. I'll see you at home."

And then I turn and run down the street, past the lights and music, into the darkness and as far from my family as I can get.

## Chapter Ten

MASON

I stand there, half in shock, trying to figure out how we went from nearly kissing to Tinsel literally running away from me.

The jingle of Santa's sleigh bells fades and I know he's reached the front of the tree. Any second, he'll dismount, deliver the Christmas speech, and cue the countdown—the same way it's been done for the past five years. Normally, I'd stand shoulder to shoulder with the rest of Winter Key, grinning through the motions and breathing in the holiday cheer. But this year... I can't. Not with her gone. Not with that look still haunting me.

Because when those bells rang, something shifted in Tinsel's eyes. She was afraid, like she'd seen a ghost and before I could move, she was gone. One heartbeat, she was there, the next, she was nothing but a blur disappearing down the street.

I kick off my flip-flops and take off after her, not even thinking about where they'll end up. Someone will toss them into Candace's lost and found at *Last Call*, right alongside the town's forgotten odds and ends. Sunglasses. Jackets. Water bottles. And now, apparently, my shoes.

"Tinsel!" I shout, but the street is too loud. Though, even if she heard me, I doubt she'd stop. She's fast. Too fast, and it takes everything I have to catch up to her near the stop sign at the end of the block. I grab her wrist, and for a split second, pure terror flickers across her face again.

"Let me go!" she yells, her voice cracking with panic..

I drop my hand immediately and lift both palms in surrender. "Hey, it's me," I say, softer now, easing closer as I touch her elbow. "Just me."

Tinsel shakes free of my touch and recoils into herself. "What are you doing, Mason? Go back to the tree lighting."

"No." I plant my feet, refusing to let her shut me out. "What's wrong?"

"Nothing's wrong. I just—" She exhales sharply, her chest rising and falling too fast. Her eyes dart around like a trapped animal searching for an exit, her fingers twitching at her sides as though she's already halfway to running. "I can't be there. I shouldn't even be here."

A spark of panic flares in my gut at the realization she might bolt. Might leave before I've even had the chance to figure her out. It's crazy, but I like having Tinsel around. I like the way the hollow parts of me don't feel so empty when she's near. I can't explain it. It doesn't make sense. But then again, nothing about girls ever has.

Still, the fear in her eyes isn't about me. It's about whatever she's running from. And for the first time, I'm scared she'll disappear before I can get to the bottom of it.

"I have to ask you something," I say, my voice low and careful. "And I know it's going to sound insane, but I need you to tell me the truth."

Her eyes snap back to mine, wild and defensive. "What?"

"Were you in a cult?"

"What?" She lets out a startled laugh that sounds more like a choke than amusement.

"I'm serious. Was that Santa one of the cult members? Is that why you're running? Are you afraid he's going to drag you back to wherever you're from?"

Tinsel's lips part like she wants to yell, but instead she exhales hard and tips her head back toward the sky. Her hands twist together, then release, then twist again. Her whole body telegraphs flight—shoulders tight, eyes darting like she's measuring the distance to the nearest escape. "No. It's not that. I just..." Her frustration ripples across her face, but the words won't come.

I take a cautious step closer, lowering my voice. "Hey. It's okay. You don't have to explain. Whatever you're running from... you're safe here. I'm not going to let anything happen to you."

"I don't need you to save me," she fires back, chin lifting, arms crossing like a shield.

"Maybe not," I admit quietly. "But that's who I am. I look out for people I care about."

"And why, exactly, do I fall into that category? We just met. You don't know me."

"True." I shove my hands deep into my pockets to keep from reaching for her, grounding myself. "But I want to know you."

She narrows her gaze, still skeptical. "Why?"

"For starters?" I take a breath, searching for the words. "I don't usually feel comfortable around people. Not anymore. But with you..." I trail off, shaking my head a little. "With you, it's easy. I don't have to force it."

Her expression softens, just barely, so I keep going.

"It's the little things like the way you wrinkle your nose when you think something's ridiculous, or how you talk about hating Christmas, but still manage to make the world feel a little brighter anyway. When you're around, the weight I've been carrying is still there, but it doesn't feel so heavy."

A quiet laugh escapes me because this is embarrassing. "That's all I meant. You make things easier, Tinsel. Lighter. And for me, that's... not normal. But it's nice."

She stares at me, and I take a shaky breath, pushing past the lump in my throat.

"My dad died earlier this year," I hear myself say before I've even decided to. "He was sick for years, and then... suddenly, he was gone. I should have had his legacy to keep me going, but I was too focused on trying to make him better and ran his bait shop into the ground. I've drained my savings trying to stay afloat, but somehow I still ended up with a foreclosure notice. On top of it all, I backed myself into a corner that's going to make everyone hate me, and most days I'm just waiting for the shoe to drop and for what's left of my paper house to come crumbling down."

I swallow, my throat dry, but the words keep coming. "But when I'm with you..." I shrug helplessly, palms open like I can't stop the spill. "I don't care about it all. I almost feel like myself again, and selfishly, I'd do anything you need if it means spending one more day with you."

Silence falls between us, heavy and charged. My pulse hammers. *God, did I say too much? Too soon?*

I let out a short, nervous laugh. "This is the point where you tell me I've overstepped. That we just met and I'm crazy for unloading my life on you. You wanted a vacation, not me or my baggage. So, say the word and I'll back off and let you enjoy the rest of your time without me hanging around."

I hesitate, heart in my throat, the leash on my thoughts fraying. "Or we can..." I trail off, realizing how reckless my own mind is. *Or we can live in a bubble of happily-ever-after for a week. We can get to know each other emotionally. Or physically. Maybe even both.* I rein it all back and settle for, "Or we can go back home, put on a scary movie, and see what happens over the next few days."

"See what happens?" She echoes. "What do you want to happen?"

A dozen answers burn on my tongue. *I want to pull you in, kiss you until I forget how to breathe, lose myself in your laugh, your touch, your skin.* But I've already opened the door and revealed too much. If Candace knew what I've just done, she'd smack me over the head and call me an idiot. Girls don't want emotionally unstable men who are borderline clingy. They want independent assholes who treat them like shit because there's a stigma that fuckboys sling the best dick. Who knows. Maybe it's true. But this is me. I'm a mess.

I'm letting Tinsel see how much of a mess I am.

Now it's up to her to decide what happens next.

I let out a sigh, fully prepared for this to be where we end. But I keep my gaze on hers, steady, even as my heart pounds. "I just want to get to know you."

Tinsel's lips twitch, like she's holding back a smile. She studies me for a long, quiet moment, then finally asks, "What movie did you have in mind?"

## Chapter Eleven

TINSEL

I'm staring at my clothes, trying to figure out why I hate everything that I packed, when there's a knock on the door. I open it, not even thinking about the fact that I'm not wearing a bra under my red silk pajamas, until Mason's gaze dips to my chest. His eyes linger for less than a heartbeat, but it's enough to make my heart skip. I cross my arms, acutely aware of my hardened nipples and the way his eyes darken before he clears his throat. That low, rough sound sends a shiver straight through me.

"Morning," he says, voice gravelly with sleep. He shifts, rubbing a hand against the back of his neck like he's trying to play it cool. "Candace said something about you wanting to go to the Reef Club?"

"Oh, yeah. I need a bathing suit. She said that was probably the best place."

"She's right." He leans against the doorframe. "But it's probably gonna be more expensive than the tourist shops down US-One."

"How much more expensive?"

"Depends on what you pick out," he admits, the corner of his mouth tugging into a grin. "But I've got a buddy who lets me use his employee discount."

"You don't mind?" I ask, watching that grin stretch a little wider. And suddenly I'm not thinking about the Reef Club at all. I'm thinking about last night. His voice. His confession. *I just want to get to know you.*

No one has ever said anything like that to me. Not without an angle or expectation attached. Mason's words were simple, honest. Not manipulative or performative. Just real. And somehow that made them the sweetest thing I'd ever heard.

My experience with boys is minimal, at best. Chris had a habit of chasing them off, even when he didn't actually want me. It wasn't protection, it was possession. He said he was looking out for me, that the guys only wanted to see what was under Mrs. Claus's skirt. Maybe he was right. Maybe they did. But that didn't give Chris the right to decide for me.

Unfortunately, the few who slipped through his radar didn't last. They ghosted me after getting what they wanted, just like Chris said they would. So I learned not to expect much, and what little I did give away was always transactional—something temporary, something that could never lead anywhere.

Which makes the idea of Mason dangerous.

He's handsome and kind. Steady in a way that makes me ache. It wouldn't be impossible to turn this into a harmless holiday fling. I could set the rules: no promises, no future, no strings. Just pleasure and laughter and maybe, if I'm lucky, a few stolen breaths that remind me what it's like to *feel* again.

He chuckles lightly. "Tinsel?"

"Huh?" The deep rumble of his voice has me swallowing a knot in my throat.

Mason reaches out and trails his fingers down my arm, just barely touching me, but it's enough to make me break out in goosebumps. "Do you want to go with me?

"Where?"

"To the reef club. I need to grab Candace's Christmas present."

Right. This conversation started because I needed a bathing suit. Not because I was daydreaming about orgasms with a very handsome, very off-limits man. "Oh, sure."

"Can you be ready in an hour?"

My chest squeezes, and I hear myself whisper, "Yeah."

Mason's grin turns boyish, bright, and infuriatingly attractive. "Cool. See you soon."

He taps the doorframe before walking away, and I'm left leaning against it, wondering how the hell he makes breathing feel like work.

Mason's truck rumbles down the highway, the windows rolled low and salt air rushing in. The warmth on my skin is a novelty, and I let my hand hang out the window, fingers slicing through the wind.

"This is nice," I say, glancing at him.

He grins, still watching the road. "Glad you think so."

Conversation flows easier than I expect. It's light and unforced. The kind that happens when the silence between two people feels comfortable instead of awkward. Mason asks about snowmobiles, and I laugh, telling him he's never truly suffered until he's tried hauling groceries through six feet of snow with frozen lashes and numb toes.

"Hard pass," he says, glancing at me, the corner of his mouth tilting up.

Before I can come up with a comeback, a familiar song filters through the static of the radio, something upbeat and old enough to make me hum under my breath without thinking.

Mason's grin widens. "You sing when you're distracted."

"I do not."

"You do, but you have a nice voice."

Heat rushes to my cheeks, and I look out the window, pretending to watch the palms blur past. A low chuckle resonates between us, soft and unguarded, and for a second, the truck feels smaller. Mason's hand shifts, turning just slightly and I take a chance. I slip my fingers between his and allow myself to pretend this thing building between us stands a chance.

Mason taps the volume button on his steering wheel, and a familiar eighties ballad fills the cab. Without hesitation, he starts belting it out, voice low and a little rough around the edges.

"Wow," I tease, glancing over at him. "You're really committing."

He grins between verses. "Go big or go home."

I roll my eyes, but find myself singing along when the chorus hits. The two of us are off-key and laughing through half the lyrics, but it's fun. Easy. By the time the song fades into another station, my cheeks ache from smiling, and the sound of our laughter lingers even after we fall quiet.

The drive isn't awkward like I feared. It's comfortable. Too comfortable, maybe. And when Mason turns the volume down and lets go of my hand as we roll up to the Reef Club's guard gate, a small, stupid part of me misses the contact.

"Mase!" the guard calls, stepping out of the booth with a wide grin. "Long time no see, brother."

"Jeff," Mason says, matching the grin as he reaches out to shake the man's hand. "How've you been?"

"Oh, you know. Same thing, different day." Jeff wipes his palms on his shorts, then adds with a grimace, "I'm sorry to hear about your dad. I would've come to the funeral, but—"

"We didn't have one," Mason cuts in quickly. His tone is gentle but final, the smile on his face dimming. "So don't sweat it."

Jeff nods once, awkward now, the easy warmth between them fading into something heavier. "Yeah. Well... he was a good man."

Mason nods too, his jaw working like he's holding something back. "Yeah. He was."

For a moment, the only sound is the low hum of the truck's engine. I glance at Mason's hand gripping the wheel—his knuckles white, tendons tight—and something twists in my chest. I want to reach for him, but don't. Not yet.

"I need to grab a few things from the gift shop," Mason says, his voice softer now.

Jeff clears his throat, shifting back toward the booth. "Go on back. You know where it is."

He presses a button, and the gated arm swings up with a metallic creak.

"Thanks, Jeff." Mason lifts a hand in a casual wave and drives forward.

As we roll past, I can feel the air between us thicken again. Mason doesn't say anything, his eyes are fixed on the road ahead, but the muscle in his jaw still ticks. I want to tell him he doesn't have to hide it—that grief doesn't scare me, but instead, I just sit quietly, the words caught somewhere between my heart and my throat.

My phone rings, sharp and unexpected, and I jolt like I've been caught doing something wrong. I'd completely forgotten it was even in my purse.

Without thinking, I slide the bag under my leg, pinning it there like I can smother both the sound and the reason it's calling. The vibration buzzes once against the seat, then stops.

Mason cuts me a quick glance from the corner of his eye. "You gonna get that?"

"Nope," I say too fast, gripping the seatbelt's strap like it's suddenly the most interesting thing in the world. "Probably spam."

He raises an eyebrow but doesn't call me out. "Suit yourself."

We park at the far end of the employee parking lot and walk side by side to the first building. Mason doesn't reach for my hand, but he does open the door for me. I smile and mutter a *thanks,* but my words barely register. Mason is deep in his thoughts, pulled down by the grief Jeff uncovered, and I don't know how to help.

I decide space is the best thing for him right now and turn my attention to the Reef Club, which is ridiculously huge. We cross through four buildings, passing by towering condos, a manicured beach lined with private cabanas. It's the kind of place people like me only ever see on postcards. Each door whooshes open, blasting us with cold air, offering a slight reprieve from the hot Florida sun. Unlike Winter Key, we aren't sheltered by overgrown oaks. The sun shines down on us, unfiltered, and it's almost too much to bear.

By the time we reach the gift shop, a steady line of sweat has dripped from the back of my neck, down my shirt. I'm sticky and clammy and half tempted to throw myself on the shiny tiles to cool myself off faster. I don't, mostly because I'm in awe at everything inside.

The gift shop is massive. Bright lights, gleaming shelves, racks of clothes that cost more than my monthly rent, and enough over-priced trinkets to make a magpie cry. It's the kind of place that screams *vacation money,* and I can't help feeling a little out of place... but also a little enchanted.

"Bathing suits are over there." Mason points me toward the women's section, barely stopping before crossing the store and leaving me alone.

"Thanks," I say, but he doesn't hear me. He heads straight for the bathroom, and the door swings shut behind him with a dull thud that seems louder than it should.

I linger where I am, pretending to study a rack of sun hats, but my eyes keep flicking toward the closed door. The heaviness in my chest catches me off guard. I shouldn't care this much. I barely know him.

But I do.

Mason looked wrecked when Jeff mentioned his dad, like he'd taken a hit straight to the ribs but was too proud to show it. Now, standing here under bright fluorescent lights and fake beach music, I can't shake the worry gnawing at me.

After a few minutes, I realize he's not coming out for a while. I shift my weight, tell myself to move, to shop, to breathe, but my feet won't cooperate.

It's ridiculous. I'm not used to this...the urge to check on someone, to make sure they're okay. It's not something I've ever had to learn.

And yet here I am, staring at a bathroom door, hoping a guy I've only known for four days isn't falling apart on the other side of it.

Eventually, I make my way to the bathing suits. I flip through a rack, nearly choking when I see the cost of a bikini. Three hundred dollars, and the one piece beside it is almost five. I think about the cash I have in my purse. I've only spent about fifty dollars the last few days, but blowing half my budget this afternoon feels reckless. Especially when I can lie on the dock in shorts and a shirt. It might not be a bathing suit, but I'll feel the sun all the same.

"That one's nice," Mason says from behind me.

I startle, nearly sending a hanger flying, and whip around to glare at him. "You can't sneak up on people like that."

He smirks, not remotely sorry. "You're just jumpy. But seriously..." He reaches for the solid green one-piece wedged between a yellow polka-dot two-piece and a black bathing suit that is more strings than fabric. "This would look good on you."

"It would also require me to sell a kidney," I deadpan.

"Well, we can't have you auctioning off pieces of yourself now, can we?" he says, voice light and teasing. He holds the suit up like he's seriously considering it, and for a moment, it's hard to believe this is the same man who looked gutted minutes ago.

Mason's smiling again. Easy. Effortless. Like he can just tuck his grief back into his pocket whenever he wants. And maybe that's how he copes. I want to ask, to press, but something tells me he doesn't need questions right now. He just needs someone who doesn't make him talk about the pain. "Let me buy it."

My mouth drops open. "No. Absolutely not."

"Consider it a Christmas present," he says, unfazed, already flipping through more suits. "How about this one? Or this? You could grab more than one if you want."

Mason is impossible. And the worst part? I actually like the suits he's picked. He's got good taste, probably infuriatingly good. My pulse kicks up as I look at the handful he's holding, then before I can stop myself, the words tumble out:

"Well... if you're going to buy it, maybe you should see what it looks like on."

For a split second, surprise flickers across his face, then that slow, wicked grin takes over, stretching wide and smug and sinfully handsome.

"If you insist," he says, voice dropping just enough to make my stomach flutter.

My pulse hammers as I grab three suits—a safe green one-piece, a sleek black two-piece, and the scandalous red string bikini—and head to the dressing rooms. Inside, the small fitting room smells faintly of sunscreen and coconut lotion. I drop the suits on the bench and brace my hands on the wall. *What am I doing?*

Why do I care what he thinks? Why do I want his reaction so badly?

But I do. God help me, I do.

I pull on the green one-piece first, the fabric smooth and cool against my skin. It hugs my curves and cinches in just right, making my ass look better than I expect. I stare at my reflection for a beat, cheeks flushed, heart racing like I've just done something forbidden. Then, before I can overthink it, I take a steadying breath and push open the door.

Mason's sprawled in a chair across from the dressing rooms, phone in hand, ankle propped on his knee like he owns the place. He glances up and freezes.

His gaze drags from head to toe, slow and deliberate, and for a long, suspended second, he forgets to blink.

"Wow." His eyes rake over me before he shakes his head, like words fail him. "Tinsel, you look..." His mouth shuts, but I don't need him to finish. His expression says it all.

"It's just a swimsuit," I mumble, suddenly unsure where to put my hands.

"Not on you," he mutters, still shaking his head, his tone somewhere between disbelief and appreciation.

Something tight coils in my stomach, hot and alive. It's the kind of tension that demands to be acknowledged, and I can't tell if it terrifies or thrills me more.

Before I can come up with a response that doesn't sound like a squeak, Mason's phone buzzes, slicing through the moment. He frowns, answers, and his tone shifts instantly.

"Yeah?" A pause. His jaw tightens, eyes narrowing in concentration. "Shit. Okay, I'll be right there."

He ends the call with a sigh and pushes to his feet, all business now. "AC went out in Villa Three. Brenda's freaking out."

"Oh." The bubble around us pops, and reality rushes back in like cold air through a crack in the door.

"I can drop you at *Last Call* on my way," he offers, already pocketing his phone. "Candace should be upstairs if you need anything."

"Upstairs?" I blink.

"Yeah. She lives in a two-bedroom apartment above the bar." His grin returns, softer this time. "It's why she's always there. She cooks downstairs so she doesn't smoke herself out when she burns something."

That makes me smile despite myself. "For some reason, I can see that."

Mason's gaze lingers a little longer before he clears his throat. "You sure you don't want any of the other ones?"

I glance at the suits hanging in the fitting room behind me. "There was one more I wanted to try on."

Mason's mouth curves into that crooked, dangerous grin that does strange things to my stomach. "If it's anything like this one..." He pauses, eyes dragging over me once more before flicking up to meet mine. "Tell you what. Why don't you show me what it looks like at the house, when I've got more time to appreciate the view?"

The air between us thickens, every word hanging heavy with implication. There's an opening there. A line I could step across if I wanted to. And I do. *Reindeer*, I do.

But before I can say anything, Mason's phone buzzes. He glances at the screen, curses under his breath, the spell breaking in an instant. "Guess our time's up."

I nod, trying not to show how disappointed I am or how my pulse still hasn't slowed from the way he looked at me. "Guess so."

# Chapter Twelve

## TINSEL

I am a lobster.

I am a char-boiled, twice-overcooked, burnt lobster. My skin hurts so bad, even the cool AC blowing on it stings. I attempted to take a shower when I first came in, but even the cold water hurt.

I should have known better than to spend all afternoon in the sun. But Mason took off fishing first thing this morning and I really wanted to test out my new bikini. My pasty skin needed some sexy tan lines, but I was going for a light sun-kissed look. Not achy, red, and crispy.

Now I'm lying face-down on the couch, groaning into a cushion, phone in hand, while I *Google* remedies for sunburns. Nothing's holding my attention—not the whir of the AC, not even the dull TV chatter—until I hear the front door creak open and Mason's voice boom across the space.

"Tinsel?"

"In here," I mumble, dropping my face back into the couch. My phone slips from my hand and hits the floor with a dull thud. I don't even care enough to look for it because that would require moving. And I want to melt into nothingness until my body stops hurting.

Mason's flip flops smack against the tile floors with each step he takes. I count fifteen before there's silence, and then, "You look miserable. What happened?"

I lift my head just enough to wince at him. "I might have fallen asleep while sunbathing on the dock."

"Might have?" Mason's voice arches in disbelief.

"Fine," I groan, dropping my forehead back onto the cushion. "I fell asleep for an hour and now everything hurts."

He huffs out a laugh, crouching beside me. I turn my head and am met with blue eyes that are filled with equal parts amusement and concern. "Ibuprofen and aloe are about to be your best friends, Snowflake, but you can't take the meds on an empty stomach. Are you hungry?"

"Not particularly," I admit, closing my eyes and resting my cheek on the cushion, "but I'll eat if it means feeling better."

His brow furrows and he shakes his head. "You're never hungry."

"Food is an afterthought where I come from." After chores. After work. Just... after. "There are sweets galore, but I can only eat so much sugar before it makes me feel sick. So, I learned to ignore my stomach when it rumbled, and now I don't eat that much."

"Oh, Tinsel." Mason runs a hand through my hair, pushing the strands away from my face. "You're lucky you're not staying in Winter Key permanently, or we'd be fattening you up."

Panic flares in my chest, and I open my eyes to see his reaction when I ask, "Are you saying you don't like the way I look?"

"No," Mason says, looking me dead in the eyes, and despite the flare of insecurity I felt, I believe him. "I'm saying Candace's love language is food. She loves feeding me. And given how quickly she's taken to you, I have no doubt she'd love to feed you, too, if you were staying. Which reminds me..."

Before I can respond, Mason's on his feet and in the kitchen. I drop my head back onto the cushion and close my eyes, listening to him rummage through paper bags. Cabinets bang, bags crinkle, and the pop of plastic containers fills the silence.

A moment later, Mason's back at my side. I open my eyes as he sets two plates of food on the coffee table. There are tortillas, limes, and small white chunks of something that look slightly burnt.

"Come on, Snowflake." He takes my hands and gently eases me upright.

I grimace and try not to groan, but the pain shoots through me anyway. I don't understand why the sun is so vicious down here compared to back home. An hour in the snow wouldn't do anything besides give me frostbite. Here, it wages war on the body and takes no prisoners.

"Easy does it."

When I'm upright and settled, Mason hands me the first plate. I poke at the white chunks with my fork, trying to decide if they're supposed to look like this or if the plate is filled with one of Candace's cooking mishaps Mason mentioned. "What is this?"

"Fish tacos," he says flatly before taking a bite of his own, stuffed tortilla.

"Fish tacos?" I echo, suspicion dripping from every syllable.

Mason looks at me for a beat, curiosity pushing a wrinkle between his thick eyebrows. "Snowflake, don't tell me you've never had fish tacos."

"I've had tacos. Are they the same?"

"Oh, god, no. They're not." A moment later, Mason's up again, disappearing into the kitchen. I watch him this time, my gaze trailing him as he grabs a bottle of wine, two glasses, and a squeeze container of spicy mayo from the fridge.

He brings it all back to the coffee table. He twists the cap off, pours a glass of red, sets it in front of me, and then carefully prepares one of the tacos, adding a drizzle of mayo on top. But instead of handing it to me, he holds it up. "Open up."

I stare at him, hesitating. Am I the type of woman who wants a man to feed her? It's never been an option before, and the feminist inside me roars that I can eat a taco all by myself, but there's a hungry look in Mason's eyes, something raw and unspoken, and I want to know what happens if I obey.

Slowly, I part my lips and take a bite.

Surprisingly, the taco is really good, but the way Mason's pupils darken and the slight upturn of his lips is even more delicious than the food. He swipes a thumb beneath my bottom lip, wiping away a smear of sauce. His touch lingers. His voice drops low. "I knew you'd be a good girl and like it."

The phrase sinks into my skin like heat. *Good girl.* It shouldn't make me shiver, but it does. Every instinct screams to argue, to remind him I don't belong to anyone. But the truth is, I like the way those words feel settling over me, heavy and possessive.

Defiance aside, Mason's praise stirs something I don't want to name. So, I take another bite, testing him, silently daring him to say it again. He doesn't. Instead, he presses the taco into my hand, a flicker of conflict shadowing his eyes, and distracts himself by reaching for the TV remote.

"How's your movie?" he asks, looking at me for permission to pause the screen.

"Boring," I admit. "I thought I'd switch it up. I tried a psychological thriller earlier and hated it. I wanted something lighter when I came in. Something to watch while drifting in and out of a nap, but this didn't cut it."

Mason stops the movie and takes us back to the home screen. "Are you open to a TV series? Or are you trying to stick to movies?"

"I'm not opposed to a series. What do you have in mind?"

He clicks on one of his streaming apps and settles on a show called *Dexter.* The still-shot looks positively delightful. A man with a sinister grin and a blood-covered glove is more up my alley than meta-humans fighting each other. "He's a serial killer who only kills serial killers."

"That's an interesting concept."

"There are eight seasons, I think, plus two spinoffs. So, if you like it, that could keep you busy for the rest of your stay. Maybe even beyond."

"We're not allowed to watch shows like this where I'm from," I admit, and Mason's eyes widen. "I don't even have a TV back home, so hopefully I can get through it."

There's a long pause where Mason just stares at me, and I wish I could read his mind to know what he's thinking. I take a bite of my taco, humming a moan of approval, hoping it'll draw Mason from wherever his mind is, but it doesn't. After a long, awkward pause, I ask, "Should we start the show?"

"Yeah. Sorry."

Mason presses play and we sit in silence for two episodes. The first flows into the next and I really like it, more than the horror movies I watched earlier in the week. The show is dark, and gritty, and I like that he's not killing for sport. There's a purpose for every life he takes. He's the perfect anti-hero.

When the opening credits start for episode three, I lean forward to grab my glass of wine, and a slice of hot pain shoots through my back. I must make a sound because Mason asks, "What's wrong?"

"Nothing. It's just my sunburn."

Mason looks at his watch, a frown tugging at his beautiful lips, and says, "I think enough time has passed. Hang tight." He takes our empty plates to the kitchen and comes back with a glass of water and two small pills in his hand. "Here."

"Thanks." I take them without question and swallow them quickly, secretly waiting, hoping Mason will say those words again. *Good girl.* But he doesn't. And the disappointment I feel is ridiculous. I don't need his praise. I shouldn't want it. But I do.

Sometime during the third episode, the pills kick in. The pain is tolerable, but still there, and I remember Mason mentioned something else that might help. "You said something about aloe earlier. Do you have any?"

"Oh, right. I have some in my bathroom." Mason leaves me

for a moment, then comes back with a neon blue bottle. He stands above me for an awkward second, just staring.

"What?"

"It's just... it might be better if you take your shirt off." He rubs the back of his neck, and the storm brewing in his eyes is addictive. He's wrestling with wanting me, which is great because I've been fighting with the same internal struggle. "That way I can rub it on your back."

Mason and I shouldn't happen. He's my landlord. I'm his tenant. He lives in Winter Key. I'm leaving in less than a week to go back to the North Pole. He's human. I'm an elf. And still, knowing all of this, I can't stop wondering what it would be like to kiss him.

"My legs are also pretty burnt. Would it help if I took my shorts, too?"

Mason's throat works as he swallows hard. "That... might be helpful."

I tilt my head, letting the tension stretch. "Should I lie down here? On the floor? Or would a bed be better?"

Something cracks in Mason's expression. His jaw tightens. "I want you in my bed," he blurts, and I see the instant regret as the words tumble out.

Heat shoots through me, stronger than the sunburn, because he's doing exactly what I want. Taking the opening I created. Now, I'm dying to know what he's going to do with it. "Well, then. What are you waiting for?"

# Chapter Thirteen

## TINSEL

Mason takes my hands and helps me to my feet, his palms warm and steady against mine. He doesn't let go right away, and I don't make him. My skin screams with every step—sunburn, soreness, and maybe nerves—but I'll be damned if I let my own stupidity from earlier rob me of this moment.

I've been teetering on this line since the day we met, between what I should do and what I know I want to do and now that I'm here, toes curled over the edge, I'm not backing down.

"Take your clothes off and lie on the bed," Mason says, voice rougher than usual.

My heart races at the demand because it's got the same unhinged strength as his praise, so I don't argue. I tug my shirt over my head, biting back a hiss when the fabric drags across my tender shoulders. My shorts follow, pooling at my feet, and after a beat of hesitation, I reach behind me and unclasp my bra. It slips from my fingers, landing softly on the floor.

I glance back over my shoulder, letting my mouth curve into something teasing, half challenge and half an invitation. Mason's gaze meets mine, dark and deliberate. His eyes roam slowly, reverently, and I swear I've never wanted to be seen so much in my life.

I crawl onto the mattress, curling forward, and rest my cheek on my folded arms. I close my eyes, waiting for Mason to move, and the anticipation winds tight in my chest until it's almost unbearable. After a long, aching pause, Mason climbs onto the bed, settling just behind my hips. "This will be cold. Brace your-self," he murmurs.

"Okay," I whisper.

The bottle squeaks softly, a quiet, intimate sound that makes my stomach flip. Then comes the first touch—cool aloe meeting overheated skin, his fingers spreading it in slow, deliberate circles. I shiver, caught between the sting of the burn and the heat of his hands. The pain fades under his touch, replaced by something far more dangerous. A dizzy, aching awareness that has nothing to do with the aloe and everything to do with him.

"Oh, Mason..." The words slip out before I can stop them, half a groan, half a prayer. "That feels so good."

Mason's hands continue to massage and need my back and shoulders, eliciting a little soft sigh from my lips. His body shifts as he leans to rub the tops of my arms, and I feel his hard length pressing against my ass. I don't say anything, I just let it push into me and imagine what it feel like if we could be more than just a tenant and roommate, realizing how much I want us to be more.

His hands drift lower, from my shoulders down the curve of my spine, tracing the backs of my thighs. When his fingers edge carefully between them, he pauses. "Is this okay?"

I breathe out, "Yes," and I swear I hear him grunt.

He takes his time, covering every inch of me, even the bottoms of my feet, which don't need aloe, but his attentiveness undoes me all the same.

"Mason..." I push up on my elbows, breasts pressing against his pillow, my body bare in a way I've never let it be, and look over my shoulder at him.

"Yes, Snowflake?"

I open my mouth, but the words don't come. I don't even know how to ask for what I want.

With Chris, *wanting* wasn't part of our equation. Our pseudo-relationship consisted of duty and expectation, and because of that, he never looked at me the way Mason does now. Like I'm something he's chosen.

And maybe that's what terrifies me most.

Because Mason isn't bound to me by promise or prescription. There's no pre-arranged destiny forcing us together. If he wants me, it's because he *wants* me. And the realization is terrifying.

"This feels... really good," I manage. "Thank you."

Mason's mouth curves into a lopsided grin. He bends my leg gently, running his hand down my shin before kneading my calf. "Anytime. That's what friends are for."

Friends.

The word scrapes against my heart. Because that's what we are, what we're supposed to be. Friends. And yet, lying here under his hands, I want to be so much more.

# Chapter Fourteen

MASON

What the fuck is wrong with me?

I don't want to be Tinsel's friend. Not after hearing the way my name rolls off her lips. Not after feeling her soft skin beneath my hands. No, I want to do very *unfriendly* things to her. Things that'd probably get me barred as her landlord, but God, they'd be so much fun.

I run my hands down the curve of Tinsel's hips and let them slowly creep between her thighs as I massage her leg. "Is this okay?"

Tinsel lets out a breathy, "Yes," that is a heartbeat away from a moan. My cock swells in my pants and I know without a doubt that she can feel it pressed against her ass because she shifts, rocking her hips ever so slightly, craving the friction. The first movement was subtle and may have been accidental, but the second time she rubbed against me was intentional.

"Mason?" Tinsel pushes up onto her elbows and looks over her shoulder at me. The sight of her half-naked, flushed, green eyes alight with a hunger that mirrors mine, nearly undoes me. The side of her breast is a tease, and all I want is to flip her over, take her nipple into my mouth, and worship every inch of her body until she's trembling with need.

Tinsel rolls onto her back, bringing the sheet with her, and stares at me. I clench my jaw and rub my thumb in tiny circles down her calf. The things I would do to this woman if she'd let me.

I'd give her anything and everything.

I'd give her *me*.

Every dark, messy, unfixable part of me, because somehow, she makes all of it feel worth offering. And yet, I was the dumbass who had to go and say that we're fucking friends.

Friends don't do this. Friends don't crave the sound of each other's broken breaths. Friends don't fight the urge to pull each other closer just to see if the world stops spinning when their lips finally meet. And yet here I am, pretending like this is normal. Like I'm not one look, one sigh, one whispered word away from losing what little restraint I've got left.

Thunder cracks outside so loud it rattles the walls. The sky opens up outside as rain hammers the roof, sheets of water pounding like a warning I don't want to hear. Tinsel pushes onto her forearms, those eyes following me as I climb onto the bed beside her. We stare at each other, tension building between us, hot and thick. I lean in, until my lips hover just above hers, close enough to taste the heat of her breath. We're a heartbeat away from something I'll never come back from.

And then...

There's a *boom*. Not thunder this time, but a surge that causes the lights to flicker and die, plunging us into darkness. Maybe this is fate warning me that we could be catastrophic. But I want Tinsel so badly, and I'm so close. All she needs to do is close the fraction of an inch between us.

Instead, she whispers, "What happened?"

"A transformer must've blown," I drag a hand through my hair and push to my feet. My phone's in the living room, so I have to leave her for a second to find it. The storm rattles the house as I grab it off the coffee table and thumb the flashlight on so the thin beam can cut through the darkness.

When I turn back, Tinsel is sitting on the edge of my bed, holding my sheets to her chest. She looks uncomfortable, so I grab one of my clean shirts from the dresser and hold it out to her. "Here. Put this on."

Tinsel slips it over her head and the fabric swallows her curves, hanging almost to her knees. It's just cotton, worn soft from too many washes, but on her... it looks indecent. Like one of those visions you're supposed to earn, not stumble into on a blackout night.

The urge to close the distance, to press her back against the mattress, to find out how far she'll let me go, hits so hard I almost stagger. Instead, I grip the phone tighter, jaw clenched, and try not to give in. Thunder booms again, rattling the windows, reminding me that it has and still is trying to keep us apart. "It's a gnarly storm out there."

"Are they usually this bad in the winter?"

I sit beside Tinsel on the bed, laying the phone down so the light bounces off the ceiling and walls around us. "Sometimes. Summers are wild, though. One minute the sun is shining, the next the sky opens up and unleashes unholy hell. Five minutes later, it's like it never happened. Losing power like this isn't normal, though, not unless we have a hurricane. A line must be down somewhere."

"I've never given too much thought to how power and all that works where I'm from, but we've never had a snowstorm knock it out. This is kind of scary." Tinsel hugs her knees and rests her chin on them.

A low rumble shakes the windows. She jumps slightly, and I can't help the small smile that tugs at my mouth. "Are you afraid of the dark, Snowflake?"

"No," she says quickly, but her eyes are wide, and when another clap of thunder rattles the room, she flinches again.

"Come here," I murmured, opening an arm. Tinsel hesitates just long enough for me to feel the air shift, then finally gives in and curls into my side. "You know, storms are kind of beautiful to watch if you're prepared for them. I've got some flashlights in my hurricane supply box. It's in the storage room under the carport. Do you want to watch this one with me?"

"Is it safe?" she shakes again as another boom echoes in the night.

"Yeah, but even if it wasn't, Snowflake, I'd keep you safe," I murmur, tightening my arm around her as the thunder rolls again.

Tinsel tilts her head to look up at me. She inches closer, giving me the opening I've been looking for, but I don't take it. Kissing her now would be wrong. I'd be taking advantage of her vulnerability, not her desire. And I want this woman to want me just as much as I want her.

"Come on." I stand and take her hand. "This will be fun."

The storage closet under the carport is packed tight with boxes and random junk, half of it labeled in Dad's handwriting, which I can barely read. I kneel down, moving one box to the side and then the other, searching the tiny room until…"Got it."

My fingers close around a clear tote marked *Hurricane Supplies* and I shimmy and twist to maneuver out of the tight space, then carry the box into the house. Tinsel follows me, using my phone's flashlight as a guide so I don't walk into anything. I drop the box by the sliding doors and toss the lid behind me. Inside are batteries, flashlights, and a bunch of random things we don't need, but are helpful when you're without power for a week… Like propane tanks for the little grill on the top shelf of the closet. I pull out the flashlight, click it on, and then lift out the battery box.

Tinsel tilts her head, probably never having seen one of these if she's never lost power before. "What's that?"

"A battery box. It's only a little one, but it'll charge a phone, power a fan, and light a lamp… if I had one."

Her smile is soft, approving. "That's smart."

I click on a flashlight, then head back out to the storage room for a fan. I stop at the hall closet on the way back to grab a blanket, then start setting everything up. I spread the blanket on the ground and drop a few pillows down there too, then open the big slider doors. The storm sprays rain across the floor that I'll need to mop later, but the breeze feels nice. We might not need the fan.

I check that everything is how I want it, then stand the flashlight upright so the glow bounces across the ceiling. I make myself comfortable on the floor and gesture for her to join me. "Ready to watch the lightning roll through?"

The sky cracks open with a flash of white light, and this time, Tinsel doesn't flinch when the boom echoes through the walls. She sits beside me, leaning into my side, and I wrap an arm around her. "Do you do this often?"

"Not anymore," I admit. "Dad used to love sitting out here, watching the storms roll through. But as his disease progressed, we did it less and less." My fingers trace lazy circles on her arm. "I can't even remember the last time I opened the doors like this."

"I'm sorry for your loss, Mason. Really. My parents and I might not be on the best terms, but I don't know what I'd do without them."

"Each day gets a little easier," I lie because that's what I'm supposed to say. The world expects me to just move on, but I can't. Moving on feels like letting go and if I don't hold on to Dad, who will remember him?

Tinsel's quiet for a moment, her gaze on the storm. Then, softly, "What about your mom?"

Mom's an even harder topic. She's a wild woman, drunk more nights than not, but a staple for Winter Key because she owns *Mermaid Tales*. The town loves her and takes care of her when she loses her way, but they don't acknowledge that she cheated on Candace's dad with mine. They ignore that I'm her kid too, choosing to look at me as an orphan now that Dad died rather than her bastard.

"We've never gotten along. I reminded her too much of a night she'd rather forget, so we were at each other's throats until I was old enough to choose who I wanted to live with. I chose Dad, and she never forgave me." The thunder rolls low, filling the silence between us, which is fine by me. I'd rather not talk about my family anyway. My thumb drifts higher, up the curve of her shoulder. "What about you? Since we're digging deep. Tell me about your family."

"Nothing to tell. I'm an only child. My life is what most people dream about. The end."

"Don't sell yourself short, Tinsel. There's more to you than that. You're... special." My palm slides from her shoulder to the back of her neck. She looks at me so I can see her eyes darken, and the way she lights up at my praise hits me square in the chest. She doesn't even try to hide how much she likes it. And God, I want to keep giving her that. I want to keep being the reason she feels seen.

"You're too nice, Mason."

"I'm not that nice." My voice comes out low, rough. I lean closer, the tip of my nose brushing hers.

Her eyes flutter closed. "Are you saying you're on Santa's naughty list?"

"If he knew what's running through my mind right now, I'd be a permanent resident." The pull between us goes tight as a wire. Tinsel's hand finds my chest while my thumb strokes her jaw, sliding up to cradle her face. "I shouldn't do this," I murmur, almost to myself. "There's so much I want to do to you, but once we cross that line, I don't know if I'll be able to come back."

"Do it," she whispers, and I give in to the temptation.

My hand slides to the back of Tinsel's neck. I close the distance between us and the first brush of her lips steals the air from my lungs. She's soft. Cautious. Electric. Her fingers clutch at my shirt, and I swear I feel every nerve in my body wake up all at once. I cup her jaw, angling her closer, and when her lips part, I'm gone. My tongue grazes hers, slow and searching, and she melts into me like she's been waiting for this, too.

And then—

*Thump-thump.*

*Thump-thump.*

A pounding at the front door shatters the moment.

Tinsel jerks back, startled, her lips swollen, chest rising and falling fast. The last thing I want to do is let her go, but whoever's out there shouldn't be standing in this storm.

"Stay here," I murmur, brushing a thumb along her jaw before I force myself to move. I grab my phone to use as a light and wrench open the door to find Candace standing there, drenched from head to toe.

"The power's out," she says, her voice pitched high with stress.

"No shit," I mutter, grabbing her by the arm and pulling her inside.

"The generator at *Last Call* won't kick on and a tree branch took out the power line. We're gonna lose everything in the freezers, Mase. I don't know what to do." She swipes a wet strand of hair from her face, and then she looks past me. Her gaze catches on the glow of the flashlights and on Tinsel sitting on the floor in nothing but my shirt. Her eyes narrow. "Am I interrupting something?"

"Yes." I drag a hand down my face, caught between irritation and guilt. "But we can't afford to lose the inventory, not with all the events this week. So, as much as I hate that you're here, I'm glad you came."

Tinsel stands, clutching the blanket we sat on around herself, and says, "It's been a long night. I think I'm going to head to bed."

"Are you sure?" Candace asks, her gaze bouncing from Tinsel to me. She's putting together that A... she was right. I have a thing for Tinsel and we could be epic. And B... she just royally cockblocked me.

"Yeah. It's getting late and I'm tired." She yawns for good measure, but I know that less than five minutes ago, sleep was the last thing on her mind.

"You can come with us." I don't want to leave her alone and risk ruining what has only just started between us. I'm gaining her trust, little by little. I can only imagine the damage abandoning her when she's scared will do. "This storm's probably going to roll for a little while longer. We're used to the rain, but..."

"I'll be fine, Mason." She smiles, but the expression is tight. "Besides, I've got a flashlight." She bends down to grab our makeshift lamp. "And the fan. Just lock up when you leave, would you?"

Tinsel retreats toward her room, the blanket trailing like a shadow and an unexplainable fear wraps itself around me.

"I'll meet you in the truck," I say to Candace, then rush to catch up to Tinsel before she can close the door. I don't know if Candace has turned and gone outside or if she's standing in the kitchen watching me, but I don't care. I just need to make sure Tinsel truly is okay with being on her own tonight.

"Hey." I catch her hand before she can pull away, my thumb brushing over her knuckles. Her skin is warm, but she's trembling. Whether from the storm or from us, I can't tell. "Are you sure you're going to be okay? I can call someone else to help Candace."

She shakes her head, her smile small but steady. "I'll be fine. Promise."

I don't believe her, not really. She's standing there barefoot in *my* shirt, wrapped in soft light and shadow, and everything in me wants to stay. I reach up, cup her cheek, and my thumb drifts along her jaw as I lean in. The kiss is softer this time. Slower. It's an apology, a promise, and temptation all tangled together.

When I pull back just enough to breathe, I press my forehead to her. "Just so you know, you make it really damn hard to walk away," I whisper, voice rough, and then I leave before I say something else that reveals how much I wish I could stay.

# Chapter Sixteen

## TINSEL

The red and white box has stared at me all morning, and every time I glance at it, a fresh wave of anxiety slaps me in the face, cold and unexpected, like I'm finding the gift all over again for the first time. It came out of nowhere, wrapped in a pretty gold ribbon beside my pillow, waiting for me when I woke up this morning.

At first, I thought it was from Mason, but as soon as I saw the calligraphy letters on the tag, my heart sank. I dropped the box like it was coal on Christmas and stared at it for five full minutes before walking away. I left it on the bed, intending to treat today like any other, but it haunted my thoughts. My mind wasn't still enough for a movie, and even *Dexter* couldn't hold my attention. I fidgeted on the couch, unable to sit still, until I gave up and brought the box into the kitchen.

But now that I've touched the gift, I can't bring myself to open it because I know who's who it's from. I just don't know what Chris has sent. Given the way I left the North Pole last week, I'm not sure I want to know.

The oven timer dings, startling me out of my thoughts and away from the past. I pull out the tray of cookies and set it on the stovetop beside the first two batches I made.

Baking has always been my reset button because it was the one class I never struggled in growing up. It's ironic, really, considering I'm borderline diabetic and can't eat more than two in a day.

But now that the trays are cooling, the kitchen is too quiet again, and the box is still waiting.

I toss the oven mitts aside and glance at the gift again. If Chris can make a present appear on my pillow, he could just as easily have shown up. So, why didn't he?

I cross my arms and stare at the box, letting it taunt and torture me in a way I thought Chris only knew how. *This is stupid. It's just a gift!*

I groan and pick the damn thing up. It's small, just big enough for a ring, but Chris wouldn't dare pull the same stunt twice. I pull the gold ribbon, untying the bow, and lift the red lid from its white base. Fear traps the air in my lungs and I let out a long breath when I see a single peppermint waiting for me on top of a folded note. I pick up the peppermint and turn around the candy and my fingers. *At least you remember something about me,* I think bitterly.

My hand shakes as I pick up the paper that's been carefully folded to look like an envelope and lift the first flap. The whole room spins, and I haven't read even a single letter of what's been written. I force myself to undo another flap when there's a knock on the door.

I jump, the sound splintering through my nerves. The paper slips from my hands, landing beside the open box on the counter. Heart pounding, I scoop it all up and shove it into the nearest drawer, the peppermint rattling as the wood slams shut. I just need to keep whatever this is out of sight and put it back in my room before Mason gets home. He and I are in a delicate place. My fiancé declaring his *love* for me in a note would ruin the first real spark of warmth I've felt in years.

"Hey," Candace says before I can even swing the door all the way open. She slips inside like she owns the place, leaving a trail of damp footprints on the floor. Her hair clings to her cheeks, darkened by the drizzle outside.

I glance past her to the driveway, frowning when I don't see a car. "Did you... run here?"

She waves a dismissive hand, already halfway to the living room. "About last night..." She stops short, spins on her heel, and pins me with a look that could peel paint. "Was I interrupting something?"

"Kind of," I admit, my voice caught somewhere between sheepish and defensive. "But I'm glad you did."

"Are you sure? Because if you and my brother want to hook up, I'm totally for it. It's been so long since he found anybody worth pursuing, and you..." She tilts her head. "I don't know. I like you. I wouldn't mind if you stuck around."

"That's sweet," I say, though my chest tightens. "But I have to go home on Saturday. Remember?"

"I mean, do you, though?" She arches her brow. "I'm just saying you're obviously running from something, and whatever it is has to do with your family. You could just stay."

"And what? Live with Mason?" I snort. "I don't think he'd go for that."

"I don't know," Candace sings-songs. "My brother likes you. He doesn't like many people."

"I mean, I *am* completely likable." I tease, but there's some truth to the statement. Elves are naturally likable. Irresistible, even. People are drawn to us without ever understanding why. It's instinct, buried deep, some half-forgotten part of them that still recognizes Magic when it walks into the room.

Which is exactly why I can't let a repeat of last night happen. I don't know if Mason likes *me* or if he's just caught in the pull.

Candace opens her mouth to say something, but hesitates when she looks past me to the stovetop. "Are those cookies? And why do you have so many?" She crosses the kitchen and pokes the tray that just came out, wincing at the gooey heat, then taps the first tray where the cookies have firmed, but still look soft and chewy. "Can I have one?"

"Sure." I grab a spatula and slide one cookie off the tray, then set it on a napkin before handing the treat to her. I watch, anxiously waiting for her reaction. This isn't my usual recipe for my *Blizzard Bites.* Mason's kitchen was pretty bare, but he had the basics, and after some searching, I found enough of the core ingredients to make a variation of my favorite cookie.

"Oh, my gosh, Tinsel!" Candace moans as soon as she bites into one. "This is amazing."

"They're peppermint chocolate chip, or as I like to call them... *Blizzard Bites.*" I explain, proudly. "I was looking for something to pass the time this morning, and when I saw the candy canes from the other night, I couldn't help myself. I will say, though, considering how bare Mason's kitchen was when I got here last week, I was surprised he had chocolate chips."

"Those were mine," Candace says around another bite. "I made fresh chocolate syrup for Martini's a few weeks back. It was Merrilee's birthday, and I thought she and Mase would be great together." Candace freezes mid-chew, as she processes what she admitted. Her eyes widen and she quickly adds, "Nothing happened. He wasn't interested in her."

"It's fine." I pick up my second cookie of the day and take a bite. It's warm, savory, and sweet all at once. It could have used a little more vanilla, but it's practically perfect. I try to focus on the way it tastes instead of the knife of jealousy stabbing me in the chest. "I'm sure Mason's dated plenty of women."

Though I don't want to hear about any of them.

"Dated? No. Hooked up with? Yeah, but it's been a while, like over a year since he's been with anyone. I was starting to worry he'd given up," Candace says, finishing her first cookie and reaching for another. "Seriously though, these are, like, the best cookies I've ever had. You need to enter them in the Mrs. Claus Cookie Contest tonight."

"The what?"

"That's why I came over!" she says, eyes bright. "We had to cancel the ugly sweater movie night last night because of the storm. Normally, we'd start the movie around eight, but given how the forecast looked like we decided to postpone till later in the week."

"Probably a good idea considering it knocked out the power."

"I know, right? Can you imagine everybody out there running from the rain, trying to carry their lawn chairs and Cocoa?" Candice laughs. "Anyway, today is the competition, and everyone brings their own homemade cookies, and we vote on who is the best. And *this* is by far better than anything I've ever tasted. You'd be a shoe-in to win."

"You really think so?" My cookies were never prize winners back home, but they passed the courses, and I enjoy them.

"Yes, hands-down. Please? Tell me we can enter them."

"Do I have enough?" I ask, and she looks at the nearly three dozen cookies I've made.

"Definitely! Come on. We've gotta have them checked in by three o'clock and it's already two-thirty. We start at five and announce the winner at seven." Candace grabs a third cookie and moans like it's the first, as if she's discovering the flavor profile all over again. "It's a little slow at first, but if your cookies aren't there the whole time, you're disqualified, and I can't let these babies lose on a technicality."

"Okay. Let me get changed."

"Eeek!" She squeals. "I'm so excited. I'll package them up while you get ready."

She tugs open the drawer I hid Chris's gift in, and the flash of red-and-white inside makes my stomach drop. "Wait!" I shout, reaching for the drawer and freezing mid-grab when Candace looks at me curiously. The soft close feature kicks in, and the drawer closes itself after being opened, silently hiding my secret for me. "I... um... I want to package them. I'm sure it's cheating if the host creates the presentation. Right?"

"I mean, I was just going to put them in a plastic container, but... yeah. I can see that coming back as an argument." Candace's phone rings, thankfully keeping her from looking too deeply into things. She frowns, and I quickly get a glimpse at the name on the screen—something *Realty*. "I've got to take this," she says, half distracted. "I'll be outside. Okay?"

"Perfect." I sigh, feeling slightly relieved.

As soon as she steps out the sliding doors, I grab Chris's box and shove it behind my back, in the band of my shorts, and then casually run to my room. I slip it under the mattress, so there's no risk of Mason stumbling upon it, then casually walk back into the kitchen to package up the cookies.

Candace is still on the phone, looking somewhat irritated, paying zero attention to me. I smile, relieved, as I dig through the cabinets for something to store the cookies in. I don't want my past interfering with my present. I like what I have going on in Winter Key. I like my friendship with Candace and my temporary flirtationship with Mason.

And if either of them sees whatever Chris has written in that box, it could ruin everything.

# Chapter Seventeen

MASON

I've been behind this bar all day, but my head hasn't been in it.

It's been with her.

Tinsel.

I haven't seen her since last night, and it's taken every ounce of self-control not to drive back to the house, knock on the door, and demand to know where we stand. I can't even text her to try to feel out the tone of her responses because she never gave me her number. I'd have to beg Brenda for the information, dance around why I want it, and hope I don't seem desperate when I reach out. I don't know what kind of guy Tinsel normally goes for, but I know what my sister hates in a man. Clingy and desperate are hard red flags for her, and I'm toeing that line.

I don't want to be that guy.

Still, it's eaten me alive. Every drink I pour, every laugh that carries from across the room, every strand of Christmas music dripping through the speakers, it all blurs together because my mind is circling whether Tinsel's been thinking about our kiss or has she already decided last night was a mistake?

Candace barrels through the back door just before the contest starts, with a foil-covered plate in each hand. "These," she announces, dropping them on the counter in front of me, "are literally the best cookies I've ever had in my life. Ever!"

She pulls the foil back on one plate and glances around to make sure no one is looking, then plops a whole cookie in her mouth. Crumbs scatter across the counter. I snag a napkin and wipe them away while she moans like she's dying a dramatic death.

"I mean, not only are they delicious, but they're gorgeous," Candace says, already reaching for a second.

I smack her hand before she can steal it, and she looks at me wide-eyed. "Quit. If you eat them all, there won't be any left for the contest."

"Screw the contest," She clutches the little cookie like it's the golden ring and she's Gollum, and then she groans. "Fuuuck. I can't eat them all. Tinsel is going to win this contest. Hands down."

"You can't rig the competition."

"I don't need to. These are going to win. Try one." She holds the plate out to me, and I level her with a glare.

"No thanks." I'm not the biggest fan of sweets. Too much sugar makes me feel sluggish. I'm not diabetic, but my bloodwork has been slowly creeping that way for the last five years. I've trained my body to survive on the least amount of processed crap possible. So, if I decide to try Tinsel's cookie, it's going to be in front of her, where she can see my delight and earn the compliment. "Why does she need to win?"

"Because she needs to be Mrs. Claus in the parade Friday night. That way you can be her Santa." Candace beams at me, her smile borderline insane. When I don't immediately pick up the clues she's throwing, she punches me in the shoulder. "I'm being your wingman, dumbass. Sling that dick so good she never wants to leave. I like this girl. I want her to stay."

"Please don't talk about my dick."

Candace rolls her eyes and shifts Tinsel's cookies onto an official entry container, which is just a silver platter. She's number seven in the lineup, and visually, her cookies look like everyone else's. They're round and golden, just like everyone else's. Nothing about them jumps out, making me want to try one, except that I know they are *hers*. Out of nowhere, a spike of fear hits me in the chest. What if she doesn't win? What if Tinsel's cookies are good, but not great? How do I protect her from that disappointment?

I can't. Not if I don't know what I'm up against.

I swipe an extra cookie off the second plate and my eyes widen the moment it hits my tongue.

"What did I tell you?" Candace says, bouncing on her toes.

"These are fucking fabulous."

"I know, right?" She steals the other half from my fingers and the urge to swipe it back before she eats it hits hard. "Now all you have to do is win the Sexy Santa competition."

Candace says that, as if strutting on stage, in front of the town, half-naked, is no big deal. Which, maybe, for the guys who enter, it's not. But I've purposefully *never* entered. I even make it a point to be off that night. I bar-backed the first year Candace proposed the event, and it was wild. The girls were feral, even to those of us who weren't in the competition. The tips were great, and at twenty-five, I enjoyed the attention, but I'd rather not be objectified, cornered, or touched by random women.

"You know how I feel about that charade."

"I do, which is why if you promise me you're entering, I'll do things differently this year."

"And let down all the thirsty women on this side of Key West... How dare you?" I tease, and Candace punches me again.

"This is a classy event!"

I roll my eyes and head back into the bar. The room is filling up surprisingly early this year. Maybe it's because the movie last night was cancelled, but it looks like almost everyone in Winter Key is already here.

At four-fifty-five, Candace and I bring the cookies out. We have two six-foot-long tables along the right side of the wall, each covered with a red cloth. We set twelve entries out, evenly spaced, with their place cards in front of them, and the room hums with excitement. Grown-ups and kids alike wait anxiously with their paper plates to collect cookies.

At exactly five o'clock, Candace grabs the microphone usually reserved for karaoke night and greets the room.

"Hello, Winter Key," She says, and people clap, ready to start eating. "I am so excited to kick off this year's Mrs. Claus Cookie Contest. We have twelve entries. I have personally tasted every cookie and let me tell you..." She pauses for dramatic effect. "You are gonna have a hard time picking this year's winner."

There's a murmur of excited chatter that blurs into inaudible noise.

"For anyone who is new or doesn't remember how this works, you get to take one of each cookie, and then you pick your favorite. You might have to look back at the table cards to remember what number your favorite cookie was, but then you cast your vote by writing one number on a ballot and then dropping it in the box." She points to a pre-wrapped present that has a small cutout of the top. "At seven o'clock, we will sort the entries and crown this year's Mrs. Claus. Are you ready?" She asks the crowd cheers. Candace beams at everyone and then says, "Let the cookie tasting begin!"

I press play on the musical playlist, and Candace's never-ending stream of Christmas music filters softly through the speakers. There's a slow but steady line at the tables, and over the course of the next thirty minutes, everyone grabs a plate. At this point, most people are drinking milk or water and only a handful have asked me for something stronger, so there's not much for me to do besides watch the room and search for *her*.

Nearly a whole hour goes by before I finally spot Tinsel. She looks like Christmas personified. Beautiful, warm, a little untouchable and completely unaware of the way she floors me.

She comes to my counter, with a big plate of cookies in front of her, nibbling like she's trying not to be obvious. She looks nervous, almost out of place, and the sight makes my chest twist. I slide a glass of water in front of her without her asking. She glances up, startled, then gives me a smile that nearly undoes me.

"Want one?" she asks, holding out a cookie studded with pretzels, M&Ms, and God knows what else.

I shake my head. "I'm not the biggest fan of sweets."

"Really?" Her brows lift. "That explains your kitchen."

I huff a laugh, brushing a crumb from the corner of her mouth without thinking. My fingers linger too long, and I force myself to pull back. "I hear you have a cookie out there."

She blushes. "I do, although I'm not supposed to tell anyone which one it is."

"I'm not voting, but I'd love to try it. Will you get me one?"

Tinsel bites her lip and nods. She scoots back and saunters directly to entry number seven. She grabs a small red plate and sets a single cookie on it, then practically runs back to the bar, like she's stolen someone's present from under the tree. "Enjoy," she says, sliding the plate across the wood countertop, though I can see the hesitation in her eyes.

I take a bite and don't even have to fake how much I enjoy it. The memory of her cookie doesn't do the taste justice. It's gooey and sweet, but not too sweet, with just enough peppermint to balance the flavor. It's also perfectly round and golden, and Candace is right. She's going to win. "Tinsel."

She worries her lip between her teeth and I know dragging my opinion out is mean, but I want it to really resonate when I say, "You did so good, Snowflake. This cookie is phenomenal."

That worry morphs into pride, and I love the way she lights up when it registers. "Really?"

"Truly. If you don't win tonight, the contest is rigged." I reach for her, watching closely for a sign that I'm crossing a line. There's a big difference between kissing in my living room and where the whole town can see, but I want to claim her. I want everyone to know that this beautiful, talented woman is here with me, and I want every man who sees us together to be jealous.

Tinsel leans onto her arms, giving so I'm not just taking, as I cross the threshold of the bar and kiss her. Everything I worried about is gone, turned into sand in the breeze the moment her lips meet mine. I'd keep her there forever if I could, but she startles and pulls away.

She digs in her purse and I realize her phone buzzing is what tore us apart. She silences the call and sets the thing face down on the counter. It buzzes again and the strong, confident woman I had only moments ago retreats into a guarded version of herself as her face drains of color.

"You okay?" I ask, my voice low.

"I'm fine," she says too quickly. She tries to smile, but it buzzes again and again. The more it rings, the more panicked she looks.

I reach for it before I can stop myself, but she snatches the phone up and clutches it to her lap. "It's nothing. Just my family trying to reach me."

It doesn't feel like nothing. I want to push, demand answers, and tell her she doesn't have to face whatever that is alone. But the walls are back up in her eyes and I know that if I press, she'll shut me out completely.

So, I swallow the words and stand there, useless.

Thankfully, Candace's voice booms over the speakers, cutting through the chatter and clinking glasses. "Don't forget to grab your pulled pork sandwiches before they're gone!"

The announcement draws a fresh wave of customers to the bar, and for the next hour, I'm swamped pouring beers, shaking cocktails, and trading laughs with locals who all have something to say about the cookie contest. Time slips by in a blur of foam and sugar.

Then, Candace's voice rises again from the stage. "All right, folks, time for what you've all been waiting for! Let's give it up for our cookie contest winners!"

Cheers ripple through the crowd. I pause mid-pour, wiping my hands on a towel as she calls out third place. Then second. The suspense stretches tight.

"First place goes to..." Candace pauses dramatically, grinning from ear to ear.

I glance toward my girl at the edge of the bar. Tinsel's sitting there, her fingers knotted together in her lap, pretending she's indifferent, but I see the truth in her eyes. She wants this. She's holding her breath.

Candace draws it out a second longer, then shouts, "Tinsel Evergreen!"

"Me?" she breathes, voice barely audible over the roar of applause as she looks to me for guidance.

"You," I say, grinning as I clap along with the crowd. "Go get your prize, Snowflake."

Tinsel slides off the stool, cheeks flushed a shade of red that could rival the holly berries in the garland hanging from the ceiling. The crowd parts for her, clapping and cheering as she makes her way toward the stage.

"Congratulations, Mrs. Claus!" she shouts into the mic as she plops a sequined Santa hat on Tinsel's head.

"What?" Tinsel's voice cracks, high and startled. She blinks at Candace like she must have misheard.

Candace just grins wider. "You get to be Mrs. Claus in the parade this weekend!"

The bar erupts in cheers and whistles, but Tinsel stands frozen in the middle of it all. Her smile falters, the color draining from her face until she looks like she's seen a ghost. It's that same look she gave me last night when I called her *good girl*. Only this time, it's fear, not desire, coloring her cheeks, and in that moment, I get the feeling that whatever she's running from is catching up.

Tinsel's phone buzzes on the countertop again and this time I can't stop myself. Someone named Chris is calling and when the call shifts to missed, it shows he's tried to reach her four times. I turn the phone facedown againbefore she can catch me staring, guilt prickling beneath my skin and jealousy burning hot in my veins.

# Chapter Eighteen

## TINSEL

It's like a curse I can't run from.

Candace holds up an apron in the signature Mrs. Claus red, trimmed with fluffy white garland along the bottom edge, and embellished with two big black buttons down the center. Before I can protest, she ties the apron snugly around my neck and waist, humming a little carol as though I'm her holiday Barbie to dress up.

I paste on my pageant smile, the one I've perfected from years of swallowing my true feelings, praying it hides the storm rolling inside me.

I left the North Pole to escape this. To escape the responsibilities of being Mrs. Claus—the stigma, the suffocating pressure to be the perfect homemaker wife, the relentless expectations to smile pretty and serve with grace. To escape being everyone's shining example of holly-jolly virtue.

And now, here I stand. A carbon copy of the role that seems to define me.

Is this forever my fate?

Is this Magic itself whispering that I can't run from what I was practically born into? That at the end of this week I'll have no choice but to go home, back to the life I've tried to flee, because even here, beneath sunshine and salty air, I'm destined to become Mrs. Claus?

The thought slices through the haze of Christmas lights. Especially when I let myself imagine what I'd lose: the dream of sunshowers and freedom, of laughter that doesn't come with obligation, of a handsome man who has no right to look at me the way Mason does. Who enjoys watching the way his compliments ripple across my face, like he's proud of me for just being me.

The crowd bursts into claps, pulling me back to this nauseating moment. Candace, ever the natural emcee, lifts the mic again and commands the room. "All right, folks, karaoke kicks off at eight! Eat. Drink. And then take those kids home by nine so I don't get my liqour license revoked!"

Cheers ripple around us and, with that, Candace and I step off the stage as Christmas music funnels through the speakers again. People murmur words of congratulations as we pass and head to the bar. Faces blur and names are lost. It's like I'm in a vortex of kindness, but the praise doesn't hit right. The words are empty, leaving me feeling just as hollow.

But then, I see him.

Mason stands behind the counter, grin too easy, eyes too knowing. "Congratulations, Mrs. Claus. Can I make you a celebratory drink?"

His words slither over me, sending a shiver down my spine, but not the good kind. It feels like a verdict, a reminder stamped across my skin in bold red ink. All of a sudden, the bar is too crowded. I'm hot and anxious and the urge to run is almost overpowering, but the realization that no matter how fast I run or how far I go, the curse of being Mrs. Claus will find me lingers.

"Thanks," I murmur, my smile stiff. My phone vibrates on the bar top, another reminder of my looming fate, and I feel cracks forming in my carefully crafted mask. I don't know how much longer I can keep myself together for. "But I think I'm gonna head back to the house."

"What?" Candace nearly drops the beer Mason hands her and

looks at me like I've just ruined her Christmas surprise. "You can't. This is my only night off until after the holidays. You have to stay."

"What do you mean? You were just working." And I need her to keep working so I can slip away. Gather my thoughts. Maybe read Chris's note.

The phone buzzes again. I grab it off the bar, trying to ignore Chris's name flashing across the screen, and shut it off. I don't even know why I brought the damn thing. The only people who have this number are the ones I'm trying to avoid.

"I announced the cookies, sure, but that's it," Candace says, taking a long sip of her beer. "Tonight, I don't have to cook, man the bar, or referee drunk locals. Tonight, I actually get to enjoy myself. I want to drink and sing karaoke, and I want to do all these things with my new bestie."

She takes my hands in hers, practically begging. "Please don't abandon me."

Everything in me aches to leave and to shed tonight like last year's wrapping paper, but Candace has been nothing but kind. A friend I didn't expect. What kind of person would I be if I abandoned her now?

"Tinsel, I need you in my life." She puffs out her bottom lip and claps her hands together like a child begging for a puppy.

"Fine," I sigh. "I'll stay. But not for long."

"Yay!" Candace squeals and spins toward the bar. She reaches over the counter, snatches up a clear bottle and two small glasses, then pours two neat shots into them. She presses one into my hand and grins. "To new friends and Christmas shenanigans."

"To new friends," I echo, though I could do without the shenanigans. The peppermint alcohol burns sweet and sharp across my tongue, tugging an involuntary smile from me as I swallow. Not half as bright as the grin lighting Candace's face, but real enough.

"We are gonna have such a good time tonight," Candace declares, already pouring another round like a bartender on autopilot. Her damp hair clings to her cheek, her eyes sparkling with the kind of excitement only a small-town girl on a rare night off can muster. "And as your new best friend, it is my *sacred duty* to make sure you enjoy every ounce of the prize you earned."

"I won a prize?" My brows shoot up.

"Uh, yeah." She leans in, voice dropping to a conspiratorial whisper even though half the bar can probably hear her. "Everyone paid twenty-five bucks to enter their cookies because the winner eats and drinks free until Christmas. Congratulations, you lucky bitch."

"I didn't even know there was an entry fee."

"That's because I expected you to win." Candace tips her head, smirking. "And if you hadn't, I would've covered it anyway."

I shake my head, a laugh bubbling up despite myself.

"And..." she drags the word out, her grin turning sly, "I noticed you didn't contest my title of best friend. Soooo does this mean we're officially besties? Because I feel like we're besties. We just click, you know?"

Candice is the nicest, most genuine person I've ever met. I was happy just to be her friend, but the fact that she wants me to be her best friend... Well, I'm honored. I look down at my hands, feeling vulnerable. I really like her, and it's going to suck when I have to say goodbye. "You are a pretty good friend, Candace."

"I know," she says with zero shame, flashing me a toothy grin. "Which is why I'm gonna show you the *best* night of your life."

Before I can protest, she straightens and waves at the girl behind the bar like a queen hailing a subject. "Cara! Two holiday sangrias, please!"

"Make 'em doubles!" Mason calls from the other end of the bar.

Candace shimmies onto the barstool and leans closer, whispering like we're sharing true Christmas secrets. "We put real cinnamon sticks in them. They're basically Christmas in a glass."

I watch Cara, *Last Call's* other bartender, mix red wine,

brandy, apple and orange slices, a scattering of pomegranate seeds, and cinnamon sticks that swirl like magic wands. She pours the mixture into a curvy glass and sets it in front of me.

"These," Candace announces proudly, "are even better than sex."

"Your sex life must be depressing," I mutter, though the words sting me, too, because mine's not much better.

Two men. That's my grand total. And neither managed to coax me anywhere close to the legendary fireworks I've read about. The experiences weren't bad, but they always fell short. Always left me waiting for a spark that never lit.

Candace snorts. "I'm on a six-month dry spell. There are no eligible bachelors in Winter Key or Islamorada, and I'm not about to widen my distance on the apps. Not worth it. The men I've tried opening myself up to in the past have been nothing but a headache, which is why I've got a pink little vibrator upstairs that's one hundred times more reliable than the guys who've tried to get me off. It's sad, really..." she trails off, then jumps back into the conversation a few seconds later. "But what's a girl to do?"

I take a sip of the sangria and almost moan. Candace is right. This cocktail's an orgasm in a glass. Sweet, spiced, and just enough kick to promise I'll feel it later. My insides warm, heat trickling outward like melted cinnamon sugar.

Not better than sex...but maybe better than any sex I've had.

Or maybe this heat isn't from the drink at all.

Because, behind the bar, a certain blond-haired man is watching me. And the way his eyes trail over my body, like he's unwrapping me one slow layer at a time, makes me want to stoke that fire tonight instead of putting it out.

# Chapter Nineteen

## MASON

I watch the girls from behind the bar, pretending to keep an eye on their drinks while Candace glides around the room with Tinsel at her side. But the truth is, I'm watching *her*.

Her smile.

Her laugh.

The way her lips purse together into a tight grin when she's nodding along, but she really wants the conversation to end. How she tucks her hair behind her ears to hide her discomfort when she's being hit on. The subtle sway of her hips when the speakers stream a song that she likes.

And most of all, I'm waiting for the moment her eyes to find mine again because ever since last night, I can't stop replaying that kiss.

It wasn't planned. Hell, it wasn't even smart. But now that I've had a taste, it's all I've thought about. Every time Tinsel laughs, I remember how her lips felt against my mouth. Every time she looks at me, I wonder if she's thinking about it too.

This girl turns me inside-fucking-out. I don't know what it is about her, and at this point, I don't care to figure it out. She's warmth and sunshine, and somehow, the time I spend with her makes everything else bearable.

The small comments that have filtered into conversation tonight—*sorry to hear about the bait shop, or damn, another piece of our town is gone. Won't be long until we disappear, too*—are meant to be comforting, but each failed attempt at kindness creates a new ache in my chest. Sometimes, I feel like I'm drowning in the weight of my failures. Though everything I've fucked up is trivial compared to what's coming. Any day, the town will discover that I'm a sellout.

I sold the deed to *Hook, Line, and Sinker* to save Dad's house. And even though *Hoeper Industries* claims they're going to restore the bait shop to its former glory, there's still a chance they'll tear it down and build... I don't actually know what they'd build. The plot is barely a quarter acre, but they'd build something. And that something will piss everyone off, even if it could help bring tourists around.

But then Tinsel smiles at me and it's like taking a breath after drowning. I know she's leaving. I know this week is all I get. But after watching her tonight, seeing how people gravitate toward her, how she brightens everything she touches. I'm done pretending that I don't want more.

Candace was right. Tinsel and I could be great. I just have to convince her that last night wasn't a mistake. That it's *the beginning.*

Cara sets another sangria in front of her just as Tinsel slides onto the stool across from me. She's tipsy, cheeks flushed, eyes glassy and bright. She leans closer to the bar top and shouts, "This is fun!"

Before I can answer, Tinsel's attention shifts to the stage. She sets her drink down and claps as Candace takes the mic to belt out her third Kelsea Ballerini song of the night. She's not half bad despite being drunk, and the crowd claps along, eating it up. When she finishes, Tinsel is the first one on her feet to hug her, and the sight of the two of them laughing together almost makes me forget I'm supposed to be pouring drinks.

Almost.

Right as they're making their way back to their drinks, a woman leans across the bar, cleavage front and center as she locks eyes with me and asks, "What's your special tonight?"

"We've got a Holiday Sangria and a Gingerbread Old Fashioned," I say, keeping it friendly.

"Can I have a glass of sangria?"

"Sure thing." I paste on a polite grin, but my eyes flick toward Tinsel only to see that Candace is not so subtly glaring. She's practically ready to throw hands and the poor woman hasn't done anything but flash a smile.

The woman takes her first sip and lets out a low, exaggerated moan. "Mmm, this is amazing. You sure know how to use your hands, don't you?"

Tinsel's head snaps toward us, and that's it. Game over. Her frown is instant, sharp enough to slice through the noise of the bar. Her lips press into a thin line, jealousy flashing across her face before she schools it away. It shouldn't make me grin, but it does. Because that look? The heat in her eyes, the way she's pretending not to care?

I love it.

"Are you opening a tab or cashing out?" I ask, trying to be as curt as possible without coming across as rude, but Tinsel's eyes haven't left me. Her mouth is set, her cheeks pink, and I swear she looks like she might hurl that sangria glass at the woman if she lingers much longer.

The woman pouts but gets the message, tossing a bill on the counter before drifting back to her table.

Candace grabs Tinsel by the hand, and they wiggle their way down the bar to take the newly open space in front of me. She's already grinning like a cat with cream, which should've been my first warning. I hand Candace a drink—water, not alcohol—and she glares when she realizes what it is.

"This isn't one of your secret masterpieces."

"Nope. Hydration is key," I say, smirking. "Someone's gotta

keep you alive through karaoke night. And who else will take care of you if I don't?"

Candace and Tinsel exchange one of those silent, conspiratorial looks only women seem to understand. A half second later, Candace groans dramatically. "If that girl flirted any harder, she'd have climbed over the bar. She was practically undressing you with her eyes. Should I kick her out? Because I *will*."

"Easy does it." I grab Candace's wrist as she sets her drink on the counter, fully intent on storming the woman's table. "It's fine. She got her drink and left to go hang out with her friends."

"Thirsty bitches get served," Candace says, trying to sound tough.

I laugh and shake my head. *This, ladies and gentlemen, is my sister. Slightly unhinged. A meddling menace. And forever a pain in my ass.* "Do you really want the PR nightmare you're about to cause? Winter Key is trying to draw in outsiders. What will everyone think when they discover you banished six newcomers because you were drunk? What will those girls tell the people wherever they're staying about us?"

Candace slumps, defeated but not defused. "Fine. But you owe me. I'm staying classy for *you*, not Winter Key."

"Whatever you say." I resign to wiping water rings from the counter, relieved.

"And I know exactly what I want," she says suddenly, and that tone has me hesitating.

I meet Candace's gaze, noticing how her eyes have shifted from *psycho bunny with a pitchfork* to *deranged rabbit with poisoned candy*. "What did you do?"

She smirks, and I already know I'm going to hate whatever it is that she says. "Don't hate me, but I might've signed you up for a song."

I groan. "Candace."

"Not just you." She bats her lashes, innocently. "The song I picked is a duet."

My stomach drops. "With you?"

"Nope." Her gaze swings mischievously toward Tinsel.

Tinsel's eyes go wide when she realizes what's happening. "Oh, no. Absolutely not. I can't sing."

"Neither can Mason," Candace chirps.

"Gee, thanks," I mutter. And it's not that I can't sing. I just prefer not to do so in public. Car-ride Karaoke the other day was a one-off that I don't regret. Tinsel and I were having fun. Bonding. And most importantly, not in front of half the town.

"It'll be fun!" Candace insists. She scoots off her chair and rounds the bar, then literally pushes me to stand beside Tinsel, though she doesn't have to work too hard to get me there. "The DJ's already got you queued up."

Sure enough, less than a minute later, the voice over the speakers calls out, "Next up, Mason and Tinsel!"

*Damnit, Candace.* This was probably her plan all along. Force us into some Hallmark-esque situation to kick-start our relationship. Well, the joke is on her because I did that last night. And while I'm not opposed to another catalyst to bring Tinsel and me together, I really wish Candace's meet-cute, or whatever, for us wasn't singing-related.

"Guess that's our cue." I smile down at Tinsel and the poor thing looks like she might bolt. I extend my hand in hopes of comforting her, even though I'm not so keen on this venture either. "C'mon. What's the worst that can happen?"

Tinsel's eyes narrow, but after a long second, she takes my hand. She's trembling, just slightly, but she doesn't pull away. Not as we wiggle through the crowd of people or even when we climb the three steps to the stage.

The DJ hands us each a microphone and if he hadn't, I think she would have been at my side for the whole song. But she steps to my right, letting me go, and the screen behind us lights up: *Baby, It's Cold Outside.*

"You've got to be kidding me," Tinsel mutters and to her credit, it's the first Christmas jingle of the night.

I lean closer, covering my mic with my hand. "Think Candace is hinting at something, Snowflake?"

She shoots me a look that's half disbelief, half panic, but before she can say anything, the music starts. I launch into the opening line, looking at her, ignoring the room and everyone watching us, because I want her to feel these words.

I need her to understand how much the singer wants the girl in the song to stay and give him a chance, despite all the reasons not to.

How much I feel the same way.

Tinsel bites her lip, shakes her head, and then joins in. At first, we're both stiff, awkward and trying too hard not to look at each other too much, but then the crowd starts clapping along, and something shifts. Tinsel rolls her eyes at one of the cheesier lines, and I grin back, hamming it up. Her laugh slips into the lyrics, bright and genuine, and damn if it doesn't feel like the whole bar notices the spark between us.

By the second verse, we're not just singing. We're *bantering.* Trading lines like flirty jabs. Tinsel's voice is soft and hesitant at first, but it grows stronger with every note. My grin widens, my tone deepens, and before long, it feels less like a performance and more like foreplay.

When she sings *"The neighbors might think..."* I can't help but murmur, "Let them."

Her cheeks flush scarlet. The crowd goes wild.

By the time we hit the last line, she's laughing, I'm grinning, and the entire bar is cheering. The moment stretches, warm and electric.

Tinsel dips into a little mock bow, and I lean down, my breath brushing her ear. "You are beyond stunning," I whisper, before pressing a quick kiss to her cheek.

She startles, eyes wide, and there's no mistaking the spark that flares between us. Before she can respond, the DJ calls the next name. The spell ensnaring us breaks as we step off the stage and make our way back to the bar, but the electricity between us still hums like the last note of a song that refuses to fade.

# *Chapter Twenty*

MASON

"When do you get off work?" Tinsel asks, her tone all casual curiosity, but her eyes say something else entirely. They've got that spark she gets when she's up to trouble. The one that always manages to undo me.

I tug my phone from my back pocket, glance at the screen, then shove it back like I didn't just check it for the tenth time tonight. "Not for about two more hours. Why?"

Her lips curve, then push into a pout that could bring a grown man to his knees. "That just won't do."

"Oh, won't it?" I tease, cocking a brow, trying and failing to sound unaffected.

Tinsel shakes her head slowly, deliberately. "Nope. Because I want to fuck you, Mason. And I want to fuck you right now."

It takes my brain a full second to process the words, because she just made the move I've been imagining all damn day. Bolder and braver than I ever would've dared. I would've worked my way toward this by Thursday, hoping time would let us ease into it. But Tinsel? She just tore the wrapping off, so to speak, and left the box open for us to discover what's inside.

"Tinsel," I murmur, her name vibrating between us.

"You are relieved of your duty," Candace says, walking up to us and waving her hands like she's the queen of this castle, and I am a soldier she can command. I arch my eyebrows at her, tempted to open my mouth and challenge her less-than-sober declaration until she says, "Go fuck my friend. I don't want any details, but you better do her good."

Candace flicks her fingers at me, literally shooting me away. I laugh, not sure I want to know how they came up with this plan, when Tinsel grabs my hand. She pulls me from behind the bar and out into the parking lot, and I don't dare try to stop her.

"What are you doing?" I ask, a smile tugging at my mouth as I watch her cross the yard.

With every step Tinsel sheds something—her shorts here, a shoe there, her shirt fluttering down like a flag of surrender. One earring catches the light before it slips into the grass. I bend down and grab it, along with every other article she's dropped, but the second earring is lost. Hopefully it wasn't expensive.

I follow her trail of clothes, collecting as much as I can hold as she strides barefoot to the dock.

"I want to swim," Tinsel shouts, pausing at the edge, the moonlight catching on her hair as she throws me a look over her shoulder. "Wanna join?"

"Probably not a good idea with our new tattoos."

Tinsel's hands reach behind her, unclasping her bra. The straps fall, and the delicate scrap of lace drops to the wooden planks with a whisper. I only glimpse the side of her breast teases me in profile, but my breath catches.

*My God.*

"Tinsel..." I warn, voice low, but she only smirks.

She stands there in nothing but her panties, every curve of her body illuminated, and I swear I've never seen anything so breathtaking.

"Don't dive. It's shallow," I manage, my voice rough. I set her clothes on a piling and yank my shirt over my head.

Tinsel lowers herself into the water slowly, sinking down until only her head remains above the surface. Ripples shimmer around her like silver. I kick my shoes off, empty my pockets, loose my shirt, and jump in beside her. The ground is squishy muck beneath my toes. The water is warm but still a brisk shock against my skin. I shiver.

"Cold, sweetheart?" Tinsel's lips curve upwardas she reaches for me. Her fingers trail down my arm, and then she presses herself flush to my chest. Her legs coil around my waist, locking me in, though I wouldn't dare try to go anywhere.

"Better now," I murmur, gripping her tightly.

She leans in, lips brushing my ear, her breath featherlight. "Don't tell Santa, but the things I wanna do to you will put me on the naughty list."

Then her mouth closes over my earlobe, sucking gently, and I groan, holding her tighter. My lips find her shoulder, tasting salt and heat, and she tips her head back to the sky.

"Mason." Tinsel trails her fingers across my back and arms. I nip lightly at her collarbone, then pull back just enough to admire the purple mark blooming there.

She cups my face and kisses me, hungry and unrestrained. I kiss her back, harder, and the longer it goes, the more her hips grind against me. She breaks the kiss with a ragged breath and presses her forehead to mine. "I think I wanna go inside now," she whispers. "Someone's got me all wet."

A low laugh escapes me, rougher than I intend. *This girl is a dream. Too perfect. Too damn good to be real.*

Tinsel untangles herself from my lap and wades toward the dock. She tries to haul herself up, but her wet hands slip against the wood. Before she can try again, I step in behind her, gripping her hips and lifting her effortlessly.

I help her onto the dock, then pull myself up after her. She doesn't cover herself, doesn't retreat. She just stands there bare and confident, waiting for me like she knows exactly what she does to me.

I kiss her again, softer this time, then whisper, "You've had a lot to drink tonight."

She shrugs, a careless smile lifting her lips. "And?"

"And I'd be a shitty human being if I took advantage of you right now."

Her smile tilts wickedly as she considers my words. "What if I take advantage of you?"

Tinsel drops to her knees and with one quick touch, she's pulled my dick out of my boxers and wrapped her lips around me.

"Fuck, Tinsel," I groan. I have to grab onto the piling to stay upright, because the way she swallows my cock like it's nothing, letting it graze the back of her throat without so much as a hiccup steals my breath. I grab her hair and push deeper, and like the good girl she is, she takes it. "You take my dick beautifully."

Tinsel stops only for a second, wrapping both hands around my length, pumping rhythmically as she looks up at me and says, "Imagine how the rest of me would feel. Do you want to find out?"

"Shit," I groan and drag a hand down my face. "Are you sure you want this?"

"Yes," she whispers. "More than I've ever wanted anything."

"The house is right there," I say, my voice hoarse. "We could—"

"Here." She cuts me off. "I want it here."

Tinsel shimmies out of her panties and waits for me to ditch my boxers. I do as she wants, having a feeling that this is only the beginning of a beautiful relationship where I'd do anything she asks, for as long as she'll let me, so long as she lets me call her mine.

"All right then, Snowflake." My chest tightens. "Tell me what you want."

For the first time since Tinsel started this adventure, her confidence falters. She stammers, "I...um...I.

I stroke her cheek, then let my voice drop. "It's okay. I've got you, babygirl. Lie back and spread those long legs for me. I want to see your fingers in that pretty pussy of yours."

There's a flicker of hesitation, but then she obeys, lying back on the dock, and pushes a finger between her folds. I fist my cock, pumping slowly, eyes locked on hers.

"Like this?" she asks breathlessly.

"Yes, Snowflake. Just like that." I won't last long if we keep this up, but I don't want to deny her her pleasure either. Tinsel's eyes close as a slow, soft ripple of pleasure claims her. She bites her lips, her fingers moving faster in and out of her pussy, and it's almost more than I can bear. I want to be the one earning that look of bliss. I want her body tightening around me as she comes.

I want her.

"I need to grab a condom from the house, Snowflake." I kneel down and press my thumb to her clit. I play with her, rubbing her nub in tight, fast circles until she's gaping and on the edge of an orgasm again. Then I stop. "So, you're gonna keep touching yourself until I get back."

"No." Tinsel grabs my hand as I stand. "I have one in my purse. Candace gave it to me."

"Of course she did." I laugh, shaking my head, then grab Tinsel's purse from the pile of things I collected earlier. Sure enough, inside the first pocket is what I'm looking for.

I rip the packaging, slide the condom on, then lean over Tinsel. I kiss her softly while I press her legs open and line myself up at the entrance. She swallows hard, and I ask her one more time, "You know there are other ways to make the naughty list."

Her smile is sly. "Maybe. But they won't be as fun."

"You're right about that." I chuckle and push inside, slow and deep. Her back arches, and once I'm all the way in, she exhales my name like a prayer. "It drives me crazy when you say my name like that, Snowflake."

I lean down and kiss Tinsel, giving her time to adjust, then move my hips. She wraps her legs around my waist, locking me in, and knowing this is where she wants me is almost enough to do me over, but I can't lose control soon. Not when I haven't had a chance to prove to her why she should let me do this again. I take her ankles and hold them, pressing her knees to her chest. I want to go as deep as I can, though even like this I'm not all the way in. She's so tiny. So tight.

So perfect.

"Oh, my reindeer, Mason!" Tinsel cries, and I feel her body tightening and then releasing as her first real orgasm claims her.

I try to memorize this moment. The sight of Tinsel's soft hips in my hands. The little sounds she makes as I thrust into her. How her fingers clench into fists every time I find the spot that draws a breathy gasp from her lips. And then I remember what really does it for her.

Being told how fucking wonderful she is.

"That's right, baby," I tell her. "You're doing so good. Such a naughty little Snowflake, fucking me out here for everyone to see."

"God, Mason," Tinsel pants and I slam into her harder, grunting with each stroke.

Just as I hoped, the praise sends her over the edge again. Her beautiful pussy squeezes me as she comes, and I can't hold back anymore. I empty into the condom, each stream of seed milked from my dick as she pulses around me.

I bend down and kiss Tinsel's inner thigh as I pull out. She rolls onto her back and I take the spot beside her, pulling her to my chest as we both come down from the high of discovering each other, but this is the part I don't do.

I don't let girls linger. They aren't welcome to stay the night. And I damn sure don't cuddle.

But the thought of leaving Tinsel alone makes me queasy. I want her in my bed tonight, tomorrow, and every day she'll give me until we say goodbye. I want the cuddles and the conversations. The *how's your day* text messages and phone calls just to say *hey*.

I want more than Tinsel can give me and the only part of all of this that scares me is knowing that at the end of week I'll wake up and she'll be gone.

The darkness I've been fighting for months seeps into my thoughts. It taunts me with false hope that I can convince Tinsel to stay in Winter Key and a suffocating sadness reminds me she will never stay. She can't.

It would be so easy to let those thoughts ruin this moment, but I refuse to let the darkness win today. So, I ignore the heaviness falling over my chest and kiss the crown of Tinsel's head. "You are perfect, Snowflake."

She tilts her face up, smiling, eyes glittering in the dim light. "You're not so bad yourself. That was fun."

"How'd I do?" The question is meant to be a joke, but the words come out rougher than I intend because a part of me doesn't want the answer. I already know how her body responded to mine, the way she came undone around my cock and in my arms. But if I could do better—if I could make every second of our time unforgettable—maybe she'd give us a real chance. Maybe she'd come back to me.

Tinsel bites her bottom lip, the corners of her mouth tugging into a teasing grin. "I'll put it in my top five."

"Top five?" I roll onto my back and clutch my heart in mock pain. I turn my head to look at her and push, "But not number one?"

Tinsel stays quiet, refusing to answer, and that silence stings in a way I didn't expect. I lean over, capturing her lips in another kiss, softer this time, but threaded with determination. "Well, I guess that means you've gotta let me try again."

## Chapter Twenty-One

TINSEL

I wake to the smell of something burning.

Not just a little burnt, but an acrid, charred burning that stings my nose and jolts me upright before I'm even fully awake. Instinct has me out of bed, bare feet hitting the cool floor, and fumbling through my sleepy, blurry vision for the source. As soon as I shove open the bedroom door, a wall of grey smacks me in the face, and the smoke alarm wails like a banshee.

"Sorry!" Mason shouts, dropping the scalding-hot frying pan into the sink with a hiss.

Water blasts from the faucet, steam billowing up and mixing with the haze that's already there. I cough, wave my hands, then yank open the sliding doors to let in a rush of fresh air. The ceiling fan groans to life when I flick the switch, and the blades cut through the smoke.

Meanwhile, Mason drags a stool across the floor and hops up, broom in hand, jabbing at the smoke alarm until the shrill beeping finally dies.

"I tried to make you breakfast," he mutters, looking both sheepish and defeated. "Did you know eggs can burn?"

Despite the chaos, I bite my lip and try not to laugh. "Yep."

"Well, I didn't. Now, bacon...I knew that could burn." He

gestures at the blackened skillet with mock horror. "I just didn't think it would happen so fast."

That's it. I lose the battle against my laughter and press a hand to my mouth to smother it. My giggles only grow worse when I notice he's wearing the Mrs. Claus apron I won last night, the ruffled red trim looking ridiculous against his bare, broad shoulders.

"It was a good effort," I manage between laughs.

"You mean a spectacular failure," Mason says, but his dimples are in full force. He's taking this failure lightly, which feels like a big step. Last night, Candace told me that Mason took his dad's death as a personal failure and that he's been hard on himself ever since. So watching him smile now, in a kitchen still hazy with smoke, feels like more than a small victory.

"Good thing I'm not much of a breakfast eater anyway," I tease.

Mason's grin turns wicked. "I told you I was gonna change that."

"That's right." I cross my arms, pretending to think it over. "You just wanna fatten me up so I can't leave."

"I mean..." He shrugs, all casual bravado, but there's a flicker of honesty in his eyes that steals my breath. "If that's what it takes to make you stay, guess I'd better learn how to cook."

As much as I don't want to bring anything serious into our fun, there are some hard truths we have to face. "We should talk about that."

Mason exhales heavily, like I've struck a nerve, then leans down and presses a quick kiss to the tip of my nose. "There's nothing to talk about, Snowflake. You go home in a few days and I stay here."

"And that doesn't bother you?" I ask, even though I don't want the truth. I want a lie, wrapped in a bright ribbon, so I can keep living in this fantasy for a few more days.

"Nope. Not if it doesn't bother you."

It shouldn't bother me. I know it shouldn't. But the thought of going back to the North Pole sends a ripple of sadness through my chest. I force it down and smile. "No. So we agree, then. Neither of us gets attached. We just have fun."

"I like fun."

"I like you," I blurt before I can stop myself. The words hang in the smoky kitchen, reckless and terrifying, but true. I *like* Mason more than I've liked anyone in my entire life. The realization should scare me, but honestly, it just makes me sad.

"I'm pretty likable," he says after a beat, voice low, teasing just enough to make it easier to breathe again. Then he clears his throat and hitches his thumb toward the door. "It's still early. I bet Candace will make you breakfast if she's not too hungover."

"I told you, I don't need breakfast. I'm not even hungry."

"I am," he counters, like that settles it.

"Well, I've got something else you can eat." I hop onto the counter and spread my legs, challenging him. Mason freezes for half a second, then that slow, dangerous grin spreads across his face, and believe me, he does not disappoint.

It's nearly noon by the time I wander into *Last Call*, and now I actually am hungry. The lunch crowd has filled the place with a steady line of locals waiting for their takeout orders. A couple of people have claimed the high-top tables near the windows, picking at their sandwiches and chatting while they eat, but most are here just long enough to grab their food and go.

I squeeze past them, ducking behind the counter like I belong there, and pour myself a glass of water. Candace catches me in the act, flashing a grin while handing over a paper bag to a customer.

"Someone slept in late," she teases, wiggling her eyebrows.

"Can't say there was much sleeping." I look over my glass of water to see Candace pretend to gag dramatically, like she didn't orchestrate the whole damn thing herself.

"That's my brother. I don't wanna know." She laughs, then softens, sliding another bag across the counter. "Though, I've gotta ask, did he at least show you a good time? I told him he needed to dick you down good enough to make you stay."

"Candace, I can't stay." My voice comes out softer than I mean it to, barely audible over the clinking glasses and low hum of the bar. "I have to go home on Saturday."

"I know." She exhales, a wistful sigh that sounds like she's trying to let go of something, too. "But a girl can dream, right?"

"Yeah," I whisper. "A girl can dream."

But dreaming doesn't change reality. Staying here would only ever be that...a dream. Because when push comes to shove, I know I can't. As much as I don't want to marry Chris, and as much as I don't want to be Mrs. Claus, my choices were written long before this week. Still, in some alternate world, maybe I'd stay. Maybe Candace would be my lifelong best friend and Mason my something more. Maybe I'd discover who I am without Christmas titles and traditions because I like the girl I'm becoming here, and I'd love to discover everything about her.

"What?" I ask.

"Nothing," she says, though the smirk tugging at her lips betrays her. "I was just noticing that you're wearing Mason's shirt."

I glance down, tugging self-consciously at the oversized fabric. "So?"

"Well, I don't know about where you're from, but around here..." She leans in conspiratorially. "That means you've been claimed. Guys will know who you belong to. Respectful ones won't even bother hitting on you. It's a man's shirt, and it says everything."

"I...didn't mean anything by it. I just grabbed the first thing I saw."

"Sure you did." Candace's grin widens. "Doesn't change what it says. Everyone who sees you is going to *know.*"

"I don't belong to anyone," I shoot back, but I don't think I'm convincing anyone.

Candace arches a brow, her voice softening as her smirk lingers. "No, you don't. But you don't look like you hate the idea of belonging to Mason, either."

I don't answer. Because the truth is terrifying, she's not wrong. I don't mind the idea of being Mason's, even if it's just for the week.

"Speaking of my brother," Candace says, changing gears, "Where is he? Clearly, he's not keeping you occupied."

"He had a call around nine. Something about burst pipes."

"Oh, that's probably the Jenkins's place." She rolls her eyes. "Their pipes have been rattling for weeks."

"And they called Mason instead of a plumber?"

Candace shrugs. "They'll call one eventually. But ever since Mason's dad got sick a few years back, people started leaning on him. First, it was just the family trying to keep him busy. Mason gets a little lost in his head sometimes, but then the whole town caught on to his struggles. Now he's basically Winter Key's handyman, even when the job's out of his league."

"He mentioned his dad died, but he didn't get into the details. How long ago was that?"

"Earlier this year," Candace says quietly. "Mason took it hard. Everyone was worried for a while. And then the bait shop closed last week..." Her voice trails off as concern colors her features. "Honestly, I thought he'd spiral again, but he's holding it together better than I expected."

Candace grabs a carton of orange juice and fills a glass, then tops it with champagne. She must need a drink for this conversation, and I don't blame her. She took a risk telling me Mason's secret, but I see his faults and I accept them because our struggles are what makes us strong.

And Mason... he's got to be the strongest person I've ever met.

Chapter Twenty-Two

MASON

"I went by *Hook, Line, & Sinker* earlier," Kevin says, nodding his thanks as I slide a beer his way. "Heard a rumor it shut down. Didn't even realize it was closed, man. When'd that happen?"

"Last week," I grunt. Kevin is the third person to bring up the bait shop tonight. Eighth since the cookie contest last night, and it's only Tuesday. Either the gossip mill's churning and my secret is about to come out, or everyone's waited until today to twist the knife of defeat in my chest.

Kevin frowns and shakes his head. "Damn, dude. That sucks. Why'd you close up?"

"Because it was haunted," I bite out. *Is he really this dense or is he just cruel?* "Why the fuck do you think?"

Kevin's face drains of color, and I feel somewhat guilty because, clearly, he's an idiot. He doesn't know what I've done yet. "Sorry, man," he mutters before retreating down the sidewalk.

I run a hand through my hair and take a deep breath. I'm fine. In fact, I'm probably overreacting. It's just a coincidence that people are coming up to me today, now that the building has passed inspection, and my window to change my mind is closing.

I need to just chill out and make it through the night so I can get home to Tinsel.

The feat grows harder with every drink I pour because every time someone opens their mouth, I expect another comment about the shop. Another reminder of what I lost, or worse, what I sold. I can *feel* the questions behind their eyes. *Why did Mason give up so easily? Who did he sell to? What's going to happen now that the first parcel of land has sold? Have the floodgates opened? Is our town ever going to be the same?*

I tell myself their unasked questions don't matter. That I did what I had to do to keep Dad's house, even though it meant losing the shop, but the words sound like bullshit, even in my own head.

I twist an empty shot glass between my fingers, the urge to pour something strong crawling through me. I want to drown the noise, dull the ache, and forget the looks. But I know better. Drinking when my head's like this never ends well, and I've already torched enough bridges this week...even if no one realizes the ground we're standing on is scorched.

"You okay, baby brother?" Candace's voice cuts through my thoughts. She leans on the bar beside me, hair tousled, eyes sharp and searching for a crack in my mask.

"Oh, you know. Just another day in paradise," I tease, but she's not buying it. I can tell by the way her mouth presses into that tight, knowing line. Candace could always see through me. She's got a sixth sense for bullshit, especially mine. I grab a rag and start wiping down the station, pretending to be busy, hoping she'll go away.

She doesn't.

"You know Tinsel only has a few days left," she says casually, though her tone's anything but. She's testing me. Watching for the reaction I'm trying my damndest not to give her. "Why don't you let me cover your shift tonight? I can probably get one of the girls to pick up your others this week, too."

I freeze mid-wipe. "You don't have to do that."

"I know I don't have to." Candace tilts her head, softening her tone as she adds, "But maybe you *should* take a break. Go see her. You've been moping around here like someone stole your favorite wrench all night."

Her teasing lands gently, but it still finds its mark. The thought of seeing Tinsel, of holding her again, of hearing that laugh that feels like sunlight, hits me in the chest hard enough to steal my breath. I want to ditch my job and find her, and that desire scares me. Not because I want her, I'm comfortable with my feelings, but because I'm afraid of what this ache will feel like when I can't satiate it.

"I don't need a break," I mutter, though the lie scrapes my throat raw. "I'm fine."

"Uh-huh. Sure you are." Candace plucks the rag out of my hand and tosses it in the dirty-dish bucket behind us. "You might be fooling everyone else, but you're not fooling me. You've been quieter than usual tonight. Darker. And it's time that mind of yours finds some light."

"I'm fine," I repeat, but the word comes out rougher, more defensive than I mean it to. "I'll stay."

She studies me for a moment, then sighs. "Suit yourself, but if some other loser curls up to your girl during the movie and steals her away, that's on you."

And with that, I lose all my fight.

"Okay," I conceded. "Thank you."

"Of course." Candace grins, victory glinting in her eyes. "What's family for, if not to help you get laid?"

I wrinkle my nose, but Candace just laughs. She walks around the booth and grabs my arm to pull me out of it. "Go. I've got this."

I stop fighting myself and wind my way through the crowd. The whole town's turned out for movie night, and given the number of faces I don't recognize, we've got some outsiders, too, which is great. That means Candace's social media plan to increase our exposure is working. But it also sucks because people are everywhere, and I can't find Tinsel. Dozens of blankets are sprawled across the square. Kids are running wild. Couples are curled together under the glow of string lights. It's a beautiful scene, but the more I wander through the street, the more anxious I feel.

Until, finally, I spot a familiar flash of white-blonde hair streaked with red and green. She's sitting on a blanket near the center, laughing at something the woman next to her says, wearing *my shirt* from this morning like it belongs to her.

A smile tugs at my lips. For a second, I was worried I blew it last night and Tinsel might have left without saying goodbye. Instead, she's at the center of everything, showing everyone that she's mine.

I take her in again, letting my gaze memorize the sight when I notice she's sitting on the hard concrete. The blanket under her is a thin beach throw that will keep her clean, but not comfortable.

I double back to *Last Call* and use the back entrance to get into Candice's upstairs apartment. She'll be mad when she notices her couch pillows are missing, but I steal two before heading back down.

I decide to go out the front door to see how Cara's doing manning the bar on her own. The place is nearly empty. Only two people are inside, lingering with beers because most everyone in town is out in the street for the movie.

Josh, our bouncer, leans against the doorway, arms folded, and nods when he sees me. "Are you heading out to watch the movie?"

"Yeah." I hold up the pillows I stole. "Tinsel's out there, and I know my ass won't survive two hours of concrete. But...uh... don't tell Candace I swiped these."

"I'll take your secret to my grave." He chuckles. "You look happier with that girl, and she seems pretty awesome."

"She is," I admit quietly. "It's gonna suck when she leaves."

Josh's smile fades and it feels like he can see right through me, to my demons trying to claw their way out of the box I'm fighting so hard to keep them in. "Don't focus on that, man. Enjoy the time you've got."

I nod again, throat tight. "Yeah. You're right."

"Hey," he adds as I start to walk away, his voice lower now. "For what it's worth. You're doing good, Mason. Even when it doesn't feel like it. You are stronger than you think you are."

That one lands deep. I give him a quick nod, then escape before I say something stupid, like admit how much I needed to hear that.

Out in the street, the crowd's settled as the first credits flash across the screen. I weave through blankets, making my way back to tinsel Tinsel. She's sitting knees tucked up close, her chin resting on them. I allow myself one minute to bask in her beauty, then walk around the last few blankets to join her.

"Hey, Snowflake," I say, as I crouch down to kiss the side of her cheek.

Tinsel's shoulder pinches up, and she giggles, then turns her head to look at me right before she presses a quick kiss to my lips. "Mason. I didn't think I'd see you until after the movie."

"Do you want me to go back to work?" I move to stand and she grabs my wrist and tugs me back down.

"Absolutely not."

"Good. I wasn't planning on leaving." I grin and hand her one of the pillows. "Here. You should sit on this. Concrete gets hard after a while."

"It's *already* hard," she says with a playful groan, shifting to get comfortable on the encased fluff. "My ass is killing me. You might need to rub it later."

"I'd be honored."

"So, don't judge me." Tinsel bites her bottom lip as she adjusts the pillow beneath her, "But I've never seen this movie."

"You've *never* seen *Elf?*" I blink. She's joking. She has to be. *Elf* is a classic, like *A Christmas Story* and *The Santa Clause*. "Do you guys not watch Christmas movies where you're from?"

She shakes her head, smiling faintly. "Not really. They're kind of redundant and a little insulting."

"You're kidding."

"I wish I was," she says, tucking a strand of red hair behind her ear. "My family takes the Christmas business pretty seriously."

"Well, luckily, this movie barely takes place in the North Pole, with even less Santa exposure," I tell her, leaning close enough that my breath stirs her hair. "Hopefully, minimal offense will be taken."

Tinsel looks into my eyes, teasing me with her closeness, only to brush her shoulder against mine, then pull away. "I'll trust your expertise, then."

The movie starts, but as the story unfolds, my attention drifts. I've seen *Elf* a dozen times. I know every punchline, every scene, every bit of holiday chaos that's supposed to make people laugh. But tonight, the real show isn't on the screen.

It's sitting right beside me.

Tinsel's nose wrinkles every time Buddy yells excitedly about Santa, and she shakes her head like she can't believe anyone would find it funny. Sometimes, her lips even curve into a smile when the crowd laughs, and twice she even lets a laugh slip free. And each time I hear it, something in me eases. The tension. The weight. The guilt. All of it.

Tinsel catches me watching her more than once, but I don't look away. I don't even try. I just grin, and she rolls her eyes with a tiny, knowing smile before turning back to the movie.

She watches the screen and I watch her.

"I liked it more than I thought I would," Tinsel says once it's over and we're walking toward my truck. "It was surprisingly cute, though completely inaccurate."

"Is that so?"

"Oh, yeah. No one at the North Pole wears hats like that. Or tights that tight."

"And you know this because...?"

Tinsel hesitates, her steps slowing to a cautious stop. When she finally looks at me, her eyes are soft, almost nervous. "Because I'm an elf."

For a beat, I just stare at her, trying to understand where this is going. But the longer the silence stretches, the more it sinks in that she's waiting for me to laugh or call her crazy, but something about the way she looks at me strikes a chord. I recognize the doubt and insecurity in her eyes. I see a version of it in my own every time I look in the mirror.

I cup Tinsel's cheek and brush my thumb across her soft skin. I will never laugh. Never make her feel like she's worth anything less than her weight in gold.

"Well," I murmur, "Even so, you're the most beautiful elf in the world. I'm lucky to have you by my side this season."

Tinsel exhales a ragged breath and shakes her head. I almost frown because usually my praise makes her glow like a Christmas light in the dark, but for some reason, my words don't hit this time. "You're just saying that because you don't know any other elves. I promise, I'm nothing special."

"That's where you're wrong, Snowflake." I tilt her chin up gently, my thumb brushing the edge of her jaw. "You are kind and beautiful and the only thing that seems to settle the noise when my world gets too loud." My voice drops lower as I give her a truth she's probably not ready for. "If I could, I'd keep you here. Not because I'm selfish and want you for myself, though there is some truth to that, but because if the people you live with can't see how truly amazing you are, then they don't deserve you."

Tinsel looks at me like I've just cracked some part of her and exposed a raw nerve that's never been seen. "You really think that?"

"I don't think it, I know it," I say. "And deep down, you do, too."

A long moment passes before Tinsel says, "I'm getting kinda tired," though her tone is anything but sleepy.

"Are you now?" I say, letting my fingers trail down her arm, slow and deliberate. "You wanna go home and lie in bed with me? Maybe let me give you that back rub you mentioned?"

She steps closer, close enough that I can feel the warmth radiating from her skin. "Since you were so honest earlier, I should probably warn you that once your hands touch me, they won't stay on my back for long."

I grin, and a low, rough hum vibrates in my chest. "I kinda hope they don't."

"Then what are we waiting for?"

I open the truck door, offering my hand like a promise I don't fully understand but know I'll keep anyway. "Let's get you home, Snowflake."

# Chapter Twenty-Three

MASON

Sleep doesn't come easily anymore. It hasn't for a while.

The fan hums above me, spinning slow circles that do nothing to chase off the weight pressing down on my chest. The air is thick, heavy with salt and humidity, but that's not what's keeping me awake. My thoughts are. They've been running in loops all week, and tonight they're louder than ever.

Beside me, Tinsel shifts under the covers. Her hair spills across the pillow like a halo of snow, the faint shimmer of it catching the moonlight. For a moment, I think she's asleep, but then she rolls over and presses herself against me, her palm finding the center of my chest like she's grounding me from myself.

"You still awake?" she whispers.

I swallow hard, eyes tracing the faint glow from the clock across the room. "Yeah. Can't sleep."

"Tell me what's wrong." She props herself up on one elbow, her gaze catching mine in the pale blue glow of the moon that seeps through the curtains.

"It's the bait shop." I roll onto my back and look her in the eyes. She doesn't have the same connection to the shop that everyone else does, but she's quickly becoming one of us. Telling her what I've done could be the nail in our coffin, but I've got to get this off my chest.

Her brow furrows. *"Hook, Line, & Sinker?"*

I nod, jaw tightening. "I listed it and had a buyer the first day. It's already under contract."

The words hang between us, sharp and heavy. She doesn't say anything for a long time, just waits for me to keep going and tell her why. To admit how much of a failure I am, even though I've tried so hard to hide this part of myself. I take a breath that feels like sandpaper scraping through my lungs and let it all out.

"I know the town's going to hate me for it. Hell, maybe they already do. They'll say I sold out. That I betrayed my dad's legacy. But I didn't have another choice. I'm one missed payment away from losing everything—this house, the shop, the boat. Everything he left me. I thought I could fix it, I really did., but the debt and the hospital bills were too much." I take a shaking breath, needing a minute to let the words sink between us because they are heavy, And I'm tired of carrying them alone. "I tried to hold on, Tinsel. I tried so damn hard, but sometimes trying isn't enough."

Silence stretches between us. The kind that feels alive, filled with everything neither of us knows how to say. Then, quietly, Tinsel reaches up and presses her palm against my cheek. I stare at the ceiling for a beat, then turn to her. "Sometimes change feels like losing everything," she murmurs. "But maybe it's just making room for something better."

"Yeah, maybe, but if I could pull out I would. There's still time, I just don't know what else to do." My voice comes out rough. "Selling the shop feels like I'm cutting off a piece of myself. Even if the town forgives me someday, I don't think I ever will because Dad's in those floorboards. In the bell on the door. And letting it go feels like I'm losing him all over again."

"You had to make a choice. Loose everything or something. Trying to save what you can doesn't make you a bad guy, Mason. It makes you resilient."

"Maybe," I say, and it's the closest I can get to *yes*. "But it still feels like failure."

"I don't think you failed. I think you did what anyone else in your shoes would have done." She kisses my temple. "Don't beat yourself up."

I close my eyes and try to let her words sink in. I know Tinsel is right, and hearing her affirm that I'm not a piece of shit sellout helps to quiet some of the voices in my head, though a few remain. *She can say this because she's leaving. She won't be here for the fallout. She can't pick up your pieces when it's all said and done.*

I roll onto my side and wrap Tinsel in my arms. That voice, no matter how much I wish it were wrong, isn't telling me anything I don't already know. I'd just rather not hear it tonight. When I open my eyes again, something I don't recognize flickers in TInsel's expression.

"Change your mind and decide I'm the villain of Winter Key?" I joke, though, that's what I feel like.

"No," she says, and the hint of a plan glints in her eyes. "I just had an idea, but I don't want to jinx it."

"What kind of idea?"

"The daylight kind," Tinsel says, her lips tipping like she's trying not to smile.

## TINSEL

When I wake, the other side of the bed is cold. The sheets are tangled, the pillow still faintly smelling like Mason's cologne, woodsy and salt-clean, but he's gone, and the quiet feels wrong without him in it.

I pad into the kitchen, hoping to find him ruining breakfast, but the kitchen is clean and smoke-free. I look out the sliding doors, checking for the boat, hoping that maybe he's steadied his mind with some early morning fishing, but it's still tied to the dock.

I peek out the front window next, half expecting to see his truck in the driveway, but it's gone. I guess I shouldn't be surprised, he's usually up early, working before the sun's even had a chance to rise. Still, something feels different today. He let me past his walls last night, and what I saw was worrisome. Mason is a broken man, stressed to the max, and worried about what everyone thinks of him. But he has a wish.

A wish the Christmas Magic can't fix.

But maybe I can.

I make a cup of tea and sit at the counter, trying to ignore the knot in my chest. My gaze drifts toward the bedroom, to the corner of my bed I swore I wouldn't lift until I was leaving. The one hiding Chris's letter.

I've avoided it for days, pretending it doesn't exist, but Mason's words keep echoing, and something in me—curiosity, fear, maybe even the need to make things right for him—wins out. I set my mug down and go to my room.

The letter's right where I left it, folded near perfectly into an origami envelope, waiting for me to untangle its secret. It smells faintly of peppermint and pine when I open it, the scent curling around me like nostalgia I don't want. Though that nostalgia is quickly smothered by nervousness as I sit down and read what Christ has in store for me.

*Tinsel,*

*I'm sorry.*

*I've spent years wanting what I wanted and calling it "tradition." I kept putting my plans in front of your voice, and then I acted surprised when you ran. That's on me, not you. I didn't listen. I broke the bridge between us one choice at a time, and then I tried to fix it with a flashy proposal you never asked for.*

*If there's still a way back to who we were before I fucked everything up—any way—I'm asking for a chance to earn it. Tell me what you need, and I will start by shutting up and listening. No speeches. No grand gestures. A walk. A call. Five honest minutes. Whatever you'll give me.*

*I know you need space. Take it. But please don't let silence be the last word between us. We're days from the ride, and the world doesn't deserve a Christmas dimmed by our stubbornness. I don't want to lose you and the season in the same breath.*

*You are my friend first, before titles, before what comes after. If all I get is a chance to fix that broken part of us, I'll take it.*

*—Chris*

Before I can talk myself out of it, I grab my phone and turn it on for the first time since I left the North Pole. It lights up instantly, notifications flooding the screen, but I ignore them and go straight to my contacts. My finger hovers over his name and a flutter of nervousness steals my breath.

If I do this, there's no unringing the bell. I'll be asking Chris for a favor, which means that any chance of me staying in Winter Key, no matter how small and unrealistic it was, will be gone. My freedom. My sanctuary. My friends. All to help a man I'll have to leave behind.

But not asking for help traps Mason beneath the weight of his failures. I've seen the ghost of his demons all week, hiding behind tired eyes and forced smiles, but last night was the first time I saw his struggles head-on. I can't walk away and let it devour him.

I press call and Chris answers on the first ring, voice low and steady. "Tinsel?"

"I need your help," I say before I lose my nerve.

There's a long pause on the other end, then the softest sigh. "Tell me what you need."

# Chapter Twenty-Four

## TINSEL

The rideshare drops me at *Island Café* in Islamorada ten minutes late, and when we pull up, Chris is waiting for me outside. He waves when he sees me, but his smile is soft, maybe even a little uncertain. He's changed since I left. Somehow, in just a week, he looks a little leaner. A little older. But those eyes—the ones that used to make the North Pole feel like home—still hold that same mix of warmth and weariness.

"You look..." he hesitates, searching for the right word. "Different."

"Florida will do that to you." I give Chris a quick hug, out of habit more than anything, then follow him into the cafe. He doesn't hold the door, doesn't pull out my chair the way Mason would, and the absence lands like a small, private ache: a reminder of what I'm about to leave behind.

The waitress seats us, almost wordlessly, and delivers us waters and menus before disappearing with the promise of coming back. Once we're alone, Chris folds his hands on the table. "You said you needed help."

"I do." I take a breath. "It's about my new friend, Mason, and his bait shop. He inherited it from his dad, but the inheritance came with more debt than he could manage. He's about to lose everything, Chris. The shop, his house, the town—all of it."

Chris takes a sip of his water and leans back in his chair. "I'm sorry, but I don't understand. What do you want to do?"

"You work with small businesses all the time. The North Pole partners with toy shops and tech companies, sometimes asking nothing in return for years. Maybe we can do the same for Mason. We could be his silent partner and offer... the worls... I don't know...free fishing lessons or something."

"Tinsel, you know that's not how our partnerships work."

"Why not?"

He sighs heavily and looks around to make sure no one is listening. "Because the Magic isn't meant for them."

I lean forward. "For *them*? You mean adults?"

He nods once. "Our Magic sustains belief. Hope. Wonder. The things children still hold onto. Adults have already let that go."

"So, they don't deserve help because they're, what, too old?" My voice rises before I can stop it. "You give kids the perfect Christmas every year, but the people who raise them—the ones who sacrifice everything—get left with nothing? How is that fair?"

"Are y'all ready to order?" Our waitress walks over, asking, likely to assess if the argument is cordial or if it needs intervention.

"Not yet," I snap at her. The woman's eyes go wide, but she walks away. When she's gone, I give Chris a pointed look, waiting for him to tell me why growing up means losing the privilege to be touched by Magic. Magic that he gives to every child, naughty and nice.

Chris's jaw tightens. "It's not about fair. It's about balance. You can't force belief where it's no longer wanted."

"That's not true," I whisper, shaking my head. "Mason believes. Maybe not in Santa or flying reindeer, but in something real. He works every day for everyone else. If that's not belief, what is?"

Chris looks at me then, really looks, and something flickers in his eyes. Sorrow, maybe? Regret? "You don't understand, Tinsel. There are rules. Magic has limits."

"Then maybe the rules are wrong," I snap. I hate this. I hate feeling helpless when Chris has Magic at his fingertips, literally, and could change Mason's life for the better.

His expression hardens. "Enough."

"No," I snap, voice trembling. "You can give billions of kids gifts they'll forget by morning, but you can't lift a finger for one man who actually needs it?"

He stands, pushing his chair back with a scrape of wood against tile. "A man. Not a boy. I guarantee this *man* isn't as great as you think he is. Belief aside, there's a reason we stop bringing Magic to adults. They lie, cheat, and steal to get what they want. They make the choices that sever the connection."

"I'm so stupid." I shake my head, and for a moment, we just stare at each other. "You almost had me fooled, you know. Your note made it sound like you actually gave a damn about what I wanted, but all you care about is having me at your side so you can inherit the season."

"You're wrong," he growls.

"Then prove it! Show me. What has Mason done to be so unworthy? Was there something specific? Or is it a switch that's flipped when kids turn sixteen?"

"You want to understand where he fucked up? Fine." Chris reaches for my arm. The touch is gentle at first, but power hums beneath his skin, alive and dangerous. The air ripples. The scent of salt and citrus twists into peppermint and snow.

"Chris," I warn, but it's too late. The world around us blurs as the restaurant vanishes into a rush of light and frost. The warmth of Florida collapses into the cold and biting air that smells like home and heartbreak. When the shimmer fades, I'm standing on solid ice.

And we're back in the North Pole.

# Chapter Twenty-Five

TINSEL

Chris's hand drops from my arm as we shimmer into the backyard of the workshop. Frost curls out from the imprint his palm left on my sleeve, like the Magic can't decide whether to cling or let go. I shiver, my shorts and Mason's fishing shirt nowhere near heavy enough for this weather, and hug myself to stay warm.

"Come on." Chris pushes the door open, letting it fall closed behind him, assuming I'll follow.

I do, but only because if he dragged me back to the North Pole, it better have been for something purposeful. Not a power play because he can.

I grab a fur-lined coat off the rack and slip it on. I don't know whose it is, and it's a little snug in the arms, but it's warm and that's all that matters. Despite us being in the main shop and away from the snow, the cold up here permeates through everything. It's a piercing chill that will freeze the marrow in your bones if you let it.

The main hall is all vaulted beams and carved ice lintels, the kind of old that wears its own authority. Elves glance up as we pass —some with relief, some with curiosity, a few with that particular brand of North Pole pity I can't stand. I lift my chin and keep pace with Chris, refusing to feel small now that I'm back in his shadow.

We take the east stairs—the ones that wind past Records—and my breath fogs in pale ribbons. The door at the end looks like a storybook should, iron-banded and heavy. Chris doesn't bother with the handle. The Magic senses him and the door swings open in his presence. It also quickly closes when it senses me. I have to scurry to squeeze inside before the room shuts me out.

The Records room isn't a library. Not anymore. The "book" everyone tells children about is a cathedral of glass and light: a domed room containing a living archive. Columns of brightness rise from the floor like frozen beams, and names drift through the air as if someone wrote on the inside of a snow globe. Every child. Every year. Soft as breath. Endless as winter.

"The Big Book of Naughty and Nice," Chris says, doing his best tour-guide voice even though he knows I hate tours. "Names you know." His mouth tilts. "And names you don't."

I take a step toward the nearest column. It *leans* toward me—as if the room just sniffed the air and recognized its own. Some-where deep, this place knows exactly who I am, even if I don't right now.

"Did you bring me here to wow me?" I ask. "Because the lights are very pretty, Chris, but I want an explanation."

"That's what this is." He moves to the central dais. "Context. A deep dive on the human you think is so special."

Chris rests his hand on the pedestal and the light changes, narrowing and sharpening until it funnels through his fingers. Glyphs spin and settle on a language we both understand, and a screen resolves out of the glow, letters steadying into a single search bar.

"Name," he says.

My mouth is suddenly dry at the sight. The Christmas Magic I stole is nothing like this. It's breadcrumbs to a bigger being, one I knew existed but never saw before today. It's beautiful, awe-inspiring, and a little terrifying. "Mason Kraus."

The archive inhales, and a bright white light dives into the snow globe, dredging up years like silt, sifting and sorting until a file surfaces. I don't want Chris to touch it, but he expands the record and lines of text blossom like frost on glass.

"Stop," I say, but I'm too late. The file is open, exposed for us all to see.

> *KRAUS, MASON CAMDEN*
> *– Minor: Possession of fraudulent identification, Age 17 (intent: entry to 21+ event), Remediated*
> *– Falsehood: Misrepresentation of age to law enforcement (same incident), Remediated*
> *– Failure to file: Late personal tax submission (Year 1), Failure to submit (Year 2), Outstanding*
> *– Domestic discord: Repeated verbal altercation with sibling (Candace Kraus), Ongoing*
> *– Civic Merit: Uncompensated assistance rendered (elderly residents, infrastructure), Ongoing*
> *– Loss Event: Deceased parent; dependent care assumed, Significant*
> *– Belief Vector: Low (Wonder attrition; practical bias)*
> *– Current Status: NAUGHTY—PROVISIONAL*

"Provisional?" I ask, latching onto the only word that isn't a verdict.

"It means the system's still weighing the inputs," Chris says, scrolling through the file. His hand waves in front of him, effortlessly moving pictures from Mason's childhood across the screen.

"Inputs?" I step between Chris and the light, making him look at me. "You're running numbers on people's lives without taking into consideration the context that earned those *inputs*." My voice shakes. "Mason takes care of everyone. The archive has that in here." I jab toward the "Civic Merit" line, the only factor that doesn't make my stomach churn. "Sure, he's not perfect, but who is?"

"Christmas isn't about being perfect," Chris says softly. "It's about worthiness."

"Of what?" I demand. "A toy train? A smartphone?" I bite off the rest because I can feel the anger rising in me like a storm. "He had to file his taxes late. He was drowning in debt and responsibility. His dad—" The word sticks, and I don't even know why. I blink hard and keep going. "His dad died . Mason put the shop and the house up as collateral to pay the bills that were left behind. He tried to keep it all, and when he couldn't, he did the only thing left: he listed the shop so he wouldn't lose the home with it. That isn't malice. That's math." The ache in my chest goes sharp. "It's survival."

Chris's jaw works once. "The system sees patterns, not excuses."

"They aren't excuses," I snap. "They're *reasons.*"

Chris looks up at Mason's file the way some people look at tombstones, trying to translate chiseled facts back into the people they were before stone flattened them. "We built this so the world could be scaled," he says finally. "So the work could be bigger than one man guessing who deserves what. Accountability matters. Choices matter."

"And context *matters more.*" I stab a finger at the oldest line. "Seventeen-year-old fake ID? Remediated. You really want to anchor a man's worth to a dumb decision at seventeen? To a fight with his sister?" My throat tightens. "To taxes when he was busy keeping every cracked pipe and broken door in his town from falling apart because everyone calls him for help before they call anyone else?"

"The file also says low belief," he says quietly.

"Belief in what?" I fire back. "He believes in *people.* He believes that if something is broken, you fix it with your hands, even if they bleed. He believes debt isn't a dragon you slay in one day, it's a thing you pay down in small cuts that tear at your soul. If that's not belief, your vector's measuring the wrong thing."

Something flickers in Chris's eyes, and I almost, *almost* see the boy I used to know underneath the mantle of Santa he's been learning to wear. The boy who could hear a crack in someone's voice and find the exact word to fill it. A boy who saw a little girl being teased, eating lunch alone because of her hair and chose to sit with her. He was my friend before he became my duty.

"Tinsel," Chris says, and my name is a plea. "Children are the point. That's who the Magic is for. To keep wonder alive long enough so they can grow into something good. Adults—"

"Adults keep the lights on," I whisper. "Adults keep the pantry stocked and the sheets clean. Adults sell the last piece of their souls to keep the roof from being taken by the bank."

I swallow a knot of emotion that's threatening to devour me. I desperately want Chris to realize he can do so much more than just bring joy to children on Christmas. He can change people's lives. "You don't have to save everyone. I'm not asking for a blizzard of miracles. I'm asking for one partnership. One chance because when Mason falls, so will Winter Key."

I look into his blue eyes, searching for some sign that my words are sinking in, but he's a blank slate. So, I keep going.

"The people there will ostracize him and boycott his bar. Candace, Mason's sister, will go into foreclosure, which means the one enticing feature that the town has to draw in tourists will be gone. Guests won't rent their villas because *Last Call* is gone there's nothing to do after dark. One by one, the people who live there will lose their homes. Eventually, the town will be bought up by developers and wiped out altogether, but we can save them, Chris." I step forward and take his hands in mine. "One Christmas Miracle can save everyone."

"No," he growls, and the word lands like a gavel.

"Because he's on a list?" I ask, incredulous. "Because a database says he's provisionally naughty?"

"Because when we bend the rules," Chris says, eyes on the

archive instead of on me, "the rules break. And when the rules break, the work fails. I can't risk the work."

"So, the work matters more than *people*." My laugh is a small, terrible thing, but I'd rather laugh than cry right now. "You know, when I left, I thought the problem was me. That I was running because I couldn't handle duty. But this isn't duty. It's cowardice dressed like order."

"I made a mistake. I shouldn't have brought you here," Chris says, and his voice has gone careful, like he's stepping around something that could explode. "I thought you would understand, but you don't. I'm not sure you ever will."

"The mistake you made was forgetting what Christmas means to people outside of the North Pole." I take another step toward the file. The light warms against my skin, aware. "It's kindness, compassion, and a light for people to grasp onto when they're lost in the dark." My throat goes raw on the last word. "This may be how your dad saw Christmas, but you have the power to change things, Chris, and it breaks my heart that you're too much of a coward to do anything."

"Tinsel—"

"No." I reach toward the dais, wondering if I can command it the way he does.

Power hums under my palm, and for a heartbeat, I see Mason's name written beside a thousand quiet kindnesses the system recognized but didn't weigh: groceries carried, midnight repairs, the way he is a hinge that keeps a whole town from coming off its frame. I don't know if it's the archive showing me or if it's something in me refusing to forget what it's like to be looked at and actually be *seen*.

Magic threads around my fingers, up my wrist, into my pulse.

"Don't," Chris snaps, catching my wrist—then jerks back with a shock, eyes wide.

The glow climbs higher, wrapping me, and the record blooms open wider than it did for him. It shows me more than the missteps that dragged Mason to rock bottom; it shows me a way out.

"If you won't help because a rule tells you not to," I say, steady now, "then I will."

Chris's gaze drops to my ring, to the gold band's faint, failing light, and panic cracks his voice. "Tinsel, you don't have enough Magic to—"

I close my eyes and think of Florida heat. Of a dock that creaks when you shift your weight and a kitchen that smells like orange peel and salt. Of laughter built on borrowed bravery and a man who looks at a broken thing and doesn't ask if it deserves fixing before he reaches for his tools.

The Magic inside the ring surges, bright and wrong and mine. Snow peels away. Bells cut off mid-ring. The peppermint air cracks, and Florida's humidity slams back into my lungs. I stumble as the dust fades away, catching myself against sun-warmed stucco, and it takes a breath to realize where the Magic set me down.

I'm downtown in the alley beside *Last Call*. The street is a river of bodies and bright, but the people I hear aren't enjoying tonight's Reindeer Games. They're angry, shouting all at once while Candace tries to control a crowd that isn't listening.

I cautiously step into the chaos, trying to make sense of what happened while I was away.

"Sold out!" a man shouts.

"Promised us!" another voice bellows, tremoring with a kind of grief I recognize.

A name hisses through the crowd, over and over until it's a tide: *Mason*.

I push forward and scan the faces around me, looking for someone I recognize, hoping they can tell me where Mason is and how everyone learned about the bait shop.

A woman jostles my shoulder, tear tracks bright on her cheeks. "He listed it," she says to no one and everyone at once.

"Hook, Line, and—he *sold* it. He let the wolves into our house, and now they'll come for us all!"

I find the bottom step and climb, wedging myself into the space beside Candace and take her hand. Her eyes cut to mine, surprise flashing, then relief so quick I think I imagined it. "What happened?"

"A man showed up tonight," Candace says, trying to hold her composure, but there's a slight shake in her voice. "He started talking about the bait shop, making plans, telling us what he was going to do to it and this town. Mason walked him out, but then Kevin started asking questions, and then Brenda..." Candace takes a deep breath. "Brenda started looking at her phone and saw that the bait shop was under contract."

*Shit.* I run my hand through my hair, trying to assess the situation. The bar is empty. The doors closed and probably locked for the rest of the night. People are scared, angry, and—

"What are you wearing?" Candace asks, noticing the coat I forgot about.

"Nothing." I push it off my arms and let the heavy thing fall to the ground beside me. "Where's Mason now?"

She tips her chin down the block, and there he is. Standing in the street in front of a man in a navy suit, shoulders squared like a pier taking wave after wave because there is no other place for the water to go. The crowd is a ring around them, hungry for something I don't have a name for.

I'm moving before I know I've decided to. The last scrap of Magic coils like a promise, hot in my palm, already swirling and ready to fix things before they become too broken.

"Tin—" Candace reaches for me.

"I've got him," I cut her off and run toward Mason because Chris can keep his rules and his lists. Everyone deserves a little Magic in their lives. It doesn't matter if they're young or old, or what they've done. Good people sometimes do bad things, but that doesn't make them bad people.

Mason's no saint—but neither am I. I broke into the sanctuary. I stole Christmas Magic. I ran.

So, if I've got one miracle left, it belongs to him.

# Chapter Twenty-Six

TINSEL

Magic leaves my body like a tide—quick, quiet, and a little cruel. What's left behind is the outline of what almost happened: wet pavement, neon humming, the ghost of a mob dissolving into small talk and laughter as people return to a night that was meant to be filled with warmth and camaraderie.

The ring on my thumb turns cold, the inscription that holds the North Pole's Magic nearly empty. I look at it, realizing that while I don't regret my decision, I don't know if I'll ever go home again. But I can't worry about that right now. Tonight, I need to get to Mason. I need to figure out exactly what the Magic did to the people of Winter Key. And, most importantly, I need to come up with a plan on how to save *Hook, Line, & Sinker*.

The man in the navy suit blinks and looks between Mason and me, confused. "What was I saying?"

"That you were leaving." I slip my arm through Mason's and give the kind of pageant smile that doesn't invite debate. "See you soon. Yeah?"

"Yeah." The guy rubs the back of his neck, then looks at Mason. "I'll call you Monday to finish that conversation about moving the closing up."

"Sounds good, Jeff," Mason says, but his words are hollow.

We stand there while Jeff climbs into his SUV. Headlights sweep over us, bleach out the street, and then he's gone. The quiet that follows makes my ears ring.

That was too close.

The Magic stole an hour or so of time from everyone it was close enough to touch, everyone who wanted Mason's head on a spike but it didn't save the bait shop.

All it did was give me time.

Mason's arms find me like a dock in a storm, solid where everything else is moving. "Where were you today?" he asks into my hair—no accusation, just the frayed edge of a long night.

"Dealing with some Christmas chaos," I say, truth wrapped in something gentler. "Nothing I couldn't handle."

"Does that mean you're leaving?" He asks, and the question lands between my ribs.

"Not tonight," I tell him and pull him close. "Not tonight."

When I wake the next morning, Mason's long gone and by the looks of things, so is his boat. Judging by how cold the sheets are, I'd say he left hours before the sun came up. I roll onto my back and stare up at the ceiling.

At some point, Mason might remember everything that happened last night. It might not be today, or tomorrow, or even next week, but eventually the memories will come back. I need a plan to save the bait shop before that happens, but I'd like to bounce ideas off of Mason. He knows more about this world than I do. He lives it every day, while I'm just visiting.

So, I decide to wait for him. I try to distract myself with TV, but I can't focus on the storyline. Any storyline, really. Murder. Romance. Animation. About ten or so minutes into everything I try to watchmy mind wanders to Mason and, even more frustrat-ingly, to Chris.

His whole view of Christmas is flawed. Kids deserve to feel the Magic of the day, sure, but what about their parents? Or the people working day in and day out to barely make rent. Don't they deserve some happiness too? I just don't understand how our holiday shifted from worldwide joy to a pure of heart checklist and an aged-out clause.

After an hour of trying and failing to force everything Christmas from my mind, I walk to the kitchen and open the pantry. Baking has always helped clear my head, but I used all of the flour and butter when I made cookies on Monday.

I lean against the counter and drop my face in my hands. I have to do something. I can't just sit here all day waiting for Mason to get home. So, I do the only other thing I know how to do.

I clean.

I sweep and mop and dust every inch of the house, but somehow sand still finds a way back inside because that's Winter Key's love language. Cleaning kills another hour, but when I look at the clock, it's only ten in the morning. If Mason follows his usual schedule, I should see him close to lunch.

I think about texting him to see if he's okay, and don't. I think about calling Candace, but I'm afraid she'll have fragmented memories of last night and start asking questions, so I don't do that either. I just stand there and clean the same counter twice, my rag working in circles to erase problems that Windex and terry cloth can't fix.

By ten-fifteen, worry has set up camp in my ribs. By noon, it's put down a welcome mat. I pace the house, walking from the kitchen to the big sliding doors and back before I finally come up with a useful idea. If I can't make my mind stop circling, I can at least have it circle something useful.

I pull out my phone and start hunting for solutions: small business loans, bridge loans, refinancing, or anything else. But every form wants the same things I don't have—a social security number, credit history, employment verification, and a permanent address. None of which I have."

I try to type *North Pole* into the residency field, and my phone autocorrects it to *Nope*, which feels rude but accurate.

Living in the real world is hard, and these forms have more rules than my mother.

I make a list of people I can call and maybe beg to help—*banks, grants, pop-up partnerships, Mom? (No), Chris? (Hell, no)*—and then rewrite it twice so it looks like progress and not a depressing account of my dead ends.

The hours stretch, sticky and slow, with me doing nothing but staring at my phone screen and searching for workarounds. I'm passively looking into how much kidneys go for on the black market when the front door clicks and Candace lets herself in like she lives here.

"Knock knock," she sing-songs, then stops dead in the doorway like she's walked in on a crime scene. Her eyes travel from my hair, which is in a questionable bun, to my outfit, which, considering the way Candace is staring at me, is even more questionable.

"What on God's earth are you wearing?"

I look down at the Jack Skellington pajama pants paired with a red *Merry & Bright* T-shirt I found at the back of Mason's drawer and shrug. It doesn't match. At all. Which is exactly why I put it together. "It's festive."

"It's psychotic. Those things do not go together."

"According to Mason, Jack Skellington *is* Christmas," I argue, spreading my arms like a Vanna White of bad choices. "You said I needed to be more festive. So, here I am being festive."

Candace's stare could melt the North Pole frost. "Honey, no. I meant you need to don a little red dress, candy-cane stockings, and a Santa hat. Sexy festive. Not...whatever that is."

"First of all, Santa would never be hot in candy-cane stock-ings." I pause, imagining what that might look like. Chris in his red coat, unbuttoned so it's his face I see, and not an old man's, with candy cane stockings under matching shorts and the signature black boots. It's quite the sight. "Although now I kind of want to give Chris a pair just to see what he'd do. I bet he'd wear them with pride."

"Who's Chris?" Candace asks, and wave of guilt sends a shiver through me.

"No one," I say, because of all the truths I've shared, that's one I can't quite let go of yet.

"For the record, this conversation isn't done, but for right now..." She shakes her head and tosses a bundle at me. "Put this on."

It's a red dress. Short. Tight. And bold enough to make me hesitate.

"No," I say automatically, throwing the dress back at her. "Absolutely not."

"Absolutely, yes!" Candace counters, volleying the scrap of fabric back at me. "You have to judge the Sexy Santa contest tonight. It's the most coveted privilege of being our Mrs. Claus."

"I thought the free drinks were the big prize?"

"Oh, people want those, too." She laughs, then pulls out the counter stool to sit on. "But having final say in who rides in the float beside you is a big flex, too."

"What if I told you I absolutely, one-hundred percent did not want to be Mrs. Claus this year?" *Or ever.*

Candace stares at me for a really long time. The silence that stretches between us is heavy and uncomfortable. When she finally speaks, she asks, "Do you...hate Christmas?"

"What? No. I love it. I just don't love the...job description." I sigh. How do I explain this? To her, being Mrs. Claus is an honor, but to me, it's an unreachable standard. "It's the cookies, spectacles, and endless cheer that I don't like. When I step into the role, I'm expected to be Santa's pillar of support but not his equal."

Candace reaches across the counter and touches my hand. "This has something to do with your family. Doesn't it?"

"Yeah. Sorry. I word vomited there for a minute." I look at the dress again and imagine what it might look like on. It's a beautiful piece that would probably highlight every curve and angle I have. Mason would love it.

*If only I knew where he was.*

"So," Candace says hesitantly. "I may have picked that dress for you tonight with Mason in mind. Just wash it before you give it back. Okay?"

"You are the weirdest sister I've ever met, but sure." I bite back a laugh. "Speaking of Mason, have you seen him today?"

"Yeah. He strolled into the bar a few hours ago to work. Why?" Her eyes go wide. "Did you two have a fight?"

"No, he just didn't come by for lunch like he normally does." *Tread lightly. I don't want to trigger any memories from last night and put a crack in the Magic.* "He's just been a little down. I was worried."

"Mason has good days and bad days," she says softly, "but it means a lot that you notice." Then her grin returns, feral and bright. "Which is why he needs you to pick him as your Santa for the parade tomorrow."

"Do I have to?"

"Yes!" She squeals. "Unless you want to risk sitting next to some rando from another Island, Mason needs your vote. People have been prickly to him today for some reason."

A curl of worry tightens in my stomach "Fine. When does the contest start?"

She glances at the time on the clock. "In about two hours, but that should give you plenty of time to get ready."

"I only need a few minutes to throw this on," I say, holding the dress. "We can head up to *Last Call* and I'll help with setting up."

"Do you want help with your hair and makeup?"

"I wasn't planning on doing anything with it."

"You are Mrs. Claus tonight. Don't get me wrong, you're beautiful as you are, Tinsel, but tonight you should be jaw-dropping. I can do that for you. Please." She clasps her hands in prayer. "Camryn is *au natural,* and Mason never lets me do his makeup. Let me live."

I laugh. "You just want an excuse to make me your life-size dress-up doll. Don't you?"

"Maybe."

"Fine." I stand and grip the dress, the fabric cool and slippery in my hands. "Give me five, and then you can do whatever you want to me."

"This is going to be so much fun," she says, already springing off the stool. "I'll grab my bag."

# Chapter Twenty-Seven

## TINSEL

"Fuck, Tinsel, what are you wearing?" The words slither down my spine, and I don't even need to turn to know who they belong to. My stomach knots as I spin around and confirm what I already dreaded.

Chris.

"A dress," I snap, more breathless than strong. I grab Chris's arm and pull us to the corner of the bar where Candace and Mason *hopefully* won't see us. "What are you doing here?"

"You look stunning," he says, his eyes rolling over my body as if it's the first time he's seeing me. The gaze lingers, slow and familiar, and for a split second, I remember snow-lit hallways and cocoa steam and how easy it used to be to breathe around him.

I cross my arms and glare. "If you think candy-coated words are going to smooth things over between us, you're wrong."

Chris reaches for my hand and there's a tingly warmth from his touch. I pull my hand away, not wanting to feel anything more than hatred for Chris and he exhales heavily. "I'm here because of you. I can't stop thinking about what you said yesterday. Maybe you're right. Maybe our system is flawed."

I drop my arms, terrified to hope, but the feeling flutters wildly in my chest. "You're going to help us?"

"Us?" he asks, eyebrows raised, then quickly masks his curiosity, mouth schooling back into neutral. "I want to see what makes this town so special to you."

"And you chose to come here? Tonight?." Panic surges hot and sharp. I grip his arm, my nails digging into his sleeve. "Chris, no. I'll find you in the morning, but you can't be here right now."

Before I can haul him toward the door, Candace's voice booms through the mic conspiratorially. "Well, well, well, ladies. Looks like Mrs. Claus found us a last-minute entry for the Sexy Santa Contest! Whoop whoop!"

"Oh, no," I mutter as all eyes pivot to me, still holding onto Chris's bicep like I'm mid-kidnapping attempt. He stiffens beside me and mutters a curse low enough for only me to hear. His eyes flick to mine, a dark warning hidden behind the smirk curving his lips."I'm sorry," I whisper.

Candace swoops in and latches onto Chris's collar like she's reeled him in. "Come on, handsome, you're coming with me."

Chris shoots me one more loaded look, then allows her to drag him toward the stage. He moves like he's in on the joke, soaking in the spotlight.

I find Mason's gaze again, and that fire in his eyes has shifted from anger to something darker. More primal. And I almost wonder if he's jealous.

He crosses his arms over his chest, muscles flexing as if he's holding himself back from tearing Chris off the stage by force. His eyes are pinned on me, sharp and knowing, and the muscle ticking in his jaw tells me everything. He might not know exactly who Chris is, but he's figured out this new Santa is from my hometown, and he hates that he's here.

Candace lines the men up: Chris, Mason, and two other guys. She puts the mic under Chris's chin first. "All right, sugar, what's your name?"

"Chris. Chris Kringle." He says it with a grin that earns a wild applause.

"Well, *Chris Kringle*," Candace purrs, "you can come down my chimney anytime." She winks, and the women in the bar scream like they've just been given front row tickets to Thunder Down Under.

Heat burns my cheeks while stress claws at my chest. Chris is here. Mason is glaring. The whole town is watching. And this year's Santa Claus is about to compete in a competition to prove how sexy he is. *Reindeer, help me.*

Candace works her way down the line, introducing each contestant. One's in a red Speedo with his chest painted like Santa's coat, another flexes oiled biceps. The crowd eats it up, hooting and hollering until she reaches Mason. "Well, ladies," she says, dragging out the words. "We all know this one."

Mason doesn't so much as blink at the women shouting for him. His eyes are locked firmly on mine, and the tension stretches taut enough to snap.

"All right, boys," Candace announces, tapping each man on the shoulder with an oversized candy cane. "Here's the drill. We're going to play a Christmas song, and each round we'll eliminate one Santa. You've gotta dance and strut your stuff until only the Sexiest Santa is left standing. And when we're down to two, we're gonna up the ante with a little surprise."

The DJ cues up a bass-heavy remix of *Jingle Bells*, and the Santas start moving. Chris hesitates a moment, then launches into moves I haven't seen since his senior year. He sways his hips, spins wide, arms thrown up with cocky flair. It's ridiculous, and a laugh bursts out of me despite my best efforts. Memories crash in of our candy-cane football pole and the striptease touchdown routine he thought was sexy.

I clap a hand over my mouth, but Mason has already seen the way *this* Chris affects me. This carefree, fun, gorgeous guy everyone wanted to date in High School, myself included. Not the uptight, rule-following Santa he's turned into.

Mason's gaze darkens, and the air between us tightens until I can barely breathe because Mason doesn't just dance. He prowls. Every roll of his hips is deliberate, controlled, lethal, and he never looks at the crowd. He only looks at me.

When the music cuts, I'm trembling with nerves and heat. Candace cups her hand around her ear. "All right, ladies, let's hear it for our Santas!"

The bar erupts, cheers splitting nearly down the middle between Mason and Chris. A poor guy named Fred, the one with the oil biceps, gets eliminated, and the rest move on to the next round.

"Round two. Shirts off, Santas!"

The crowd loses its mind, practically going feral. It's unsettling but amusing at the same time. I almost wonder if we should do something like this back home. Or would it be too weird because we've all grown up together? I guess it can't be any stranger than us dating each other.

I push the thought to the back of my mind when Chris yanks his shirt off with a showman's grin, and tosses it into the audience. His abs are cut, and the women scream like they've been waiting for this all year.

Mason loses his tee without the flourish, and the effect is just as devastating. It's only been a day since I held him in my arms, but seeing his body through everyone else's eyes is intoxicating. His muscles are golden, taut, and carved like something meant to be worshipped.

Candace hands out peppermint bowties, and Mason loops his around his neck like it's a collar, gaze never breaking from mine.

The music starts again, and Chris drops into a push-up, grinding his hips to the floor, and the women shriek. Mason prowls the stage with slow precision, rolling his shoulders, rolling his hips, making it impossible to look anywhere else. The other guys in the competition don't stand a chance, because as I look around the room, the girls—and even some of the guys—are mesmerized by the only two contestants that matter. Mason and Chris.

By the time the round ends, the cheers are deafening. Candace cackles like a witch at a bonfire, thoroughly amused. "Oh, this is good. This is *really* good."

The next round has a tissue box strapped to their ass while they booty pop ping-pong balls free. Chris throws himself into every challenge with reckless charm, flashing me grins like he's daring me to cheer for him. I don't. I can't. Because Mason's eyes are on me every second, possession radiating off him in waves. By the time the last ping-pong ball bounces free, it's down to just two of them. Chris and Mason.

My past and my present colliding under flashing Christmas lights.

Candace signals for the bar back to bring two chairs onto the stage. "All right, this is the moment you've been waiting for. Our Santas are gonna pick their Mrs. Claus and woo her into submission with a lap dance!"

The women surge forward, hands in the air, shouting to be chosen. Chris's eyes snap to mine. His smirk says everything: that he's about to stake his claim, and my breath stalls in my chest; horror and panic tangle. Before he can open his mouth, Mason's voice thunders through the speakers. "Tinsel. I chose Tinsel."

"What?" I squeak, heat flooding my face.

"You heard him, honey," Candace laughs into the mic. "Get your ass up there!"

Every nerve in my body goes haywire. I glance at Chris, whose face twists with fury he can't quite mask, but he doesn't stop me. So, I climb onto the stage and lower myself into the chair in front of Mason.

Candace grins, wicked and delighted. "All right, Santa, who's your Mrs. Claus?"

Chris doesn't look at her. He doesn't look at anyone but me. "That's not fair," he says, voice smooth as sin. "Every woman here is beautiful, but none of them have put in the work you have." His smile is sharp, dangerous as he swings his gaze to her. "Will you be my Mrs. Claus?"

The crowd loses its collective mind as Chris takes the mic from Candace's hand and guides her to his chair. For the first time since I've known her, Candace blushes, but she doesn't shy away from the attention.

The music slams back on, and Mason straddles me in one fluid move. "I don't like him," he growls under his breath, grinding his hips against mine.

I glare, but my body betrays me, melting beneath Mason's touch. His hands slide mine over his chest, his abs, lower still. The whole bar is screaming, but all I can hear is the pounding of my heart and the silent warning in his eyes. *Mine.*

When the song ends, Mason looks smug, victorious. Candace looks wrecked, her hair mussed, cheeks flushed like she just got the lap dance herself. "Oh my!" She clears her throat and tries to smooth her appearance. "I don't know about you ladies, but that was an experience."

She dramatically fans herself and winks at Chris over her shoulder. "Time for the hard part. We can only have one Santa in our parade tomorrow night, and the sexiest wins. You all got a candy cane when you walked through the door tonight." Candace holds up her mini candy cane, still in the wrapper. "You each get one vote." She grabs each Santa by the arm and pushes them into their chair, then takes the tissue box from earlier and sets it at their feet. "The Santa with the most candy canes at the end of the song wins."

Candace signals the DJ and drops her candy cane into Chris's box first. Slowly, everyone makes their way to the stage, dropping their candy and casting their vote. It's hard to tell who's winning. There isn't a clear line. Just a mass of people.

"Here. You need to vote, too." Candace says, striding up to me. She hands me a full-sized candy cane instead of a small one.

"Mine's bigger than everyone else's."

"I ran out of minis." She shrugs. "Sorry."

I swallow hard and walk to the front of the stage. The man I'm tied to and the man I want both stare at me. This is more than just choosing who I sit next to in a golf cart. It's like I'm choosing who I'd rather be with, and I can't make that decision.

I need Chris's help to save Mason. If I choose Chris, his ego will be stoked and I'll have more sway to win him over, but it'll crush Mason. If I choose Mason, Chris will assume my desire to save the bait shop is because of my feelings, not because I have fallen in love with this town. No matter who I choose, I loose.

The song ends seconds before I get to cast my vote, and I couldn't be more relieved. Candace picks the boxes up. She takes her time, milking the moment, pulling out each candy cane and counting it with a dramatic flourish in front of the bar. The room hushes, then surges, then hushes again.

"Uh-oh," she purrs, lips curving around the mic. "It's a tie."

My heart clenches in my chest because I know what's next.

"Mrs. Claus," she singsongs, sugary and merciless. "It's up to you to crown this year's Santa."

She dangles a Santa hat in front of her, beckoning me to take it. I walk back up to the stage, feeling like I'm walking to my death. The hat is warm from her hands and smells faintly like peppermint and cheap champagne. To make matters worse, Candace has both boys stand side by side, in front of me—north and south, past and present—everything I've been avoiding in one neat line.

"I'm sorry," I whisper—to one of them, to both of them, to myself—then rise on my toes and set the hat on Mason's head. The brim brushes my fingers, and his breath stutters, just once.

Candace lifts Mason's arm in triumph. "Ladies and gentlemen, your Winter Key Santa Claus!"

The room erupts in cheer again as the bar reverts to its natural state of chaos. But for me, everything is a hot, sticky, suffocating blur. My hands tremble so hard I can barely hold the candy cane cocktail Candace shoves into my grip; condensation slicks my fingers, the glass knocking softly against my rings.

Mason puts his arm around me and pulls me close, but I can't enjoy the moment. My thoughts are on Chris and the way my betrayal shone in his eyes. I look over my shoulder to where he was a moment ago, but don't see him. I scan the crowd, blinking through lights and bodies, dread sinking in my stomach like a stone because Chris is gone.

And that terrifies me more than if he'd stayed.

# Chapter Twenty-Eight

TINSEL

Mason left before I woke again this morning. Despite how happy he seemed last night, there was tension between us when we got home. He didn't pull me into his arms or try to steal a late-night kiss. His hands didn't roam my body, and he didn't wake me up with a teasing poke of his hard length against my backside.

He gave me a kiss goodnight, rolled over, and went to sleep.

And now, with me checking out tomorrow, he's gone again.

I push myself out of bed and walk into the kitchen. The sun has only just begun to rise. Orange and pink wisps color the sky. I make a cup of tea and walk to the dock to feel the warmth overcome the day one last time.

Tomorrow is Christmas Eve. By noon, North Pole time, Chris will be climbing into the sleigh to begin his journey around the world. I should be there. I was meant to be there. My decision to avoid the holiday felt different when I *chose* to leave, when I still had Magic humming under my skin. But now that it's gone—now that I can't stand by his side even if I wanted to—the ache is worse. There's no freedom in the absence, only loss.

The sun catches on the gold engraving on my rings, and I jerk forward so fast I nearly spill my tea. The ring is full, glistening like a star-filled night. My stomach churns in a new way as I try to figure out when and how Chris refilled it, but I'm at a loss.

I stand and walk back to the house for my phone. I should thank him, though it's the last thing I want to do. Turns out, I forgot to charge it and it's dead. I plug it in, and when the screen finally lights up, I have two text messages waiting for me.

> Chris: You were right. People are more than just inputs on a screen. I came to Winter Key to prove you wrong, ready to show you why each person there is flawed. Instead, I had more fun than I had in years. I understand why you don't want that place to change, and I think I figured out how to partner with Mason's bait shop in a way that won't trap you here or there.

> Chris: I want to do better than Dad did. I want to be a better Santa Claus, but I can't do it on my own. I need you, Tinsel. Come home so I can tell you my plan and we can change Christmas for the better.

I drop onto my bed in a daze. Chris is going to help, which is great, but I have to go home to learn how. I'm sure he has a great plan, one that would even allow me to visit Mason and Winter Key throughout the year, but the thought of coming back after I leave, of seeing the pain in Mason's eyes when he finds out I'm married, or watching him move on with someone else burns hotter than the first sip of scalding cocoa.

I close my eyes, letting the sting rise and fade, and then decide to go find Mason. He needs to know I have a plan before he does something stupid, like agree to an early closing date and lose his window to back out.

I grab a pair of shorts and slip them on with the shirt I slept in, then shove my feet into sneakers, and pull my hair into a loose knot. By the time I'm ready, the morning light has already crept across the kitchen floor, warm and gold, a reminder that time is running out.

Today is my last day in Winter Key.

And there's so much I have to fix before I leave.

As I walk up to *Last Call*, I can hear the murmur of voices through the walls, carrying onto the porch. The chalkboard sign out front says "closed," with no apology or opening time in sight, and the front door is locked. I peek through the window and see Candace and Mason in a standoff, yelling at each other, and I realize that either the threads of my Christmas wish are unbinding, or he told her.

I race down the steps and around the side of the building, my sneakers skidding on damp sand. The pulse of my ring is a faint hum that's more warning than comfort. Magic can only do so much, for so long. And I'm running out of both.

The back door to the kitchen is open, and I race through, as Candace's strained voice echoes in the empty space. "You should've told me before you made the decision."

"I wanted your hands clean," Mason answers, low and tired. "I wasn't dragging you down with me."

"That wasn't your call." She runs a hand through her hair and exhales a heavy breath.

I knock on the doorframe, knowing I'm walking into a disastrous moment. They both turn. Candace's eyes are rimmed red, her jaw set like stone. Mason looks wrecked. His hair is mussed, shoulders slumped, but there's still something steady in his gaze when it lands on me.

"The front door was locked. Is everything okay?"

"Yes," Candace snaps before he can speak. "My brother and I are having a conversation. You need to leave."

"Candace," Mason warns, and the rough edge in his tone is the only thing about him that doesn't sound completely broken.

She throws up her hands. "What? She doesn't need to—"

"She already knows." He cuts her off, tired but firm. Then his eyes soften, finding mine again. "Come in, Tinsel."

My heart hammers against my ribs as I step inside. The room smells like sugar cookies and burnt coffee, two scents that shouldn't go together but somehow do—like Mason and me.

"I might have a way to fix it," I say quietly.

Candace freezes mid-breath. "Say that again."

"My family..." I hesitate, choosing my words carefully. "We partner with small businesses all the time. I asked for help. They agreed." I look straight at Mason, trying to steady my voice. "They'll cover what you need to get out of trouble and help you stay afloat. The shop doesn't have to close. The house stays yours. It's a win-win."

"No," He says, and the word lands hard, sharp enough to sting.

I worked so hard for this opportunity. I don't understand why he isn't excited. I saved him. I gave him his Christmas wish. "Why not?"

Mason looks down for a long beat, then back at me. "Because something about those people has you spooked, Snowflake. Whatever they're involved with, I don't want any part of it."

"Mason," Candace says quietly.

"Stay out of it," he snaps, though the edge in his voice breaks halfway through.

"This is the only way," I say, stepping closer before they can spiral. "I have to go home tomorrow. I have to get my family through Christmas, and I don't know what's going to happen after that. But if you accept this offer, Mason—if you trust me—it doesn't just save the business. It opens a door for me to come back. To Winter Key. To you."

I don't add the part clawing at my throat, that a door isn't a promise of me walking through it. That love doesn't always survive the miles between worlds, but he already has enough pain to carry. He doesn't need mine added to the weight.

Mason stares at me for a long, quiet beat. His jaw flexes. His chest rises and falls too fast, like he's trying to breathe around something heavy. Finally, he exhales. "I'll think about it."

Candace swipes at her eyes, straightening her shoulders like a general in the middle of chaos. The tears are gone, resolve replacing them. "When's the deadline for the paperwork?"

"Monday," Mason mutters.

"Then we've got until Monday," she decides. "For now, we show up. We do the parade. We remind people why they love this town—and you—before the word gets out. If we can control the story, we might be able to soften the blow."

Mason's mouth twists, half a smirk, half defeat. "The parade. Right."

I step forward and brush my fingers against his wrist. His skin is warm, but he doesn't move. "Should we start decorating the golf cart?"

"Yeah," Mason says after a pause, his voice distracted and low. He gestures toward the back door I just came through. "The decorations are over here."

# Chapter Twenty-Nine

## TINSEL

The storage room under the steps leading up to Candace's apartment looks like a thrift store and a snow globe had a messy, little baby. Plastic bins that are stacked four high teeter like a Jenga tower every time Mason shifts something in the tiny space. Broken tinsel dangles from the handle of one tote, a snowman's decapitated head pokes out of another, and somewhere, under it all, I swear I hear the faint jingle of a lost bell.

Mason ducks under the low beam and yanks totes out without even checking the labels. Each one lands with a heavy *thud* that makes dust and glitter rise like ghosts. He tosses loose garland behind him, onto the floor, and I feel helpless to the storm raging inside him.

"What's wrong?" I ask.

Mason straightens, arms braced on a tote labeled **LIGHTS**, jaw set. "Nothing."

He shifts another box out of the space, and I'm not sure what else to do, so I crouch and pry it open. White and multicolored lights spill out in tangled clumps, the strands knotted together like they're fighting for their lives. I lift a handful of tangled wire, wishing today's decorating task was as light as last week's, and force a grin. "Is this our new meet cue? Untangling lights while we pretend not to like each other again?"

The quiet stretches until it starts to ache. We work side by side, the only sounds are the soft shuffle of plastic and the scrape of cords on tile. And then, out of nowhere, Mason asks, "Who is he?"

My fingers still. "Who's who?"

"Chris." Mason doesn't look up from the strand of lights in his hands. "Who is he to you?"

My heart stumbles. I should lie. Tell him it's nothing. That Chris is no one. But I can't. Not after everything. "It's... complicated."

"How complicated?" he asks, still not meeting my eyes.

"Too complicated."

The strand slips from his fingers, clattering against the floor. When he finally looks at me, it's not with anger, it's worse. It's quiet understanding as he's put together the part of the puzzle I wish didn't exist. "He's what you were running from, isn't he?"

"It's not that simple." I swallow hard because if I were only running from Chris, I could stay. I would leave the snow and expectations behind and risk insanity to stay in Winter Key because I think what Mason and I have could be real. It's messy, and scary, and doesn't make sense, but that's why I think if given a chance, these feelings could grow into something great. Something worth fighting for.

"It really is," Mason whispers, and something inside me cracks.

I step forward, before I can talk myself out of it, and slide my hand into his. His palm is rough, warm, familiar in the way a heartbeat is familiar. His thumb brushes the inside of my wrist in a fleeting touch that feels like goodbye even though neither of us says it.

We stand like that for a long time, surrounded by half-lit chaos and the faint smell of dust and salty air, both of us pretending that we don't know what comes next. That this is just another afternoon in Winter Key. That tomorrow isn't waiting like a countdown clock, neither of us can stop.

"We've got one more day." Mason's hand tightens around mine.

"One more," I echo, though we both know how little that really is.

"Then let's make it count." Mason's hand tightens around mine, and just when I think he means it, that he might kiss me, he turns his attention back to the tangled mess of lights.

My heart sinks like a stone because this is it. The beginning of our goodbye. I knew this moment would eventually come, I just didn't expect it to hurt so much.

## Chapter Thirty

TINSEL

Having spent every day of my life under the stigma of Christmas, I thought I knew what to expect from a Christmas parade.

I anticipated music, and people lined up down Main Street, filling each side of the sidewalk. I thought I'd see kids sucking on candy canes, dressed in their holiday outfits, running around as sugar causes chaos in their veins. I thought there'd be a steady stream of music, one song after another, for a seamless experience. Most importantly, I thought Mason would be in a cheap Santa suit, waving at the crowd while bellowing *ho, ho, ho* to everyone and no one at once.

But no.

Were there families waiting on the sidewalk for each cart to pass? Yes, though it seemed like most of the audience was outsiders looking for a family-friendly event to pass the time.

The music I thought I'd hear wasn't a cohesive stream of song, but loud, echoing streams that fought for air space with the golf cart behind it. Each driver had their own sound system, playing their own songs, and more lights than Santa's runway.

At one point, I asked if there was a competition for the best and worst decorated golf cart, but Mason just laughed, shook his head, and sipped on a beer.

That was the other disappointing part. Mason and I sat on a trailer that was a hodgepodge mix of lights, inflatable decorations, and our beach chairs in a giant sandbox. But the part I think was most depressing was that Mason and I were the most un-Claus-like Mr. and Mrs. Claus I've ever seen. Maybe it's because we both had a lot on our minds, but I felt bad for the people of Winter Key.

We failed them.

Even if they don't realize we did.

The block party that came after the parade is in full swing. The golf carts are parked haphazardly, providing extra decoration to an already crowded street. Pieces from each event are scattered throughout. The big projection screen from the other night has a kids dancing game streaming, keeping the children who aren't chasing bubbles busy while their parents drink and play reindeer games. All in all, it's a nice closing to the holiday season.

Tomorrow, families will start their Christmas traditions, and when the moon is high in the sky, Chris will visit each home, sharing Magic with both the naughty and nice.

"Are you okay?" Candace asks, sitting in Mason's empty beach chair. He left a little while ago to get a drink and has been mingling with people ever since.

I'm sure it's been hard for him, putting on a smile and pretending to laugh, while secretly fearing what his neighbors might know. Every so often, I catch a glimmer of the hatred and fear I saw Wednesday night, but then it's gone, the Magic keeping Mason safe for one more day.

"I'm fine." I smile as Candace hands me a cold water bottle, though my pageant mask doesn't feel flawless tonight.

"Mason won't say it, but we're grateful for what you did." She reaches over and squeezes my hand. "I know things with your family are complicated, but it means a lot that you'd stick your neck out for us. Thank you."

"He hasn't accepted the offer yet." My gaze drifts back to Mason, watching him nurse the same beer all night, while he pretends to drink with his friends.

"He will. He's just scared."

I take a sip from the bottle and sigh. "He doesn't have to be. I'm here."

"Are you though?" Candace leans back in her seat, and a similar tension to what's been building between Mason and me crackles now. "You're leaving us, but I think it's just now hitting that you're leaving *him.* We've joked about wanting to keep you here, Tinsel, but if I'm being honest, Mason doesn't want you to go, and neither do I."

"Candace..."

"Look, I get it. You have responsibilities, or whatever, back home, but this could be your new home. Go back. Clean up the mess you left behind, and then come back to start your life here. Winter Key is such a better place when you're around. I actually don't mind socializing with people."

Tears prick the back of my eyes because I want nothing more than to stay. "Candace, I can't..."

"Live with Mason, I know," she says, cutting me off. "Which is why you should stay with me. I have the extra bedroom upstairs. It's yours if you want it, and so is a job at the bar if you want to stay away from whatever deal your family is offering. I just need you to know that you have options before you run away."

She glances at Mason, whose smile doesn't quite reach his eyes.

"This might be the last time I see you, so..." She stands. "Give me a hug, but don't you dare say goodbye."

I do as she says, and her arms wrap tight around me. I squeeze her back, feeling a part of my heart break. In all likelihood, we'll never see each other again, but saying that word, *goodbye,* is too real. So, I say nothing.

"You should go." Candace wipes her eyes when she pulls back. "I'm sure you'd rather spend tonight with him, anyway."

Mason strolls up, hands tucked into his pockets, and shrugs. "Feel like watching the stars, Snowflake?"

# Chapter Thirty-One

## MASON

Is it lame to say I miss Tinsel already, even though she's sitting beside me?

Things between us haven't been the same since I let her in on my secret the other night, and I know the shift between us is my fault. I pushed her away, thinking it would make the inevitable easier, but all it's done is make being with her more painful, which is why I've spent as little time at home as possible the past few days.

But now that I'm here, I feel like I need to memorize each smile line, the sound of her voice, everything, because I know that when we say goodbye, we're done. I knew it in my bones, even before meeting Chris, though our conversation this morning only confirmed my suspicion.

She's his woman.

I don't know if they're on a break, dating, or worse, but it doesn't matter because I saw the way they looked at each other. He was enamored. She may not be in love, but there was something there all the same. Something that said I could only borrow her love.

"It's such a clear night," Tinsel whispers, looking up at the stars.

The full moon casts a warm glow down on us and she looks like an angel in the dark. She sits beside me, her hand casually touching mine, our pinkies overlapping on the worn wood. And when she turns her green eyes to me, she steals my breath, just as she's done every time we're together. My chest aches, knowing I have to let her go, but what else can I do?

Accept the offer to save *Hook, Line, & Sinker*, hoping our paths will cross again? Confess a love I don't feel, in hopes she'll choose me, knowing that while my heart isn't there yet, it easily could be? Beg and plead for a phone number I've never been given, even though our conversations would add paper cuts to my heart every time I'm left on *Read*.

I want to do all of those things, but I respect Tinsel's wishes more. If she wants to be in my life, she'll open the door. If she doesn't... Well, I'll have a story to share when I'm old and sitting alone at a bar about the girl who got away.

"I'm sorry," I say, and a small wrinkle settles between her eyebrows.

"For what?"

I let out a heavy breath and lay back on the dock. This isn't even our goodbye, but I can't barely get through the night. How am I going to survive tomorrow?

"I saw in a movie once that no matter where you are in the world, the moon isn't ever any bigger than your thumb." I squint and hold my thumb up to the sky. Turns out, the movie was right. Somehow, my thumb swallows the moon, even though it's full and bright.

Tinsel lays beside me and sticks her thumb in the air, too. She bites the corner of her bottom lip, then smiles when the perspective change proves to be right. "I'll have to try that when I get home."

"Can I have your number?" I blurt, having lost control of my thoughts. I wasn't going to ask. I was going to let Tinsel call her shots, but the mention of her going home, her leaving, cracked my resolve.

She rests her cheek on the dock and looks at me. "You can, but I don't know how much good it'll do."

"Because we're cutting ties after tonight?"

"No." She rolls onto her side and props her head up with her fist. "Because we aren't allowed to have them. That's a work phone. I may have stolen it before I left last week."

"Somehow." I laugh and grab her by the waist, shifting her so she straddles my lap. "That doesn't surprise me."

Tinsel rests her palms on my chest and looks down at me. The moonlight reflects on the white of her hair again, and this is an image I never want to forget. I cup her cheek with my palm and pull her down to kiss me. Her soft lips part the moment they meet mine, and we stay like that for a long time, drinking each other in, kissing like the weight of tomorrow isn't looming, and we have all the time in the world.

"Let's go to bed," she says, pulling back and resting her forehead against mine. "I want one more perfect night with you."

I shift, sliding my hands under her legs, and lift her as I stand. Tinsel squalls and then laughs, her eyes lighting up with pure joy as she curls her arms around my neck. I carry her into the house and we fall on the bed together. As soon as her back meets the mattress, we're kissing again.

Her hands are everywhere, on my back, in my hair, running down my sides, and her legs wrap around my hips. I try to slow the moment by breaking the kiss and nibbling on her neck, but she's not having it.

Tinsel cups my cheeks and looks me in the eyes. "I need you, Mason. Right now."

I need her, too. More than I can admit out loud because acknowledging how attached I am is terrifying. I shimmy my shorts off and grab a condom from the nightstand drawer. They're old. I honestly don't know when I bought them because I can't remember the last time I brought a girl home. But it's better than nothing.

I roll it on as Tinsel slides her panties off and pulls her dress over her head. She's naked in my bed, and it is a sight I'd give anything to see again.

Before I let my emotions ruin the moment, I capture Tinsel's face in my hand and claim her lips. We go slow, unlike the last few times we've fucked, and the careful way she lets me worship her body feels more intimate than any other time I've done this.

Her ankles hook around my waist as I push my way inside, and once we're connected, she holds me there. We stare at each other, neither one of us wanting to blink or miss a single moment. Tinsel's tongue swipes across her bottom lip, and it looks like she wants to say something, but she kisses me instead, which is probably for the best because I have a feeling that whatever is on her mind will ruin me.

I take my time, letting her guide when we switch to new positions, until I know she's satisfied in each. Eventually, I can't delay the inevitable. "I'm close," I mumble into her shoulder, my hands gripping her hips.

Tinsel looks over her shoulder and breaths my name, "Mason?"

The question in her tone has me hesitating. I slow my stroke, delaying my release just a little longer when she asks, "Will you take the condom off?"

My balls tighten, nearly ready to explode from the question alone, and I stop moving. "Are you sure?"

"Yes." She hesitates, doubt filling her eyes as she touches my soul with her gaze. "Only if you want. I've never done that before. I want you to be my first."

If it was possible to fall in love, right now, I think I might have. I've never been anyone's first anything before. And Tinsel is choosing me to be hers.

I dip my hands under her to cup her breasts, then shift Tinsel upright so I can kiss her lips. She locks eyes with me when we break and nods slightly, then crouches down again, resting her weight on her forearms while pushing her perfect, beautiful, round ass in the air.

The condom pulls off with a *snap,* and I toss it to the ground. I hesitate for a heartbeat, never having gone bareback before. There's a lot more pressure this way. A lot more risk.

But then Tinsel looks over her shoulder at me again, a sly smile lifting her lips as she wiggles her peach in anticipation, and any restraint I had is gone. I ease my way back inside her and the feeling is unlike anything I could have imagined. Her pussy is warmer, wetter, and tighter than it's ever been, and when I move my hips to give her pleasure, I'm dizzy from how good it feels.

"You feel incredible," I tell her, though incredible isn't a strong enough word to describe how amazing this is.

"Faster, Mason," she says and then sighs. "I want to know what it feels like to have you come inside me."

*Oh, goddamn this woman!* I do as she asks and pick up speed. Each thrust is heaven and hell all at once. Torture in the best way, because to give her pleasure, I have to pull out some, but then I get to go right back in.

Tinsel's fingers curl at her sides, tugging the sheet out of place as she gets close to another orgasm. She moans, "Oh, my reindeer," and then tightens around me.

I don't want to hold back any longer. I push as deep inside as I can and let myself go. The moment is everything I thought it would be. Exhilarating. Terrifying. And unforgettable.

And I don't regret it.

Not even when the awkward part comes after, when I don't know how long to stay inside her or what the minimum amount of time is to hold her in my arms after I pull out before we can get cleaned up.

Tinsel rolls onto her side and lays her head against my chest. "It was warm."

"What was?" I ask, my eyes drifting shut.

"You," she says softly. "I wasn't expecting that."

I shift and look down at her, wanting to see every micro expression when I ask, "Do you regret it?"

"No." She kisses me quickly, just a soft press of her lips to mine, and it's enough. "But I am sticky. I want to take a shower, then fall asleep in your arms. Sound good?"

It sounds like heaven.

And even though hell waits for me when the sun rises tomorrow, I'm going to take every minute of this bliss I can steal, for as long as I can.

# Chapter Thirty-Two

MASON

She's gone.

I know it before I open my eyes, the way you know a storm has passed in the night and left the air hollow. The other side of the bed is cold, the pillow flattened without her weight, the room too quiet. No humming under her breath while she steals my shirt. No peppermint-sugar scent lingering beneath the cedar and soap.

I roll onto my back and stare at the ceiling fan spinning circles that don't fix anything.

It's Christmas Eve.

I thought, stupidly, that I'd at least have today with her. Breakfast. A surprise gift exchange. One more lap between the bar and the dock. Maybe even a goodbye I could hold onto, but I guess that's what last night was.

My chest tightens. I sit up and rub my face, and that's when I see it: cream paper on her pillow, edges kissed with gold like it belongs in a world nicer than this one.

My name is on the front in careful script.

I stare at it like it might change its mind, then slide a thumb under the fold.

*Mason,*

*If I say this to your face, I won't go, and we both know I have to. It isn't because I don't want you. It's because the world I ran from is counting on me to do what I promised. Christmas doesn't stop because I fell in love with the way you say my name.*

*Last night was mine. Ours. And I won't apologize for taking it.*

*I talked to my family. The help is real, and I truly hope you take it, because it is my gift to you.*

*This was, by far, the best Christmas of my life. Thank you.*

*Love always,*

*Tinsel*

*Ps. I don't know how long I'll have it, but my number is 727-555-3110*

I read the note twice, then a third time because my hands won't stop shaking. The words blur and sharpen, blur and sharpen, until I set the paper down and breathe slowly like I do when fixing a leak and not a heart.

There's an ache in my chest that can only be described as *Tinsel,* and I don't know how I'm ever going to fill it.

After a long time of lying in bed and staring at the ceiling, I try to do something with myself. Candace expects me at *Last Call* by eleven. I need to get dressed and eat, but convincing myself to do anything but lie in bed seems futile.

I knew our goodbye was coming. I knew it would hurt when Tinsel left, but I didn't expect the pain to echo on every piece of this house or on every thought that shifts into a memory.

There's a soft knock and then the scrape of the deadbolt. I

don't even bother to lift my head to see who it is. There are only two people who walk into my house like it's their own, and the one I want to see is long gone.

"Mason?" Candace calls as she drops her keys on the kitchen counter. I count the footsteps, knowing it's only a matter of time until I'm discovered, and then, as expected, she lets out a heavy sigh. "You got a note."

I hold it in the air, then shift to sit upright.

"So did I." She pulls an envelope from her back pocket, waves it once like she can't decide whether to throw it or frame it, then tucks it away again. Her voice drops. "Are you okay?"

I make a sound that isn't a laugh and isn't anything else either. "It's Christmas Eve," I say, as if the calendar owes me an apology. "I thought we'd have today. I thought she'd at least say goodbye."

Candace crosses the room and puts a hand on the middle of my chest like she's checking to see if my heart's still beating. I'd be okay if it wasn't, because then it wouldn't hurt anymore.

"She's not good at goodbye."

"I noticed."

"Did you read it?" she asks.

"Yeah."

"What'd it say?"

"That she had to go." I swallow. "That the help is real if I want it, but it doesn't say if she'll come back or not."

Candace nods once, lips pressed tight. "Mine said almost the same. Plus a bossy list for next year's parade that made me cry in the back room and then hate her for making me cry in the back room."

"Sounds right," I say, and the breath that leaves me after is a little broken, a little relieved. "Do you think I should take the offer and let her family help?"

"Do you?"

I walk to the window to look at the dock I'll always end up on when things get too loud. The water is slate today, like the sky is holding its breath, waiting for Tinsel to come back or create a storm.

"Yeah," I say. "I think I do."

A beat passes, long enough for something inside my ribs to crack and shift into a shape that hurts less. I don't see it coming until it's already happening—the way the floor tilts and my knees go a little loose, or how my hand reaches for my curtains because if I don't touch something solid, I might not stop falling.

"Mase," Candace says softly as I crash to the floor.

I shake my head, like that will stop the tears I can't control, but it doesn't. I've been a dam for weeks—months, if I'm honest —and the first leak starts with a sound that embarrasses me before I recognize it's mine. I hug myself tight as my throat works and my eyes burn. The room blurs again, and this time I don't fight it.

For the first time since Dad died, I let my sister see me break.

She's there before I can flinch away, her arms around my shoulders, chin pressed to the crown of my head, the way Mom used to when I was someone she cared about. I fold into myself the small, stupid way men always do when the world gets heavy, then give up trying to control the damage because there's nothing left to hold it back.

"It's okay," Candace says into my hair. "It's okay, it's okay."

I don't say *no, it isn't.* I don't say *I can't do this without her.* I don't say *I just wanted one more day.* I just breathe and let the pain move through me, tidal and mean and necessary.

When it passes, I'm empty and steadier. My face is wet. Candace's is, too.

"Sorry," I mutter, swiping at my eyes.

"Don't be stupid." She digs a tissue out of her back pocket like a magician.

We stand there a minute, the house too quiet around us. The kind of quiet that doesn't feel like peace. The kind that feels like absence. "This place has enough ghosts," she says finally, voice gentle in a way she doesn't use on many people. "Don't sleep here tonight."

"I don't want to leave."

"You have to," she counters. "You need a distraction. Come to the bar and help me get set up for tonight. When the night's done, though, you're not coming back here. You're staying in my spare room this weekend."

"I'm not a kid you need to take care of," I huff, feeling defiant even though I'm grateful for the support.

"True." She squeezes my bicep and steps back, practical again because it's how we survive. "But you're my brother and I need your help. Today will be busy and miserable and over before you know it."

"I'll grab a bag," I conceded, because if anything, I can't say no to helping someone. Especially my sister.

"Good." She glances toward the bedroom. "You want me to get...?"

I shake my head. "I've got it."

I fold the shirt Tinsel wore last night and tuck it into my duffel. I fold the note, too, because I'm not the kind of man who pretends words don't matter. I look around the room once, searching for anything Tinsel may have left behind to hold onto, but there isn't even a strand of hair. She's gone, the only trace of her ever being here is the ache she left behind.

# Chapter Thirty-Three

## TINSEL

**B**ack in the North Pole, the air bites colder, the smell of peppermint and pine sap cutting clean through my lungs. Snow crunches under my boots as I step into the heart of the village, and before I can blink, Chris is there, half-staring, half-stopping like he's not sure I'm real.

"You're... here." Surprise cracks his voice. "I didn't think you'd come back."

"Me neither," I admit. "I wasn't sure I had enough dust left."

His gaze flicks to the ring on my thumb, the gold band wreathed in a faint, stubborn glow. Something like guilt softens his mouth. "You didn't," he says quietly. "I topped it off when I saw you last."

I blink. "You...what?"

"In the bar," he says. "When I took your wrist, I made a Magic transfer, just in case you chose us. Or needed a way back."

Before I can answer, Chris steps in and hugs me. It should feel like home, warm and familiar. Instead, it fits like a sweater I've outgrown. He kisses me, his lips hungry for an affirmation that even though I chose Mason in Winter Key, that I'm here because I choose him now, but I feel nothing.

No spark, no tingle, just wrongness pressing hard enough to bruise.

Chris pulls back, confusion shadowing his eyes. "What's wrong?"

"Nothing," I lie, and the lie lands between us like sleet.

His jaw works once, but he lets it go, glancing past me at the organized chaos of Christmas Eve: elves darting between sleigh bays and workshops, polishing bells, tightening reins, and checking their lists twice.

"Well," he says, voice slipping back into the steady of command. "You came just in time. We have six hours, maybe less, before takeoff." His eyes return to mine, searching.

"You should go see your dad," he says, softer. "And your mom. They've been worried."

"I know." Guilt threads through my chest.

Chris's gaze dips to my hand again. "But stop by the Starlight Atrium first," he adds, quieter now. "I want you to have enough dust in that ring. Always."

I nod, already needing air. "I'll find you before the ride."

Being home is like stepping into a snow globe that's been shaken too hard. There are flurries of motion everywhere, glittering and overwhelming. Hammers clatter, bells jingle, voices rise in a chorus of hurry. As soon as the sleigh lifts, this village will sag with relief and throw the afterparty of the year.

"Tinsel!" Mom barrels through a drift of fabric bolts, cheeks flushed, hair a storm. She squeezes me until my ribs protest. "Thank the stars, you're here! We're down to hours!"

"I know," I say, letting myself be held.

"The dressmakers are finishing your gown," she gushes,

already moving again. "You'll be stunning tonight. Picture perfect."

Oh yes. The Magic dress that turns me into the classic image of Mrs. Claus. Once I slip into the heavy red dress, the enchantment will do the rest. It will turn my hair silver, soften my waist, and round my face into a storybook image that isn't mine. Chris will fasten his coat, and the beard and belly will appear like a sigh. We'll become the archetype that keeps the myth alive for another year.

My phone buzzes, and I stiffen at the human noise in a not-human place. I turn, hiding myself from prying eyes, and peek into my purse.

> Mason: I was hoping to see you before you
> left.

My heart lurches. I can't leave him on read, not after the way I left in the middle of the night, but I can't tell him the truth either.

> Me: Had to catch an early flight. Sorry. Didn't
> mean to leave like that.

I add a shrinking emoji because I don't have better words.

> Mason: Will you come back once the holiday
> is over?

Tears sting my eyes. I want to type *I want to. I want you. I want Winter Key.* Instead, I shut the phone off before I break where my mother can see.

"You okay, honey?" Mom asks.

"Allergies," I lie. "There was so much pollen, I'm still adjusting to it not being in my system.

Mom presses a tissue into my hand, even though she knows I'm lying. "Better now than during the ceremony. Don't ruin the Magic with a runny nose."

I swallow. "About that, Mom... I don't know if I can."

"Shhh," she hushes, her hands closing around mine, firm as

faith. "You were born for this. No one else can do what you do. You and Chris will be perfect, my love."

I nod because she needs me to, and the world needs me to be the perfect version of myself, my parents crafted specifically for Chris. "You're right."

"I almost forgot, Chris wants to see you before the ride. You've got forty-five minutes." She kisses my cheek. "We're all rooting for you."

"Thanks, Mom," I say, leaving her and walking across the compound to Santa's house. I could take an ATV, but I want to walk in the cold. I need the snow to freeze my heart so I can get through tonight.

I kick the snow off my boots before stepping inside the big house and strip out of my snow suit. A small smile tugs at my lips as I remember thinking the Magic had got things wrong. I needed a bathing suit. Not heavily padded cotton. But that smile falls as I realize it knew all along that I would come back to the North Pole. It was preparing me for the journey, even before I knew what I needed.

My fingers curl around the hem of the Jack Skellington shirt I stole, the one piece of Mason I allowed myself to keep, and a tear falls down my cheek. I brush it away, and the next, before it can leave my lashes, then swallow my emotions.

Mrs. Claus doesn't cry for a love lost. She stands beside her Santa, helping bring joy to the world and making it a better place. And that's exactly what I plan to do.

Upstairs, Chris's study door stands ajar. The bay window frames the village, and it looks like a porcelain collection with all the glowing windows, sugared roofs, and tidy paths. It's picture perfect, but I know about the cracks no one cares to look for. Nothing is ever as wonderful as it seems, not even Santa's North Pole village.

Chris waits for the credenza, pouring cocoa into two mugs. There's a peppermint stick in one, marshmallows in both, and whipped cream layering the top like snow.

"Sugar-rushing for the big night?" I tease, trying to untangle the knot in my chest.

He smirks and hands me the mug. "*Our* big night."

"Our big night," I echo. *Right.*

Chris sets his mug on the desk and leans against the edge. He folds his arms across his chest, analyzing, truly looking at me for the first time since I got back. "What happened in Florida?"

I take a sip, trying to ignore my racing heart, and burn my tongue. I lick my lips, knowing it won't ease the ache, then ask, "What do you mean?"

"You look different."

"Because I am." The admission tumbles out before I can stop it. I found magic that didn't belong to sleigh bells, but sun and sand, and laughter that wasn't scheduled. Here, the weight of Christmas drains that Magic out of me like a slow leak. Even the cocoa tastes wrong.

Chris's eyes cut to my thumb again, narrowing on the ring. "I meant what I said out there. I refilled your ring that night because I wanted you to have the choice. But you didn't refill again."

"It slipped my mind." I set the mug down because my hands won't stop shaking. "I've been busy with Mom preparing for tonight."

Chris takes both cups and sets them aside, then looks at me like he's been rehearsing a line and decided not to use it. "Tinsel, I don't think we should get married next year."

My heart trips. "What?"

"This isn't love. It's duty. Legacy. Everything our parents want but without the spark. You don't look at me the way you looked at him."

"Mason?" My voice thins. "I don't—"

"You do." No cruelty, just certainty. "And I don't blame you because he does, too. Mason did in a week what I've failed to do all our lives."

"What's that?"

"Make you fall in love." There's a sadness in the way Chris

says those words that resonates with me, because for years, that was all I wanted.

I wanted Chris to look at me like I was the only girl in the room. I wanted him to choose me with every breath, even though there were always other options. I wanted him to see me for who I could be, not just who I was at that moment. And maybe he does, now, but it's too late.

Who knows, maybe one day I will fall in love with Chris, but it will never be the same kind of love as what I have for Mason. Which is *crazy* to even comprehend because I'm not in love with Mason. I never got the chance to be.

"Chris," I sigh. "If you're not married by thirty, you break the line of succession. No one's ever risked the lineage, what happens if—"

"Tinsel," He opens a drawer and lifts a small velvet box.

I freeze, my heart skipping a beat, and the air in my lungs turning to ice. "I thought you said you didn't want to get married."

"I'm not proposing." He flips the lid. Inside, a golden band glows with a warmer magic than the one I wear. "This isn't a betrothal ring. It's a key. It'll take you two places. Here and where your heart truly lives."

My throat closes at the words he isn't saying. "Why?"

"I want you to be happy," Chris says simply. "I understand now that the kind of happiness you deserve can't be with me, but I'd like you to still ride with me tonight. See Christmas the way we dreamed it would be when we were kids. And when it's over, I'll let you go back to Winter Key... If that's where you belong. If *he's* where you belong."

A wet laugh escapes me. Then tears. "You've always been my best friend, even when you weren't."

"And you've always been mine." Chris pulls me in, solid and safe in the way best friends are. "Which is why I won't ask you to be anything else."

We stand like that until the clock on the mantle cleaves the moment with a neat little chime.

"Ten minutes," he says, tugging his suspenders with a flicker of boyishness that doesn't need Magic. "How do I look?"

"Like you're about to gain two hundred pounds and sixty years overnight."

Chris's cheeks go rosy without help. "Perfect." He squeezes my shoulder and nods toward the window where the village has begun to gather, faces tipped up toward the sky. "See you at midnight, Tinsel."

# Chapter Thirty-Four

## TINSEL

Everyone gathers along the runway, breath misting in the frigid air, lanterns flickering gold against the snow. Elves press close, their small faces glowing with anticipation, while the reindeer paw at the ground, hooves striking a steady drumbeat that thrums through the icy night. Tonight isn't just a holiday tradition. It's history.

Chris's father, Nick, steps to the microphone first. His beard shines silver under the floodlights, his red coat heavy with decades of Magic transforming him into the world's Santa Claus. When he raises his hand, silence falls. Even the reindeer still, ears flicking forward as if they, too, know what's about to happen.

"Can you believe it's already that time again?" Nick's voice booms, worn but strong. "For forty years, I have been honored to be your Santa Claus. With Martha at my side, I have carried this torch, and together we've kept the Magic alive. But now the time has come to pass it to the next generation, to our son, Chris."

The crowd erupts in cheers, stomping and clapping, bells jingling wildly. My chest aches with the enormity of what this moment means.

Nick begins to undo the buttons of his coat. Each one seems to release a weight, until finally he slips the sleeves free. The transformation is immediate. His frame shrinks, his beard shortens, the Magic shedding him like wrapping paper on Christmas morning until he is simply Nick again, the man the village knows all year long.

"Congratulations, my son." Nick's voice cracks, thick with pride as he holds out the coat. "This now belongs to you. Treat it well."

Chris steps forward and slides his arms into the sleeves. The fabric molds to his frame and the belt cinches itself with a jingle of Magic. Sparkles of stardust swirl around him, racing across his hair and beard, deepening his voice and broadening his shoulders until he is no longer just Chris. He's Santa Claus.

The crowd roars. Elves shout. Reindeer toss their heads. For a heartbeat, it feels as if the whole world is cheering, as if even the stars in the sky understand what this moment means. I'm happy for Chris. This is the night he's prepared his whole life for, and yet when I catch a glimpse of the moon, I have to fight hard against the tug of a frown.

Chris takes the microphone, his new voice rich and resonant. "Thank you," he says, steady. "But as wonderful as my father's speech was, there's something he didn't tell you."

A murmur sweeps the crowd. Nick blinks, surprised.

"This is my first year as your Santa Claus," Chris continues. "And while Tinsel will be at my side tonight..." He extends his gloved hand toward me.

The hush that falls is so complete it makes my heartbeat sound deafening in my ears. I step forward slowly in my snow suit, not my carefully crafted dress, and each crunch of my boots echoes. When my fingers slip into Chris's, his grip is strong, reassuring, and yet something in my chest twists.

Up close, the transformation is surreal. He looks every bit the Santa Claus the world adores, but beneath the beard, I still see my friend. The boy who teased me through snowball fights. The man who was supposed to be my future.

"She will not be the future Mrs. Claus," Chris says.

The gasp that ripples through the crowd is sharp, followed by hushed whispers. All eyes turn to me, hot and heavy, and I want to sink straight into the snow.

"I know this isn't what you expected," Chris continues, lifting a hand to quiet them. "But Christmas Magic cannot be forced. It isn't duty or an arrangement. It's love. The kind of love that fuels joy, hope, and wonder. And while I love Tinsel, I don't have *that* kind of love for her. She'll ride with me tonight, but only tonight. After that, we each must follow our hearts, wherever they may lead us."

For a moment, no one breathes. This is unheard of. Generations of Clauses have followed the same path, but never this. And yet, there's a steadiness in his voice, a conviction that makes me believe.

"Well," he says finally, with a crooked grin, "this is awkward. Thanks, everyone. Have a good night."

The crowd doesn't know whether to clap or protest, but Chris doesn't give them the chance because he tugs me toward the sleigh and ushers me on first. The moment his boot hits the step, golden dust explodes outward, racing down the sleigh's frame, threading through the harnesses, and igniting the bells. Patterns of light etch themselves across the straps like ancient runes, pulsing with power. The reindeer toss their heads, snorting steam, eyes glowing with readiness.

With a sharp snap of the reins, the reindeer lunge forward, hooves pounding hard against the runway before leaping into a gallop. My stomach swoops as the sleigh shudders, then lifts, and the ground drops away beneath us. The village shrinks to a porcelain display, rooftops dusted white, windows glowing gold.

"Ho, ho, ho!" Chris bellows, his voice booming like thunder. "Merry Christmas!"

The crowd below remains silent, as tradition demands, watching as the sleigh carries us into the sky. The aurora ripples above us, green and violet light swirling brighter than I've ever seen, as though even the heavens are acknowledging the change.

When we're high in the sky, drifting toward the first continent, Chris ties off the reins, letting the Magic guide the team, and leans back with a long exhale. "I think that went pretty well," he says, almost amused.

I stare at him, still half in shock.

"You'll be bombarded with questions when you get back," he adds with a chuckle. "And probably with dates. Half the elves will line up for a chance, while the rest of the town tries to figure out what my rejection means."

I manage a weak laugh. "I don't want to date anyone from here."

He glances sideways at me, beard twitching with a smile. "Didn't think you would. But you'll inspire people no matter what. That's who you are, Tinsel." His tone shifts, quieter, more certain. "As for me...my soulmate's out there in the world somewhere. I just need to find her."

# Chapter Thirty-Five

## TINSEL

"So, what's your grand plan?" I ask, half-teasing, half-terrified, arms crossed tight over my chest. I'm freezing despite the heated seats. My dress would have been embedded with Magic to keep me warm, but putting it on felt like sealing myself to a fate I'd just escaped. So, I left it behind.

Chris only smiles, beard twitching, his Santa belly shaking like he's enjoying the secret too much. It's still strange to see him like this—older, rounder, draped in centuries of Magic—but his eyes are the same as always. "You'll just have to wait and see."

Hours slip past in a blur of rooftops and chimneys. Christmas Eve folds into Christmas morning across time zones. I'm exhausted, slumping against the sleigh's edge, but Chris hasn't slowed once. He moves like this is what he was born to do, dropping gifts, scattering golden dust, laughing that booming laugh. I've yawned so many times my jaw aches, and more than once I've nodded off, jolting awake when the sleigh dips.

"Are you ready?" Chris asks suddenly.

"Ready for what?" I ask lazily. We're somewhere in North America now, though I have no clue where.

"The cool thing about being Santa," he says, tightening the

reins with a mischievous glint, "is that I can find anyone, naughty or nice, anywhere in the world. All I need is their name."

I sit up straight. "Chris—"

"Oh, I know. Creepy, right? But useful. Helps me know who's asleep and who still needs a sprinkle of Sandman's dust." He smirks, and I groan.

My pulse races when I see palm trees and more ocean than land. "Chris...what are we doing?"

He glances at me, softer now. "He's still at *Last Call* with Candace. Did you know it's almost midnight in Winter Key? So many of its residents are still up. I might need to dust the whole town to sleep."

I lean forward, peering down as the village lights come into focus. Music drifts out through the open bar door, mingling with laughter. And then I see him, the Magic of the sleigh helping me to find Mason even through the wall. He sits at the bar, shoulders hunched, with a half-empty beer in hand and three more beside it. He lifts it to his lips, brows furrowed in thought, while Candace leans in, her expression tight with concern.

Chris circles lower, giving up precious minutes he should be using to spread Christmas joy. "Are you ready to tell him the truth?"

"No." My heart stutters. I grip the edge of the sleigh so tightly my knuckles ache. "But I don't have a choice, do I? How do I even start? This is breaking every rule. I'm going to land myself on the naughty list forever."

Chris lets out a belly laugh that shakes the sleigh. "Tinsel, you could never be on the naughty list. This..." he looks at me, voice gentling. "This is my gift to you."

My throat burns. "And what do I do? Run inside, drop to my knees, and beg him to take me back?"

"Call his name," Chris says simply. "Make him come outside and look up. The rest will follow. Trust me, he'll hear you."

I swallow hard, nod, and lean over the side of the sleigh. "Mason!"

Mason's head lifts, and like a man in a trance, he stands and walks out to the porch. Candace follows, calling his name with worry. When they're both outside, he looks around.

"What are you doing?" Candace asks, resting her hand on his shoulder.

"I thought I heard..." He shakes his head and mumbles, "Never mind."

"Mason!" I shout again, only this time it's Candace who hears me. Her eyes widen until they look ready to fall out of her head when she sees the sleigh floating twenty feet above her.

She smacks Mason's shoulder, then points skyward.

The sleigh dips lower, antlers glinting, bells jangling wildly, though Chris keeps us just above the string lights because there's no safe space to land without destroying downtown's decorations. Reindeer hooves spark against the night air as we hover.

"Tinsel?" Mason's voice cracks as he tries to make sense of what he's seeing. He rubs his eyes, blinks, then stares harder. "What the hell are you doing in a flying sleigh?"

His tone is so perfectly, dryly Mason it almost undoes me. He's not screaming. Not panicking. Just standing there like the world tilted sideways and he's waiting for me to set it right.

"You know how I told you my family was into Christmas?" My laugh shakes. "Turns out I wasn't exaggerating."

He drags a hand down his face. "You've got your own Santa, sleigh, and reindeer? That's one hell of a getup. No wonder every mall in Florida probably booked you all season long."

"It's not a costume." I look to Chris, unsure of what to do now. He pushes a button and a rope ladder appear off the side of the sleigh. I climb down, step by step, until my boots hit the pavement. My legs wobble when I'm finally on solid ground after flying for more than twenty hours, but I straighten. "I'm an elf."

"A what?" Mason asks, his eyes focused on me instead of the sleigh hovering above us.

"I'm an elf." I shrug. "I told you the other night, but I knew you didn't believe me. And that..." I point up. "Is the real Santa."

"Bullshit," Candace blurts.

Chris's deep, belly rumbling chuckle carries down in the night. The next thing I know, he's shimmying down the ladder, even though the suit's Magic would let him jump without injury, and looks Candace dead in the eyes. "You begged for a Polly Pocket when you were eight."

"Plenty of kids did," she shoots back. "That doesn't take a rocket scientist to figure out."

Chris chuckles again, already grinning, and lifts a gloved hand. "Ask me for something. Anything. If I'm Santa, it's in the bag."

Candace smirks, wicked. "Okay. I want a fourteen-inch rainbow dildo that sings Christmas carols."

Mason groans and looks at her for the first time since seeing me. "Candace. Really?"

Chris whistles, and his red Santa sack flies to him, then lands open and ready at his feet. If that wasn't convincing enough, he sticks his gloved hand into the back, Magic falling off the velvet like glitter. A moment later, he pulls out a box that hides exactly that, except the toy is red, white, and green with her name engraved on the handle.

Candace's jaw drops. "Okay. That's... horrifying. But thanks." She clutches the box to her chest like it might explode.

"Be careful what you wish for," Chris says, winking.

Mason scrubs his face, likely trying to sober up and sort the insanity he just witnessed. "Can someone please explain what I'm looking at, because I haven't had enough to drink for this."

"Okay, here's the truth," I say quickly. I tuck my hair behind my ear, exposing the faint point he's probably never noticed. "He really is Santa, and I'm the elf who was supposed to marry him and be Mrs. Claus."

Candace whistles low. "Talk about an age gap."

I laugh weakly. "Candace, that's Chris. He doesn't normally look like this. It's the coat. The Magic. If I'd worn the Mrs. Claus gown, I'd be gray-haired and plump right now, too."

Mason's gaze sharpens. "But you didn't."

"No." My chest tightens, the words trembling out of me. "Because my heart doesn't belong to Christmas. Maybe it never did. I know I left without saying goodbye, and I'm sorry. If I'd seen you, I never would have been able to walk away." My voice cracks. "But I had to go home. To help the sleigh and keep Christmas going, and I'm sorry."

Silence stretches, thick and heavy. Even Candace doesn't weigh in. I watch Mason put the pieces together of what I am, and as darkness clouds his eyes, I realize I'm too late.

"For the love of fruitcake, dude," Chris groans. "She gave up Christmas Magic. She gave up being Mrs. Claus for *you*. Either you accept her, or I drag her back to the North Pole, because I've got presents piling up and the clock is ticking."

Shame curls through me. I thought, despite how different we are, that Mason would accept me. That what we had was real enough, but I guess I was wrong. I shrink back. "This was a mistake. Let's just go."

"No." Mason takes a step closer, eyes locked on mine. The pain there guts me. It's heartache and hope tangled into one. "This is...a lot, Snowflake. More than I know how to process. But I like you. Too damn much. And I don't care if you're Santa's ex or an elf or whatever. I don't want you to walk away. Not again. If I'm being honest, not ever."

My breath shudders. A thin strand of hope wraps itself around my heart. I don't want to hold it too tight, fearful it'll snap, but I can't let it go either. "What if it's too much? What if I can't give you normal?"

Mason shakes his head. "I don't want normal. I want you. Complicated, impossible, pointy ears and all. You are my Christmas wish, Tinsel. You always have been."

"Awe!" Candace coos loudly, hugging her giant sex toy. "I guess you two really are endgame."

Chris grins, satisfied. "Boom. Best Santa ever." He throws the velvet bag over his shoulder and then steps onto the rope ladder. "Merry Christmas, lovebirds. I'm out."

The reindeer paw the air, gold dust swirling as the harnesses flare. The ladder hoists Chris into the sky, recoiling back into its hiding place until Santa is safe in his sleigh again. Chris cracks the reins, but not before throwing me one last look. "Bring this one to the Pole on Tuesday. We need to sort through the details of our new partnership."

"You're still helping Mason?" I ask, wiping happy tears from my face.

"No, I'm helping you change Christmas, Tinsel. Mrs. Claus or not, you were right. We aren't doing enough for the people of this world. Mason just happens to be our guinea pig." Chris winks and with a jingle of bells, the sleigh shoots forward, hooves sparking as they gather speed, then lift high into the sky. Starlight swallows them, the last echo of Chris's laugh fading into the night.

# *Epilogue*
## MASON

TWO MONTHS LATER

*Last Call* looks like a party store threw up in here.

Not in a bad way. Candace would kill me if I ever called her decorating "tacky," but in that cozy, small-town way where pink string lights are draped across every available beam, cardboard hearts hang crookedly because someone (probably Candace) didn't measure, and silver and pink tinsel touches every flat surface. Yeah, tinsel. The real kind that sheds glitter every time someone brushes against it.

I can't help but smirk at the irony. I've got *my* Tinsel behind the bar tonight, hair pulled back, cheeks flushed, laughing as she pours beers faster than Candace can yell orders. It's been a few weeks since that insane Christmas Eve, and life still doesn't feel real.

I keep waiting to wake up back in my room, hungover, and find out that Santa floating above the bar was just some wild holiday dream. That Santa never actually hovered his sleigh outside the bar. That Tinsel isn't really an elf who gave up Christmas Magic for me. That I didn't almost lose her before I ever really had her.

But then Tinsel catches my eye from behind the counter, lips curving into that secret little smile that's just for me, and I know it's real. All of it. The chaos. The Magic. The responsibility. Her. Especially her.

Candace's Valentine's Day party is in full swing. Locals and visitors fill the bar, elbow to elbow, raising glasses and yelling over the music. Somebody dragged in a small karaoke machine, and it's been crooning bad 90s country for the last hour. The air is warm with laughter and fried food, thick with the smell of whiskey and strawberry schnapps.

*"Are you sure you want to do this?" I'd asked when she told me Candace offered her the job.*

*"I need to," she'd said, chin lifted. "I need to prove I can stand on my own two feet, not just lean on you or...on the family Magic."*

So, here Tinsel is, proving it, slinging drinks in boots that make her look too damn good while I sit at the corner table pretending not to glare at the guys who flirt with her. Every time she laughs at one of their jokes, I remind myself it's just customer service. And every time her gaze slides back to me, soft and sure, I know where her heart really is.

The door swings open, letting in a burst of rare cold air and two late arrivals. Tyler strolls in, tattoos climbing his throat, leather jacket creaking. He's trouble wrapped in charm, and I swear Candace's eyes roll so hard I hear it from across the bar. He orders something, smirks at her, and for once she doesn't bite his head off.

I take a sip of my beer, watching the scene play out. Tinsel slips into the seat beside me, setting down a drink. "Break time. And before you ask, no, I'm not quitting. Your sister's a slave driver, but I like it."

"You look good back there," I admit. We have an agreement that for the four nights Tinsel works, I'm only allowed to work two of them. The other two, I'm supposed to be enjoying my freedom, but most nights I end up right here.

Tinsel grins and brushes glitter off her arm. "You just like the view."

"Guilty." I lean closer, lowering my voice. "But I still think you should stay with me instead of moving into that shoebox next week."

Her smile softens. "Mason..."

"I know. You want your space." I sigh, threading our fingers together. "I just don't want distance between us. Not after everything."

"You won't lose me." She squeezes my hand. "I love spending time with you, but we need this. We need to build a relationship, not a co-dependence. And besides..." her eyes sparkle, "You'll see me almost every night anyway since I work here."

I groan. "Which means I get to watch drunk idiots hit on you all night while I sit here resisting the urge to break their noses."

Tinsel laughs and leans in to kiss my cheek. "You'll survive. You're tougher than you look."

I chuckle, but my chest tightens as I look at her. She doesn't know how much she's changed my world.

I've carried secrets these past few weeks that no one else in town could ever dream of knowing. I know Santa Claus. I know the North Pole is real. I know what it's like to see the sleigh flying in the sky, bells jingling, reindeer soaring. And yeah, I know what it's like to meet Tinsel's parents—intimidating as hell but still welcoming once they realized I wasn't going anywhere. That was a trip I'll never forget.

Loving Tinsel means carrying all of that. Protecting it. Protecting her. And I'll do it gladly, because she's worth everything.

The karaoke machine cuts off, and for a rare second, the bar quiets. That's when it happens. Tyler leans over the counter, says something to Candace, and before any of us can blink, he kisses her.

Full-on.

Candace freezes, staring like she just got smacked, and Tyler pulls back with that smug grin.

"What the hell was that for?" She asks, once she gets her bearings again.

Tyler points up to the ceiling, where they're standing under one of two dozen cardboard hearts, and says, "Valentine's Day mistletoe." And then, like he didn't just shock my sister into submission, he grabs his beer and walks away.

"Hey!" Candace says, chasing after him. Tyler turns, and she shoves him back with a finger to his chest. "You're out of your damn mind!"

"Maybe." Tyler winks, walking backward, still smirking like the cat that caught the canary. "Maybe not."

Candace groans and turns back toward the bar, practically stomping the whole way.

I glance at Tinsel, and she's trying not to laugh. She tucks her hair behind her ear, then quickly changes her mind like she still worries I'll notice the tiny, almost non-existent point at the tip, but I don't care. She's mine. Elf ears, Christmas secrets, all of it.

"Are you sure you want that apartment?" I ask again, teasing but hopeful.

She smirks. "Yes, Mason. I want to paint the walls whatever color I like. I want to learn how to unclog a sink. I want to know I can survive without leaning on anyone. But..." Her hand slides against my chest. "I'm not going anywhere. You've got me for the long haul."

I kiss her lips, not giving a damn that she should be on duty or who's watching. Everyone in town already knows I belong to this woman, but for any outsiders who haven't gotten the memo yet, I'm writing the note in neon pink. I'm her's. She's mine.

End of story.

# Want More Holiday Magic?

You didn't think that was it, did you?

There's more mistletoe, more magic, and one very tempting bonus chapter waiting for you.

Plus, recipes guaranteed to make your kitchen smell like Winter Key. Unlock the bonus content before it melts!

Take Me Back to Winter Key

**Looking for some love in your life? Bailey's contemporary romances range from sweet to spicy, with everything in between.**

Enemies to Lovers, High School Bully, Athlete Antihero, First Love, Girl Next Door, Completed Duet

BOOK 1 IN THE BROKEN LOVE SERIES

**Piper**

Most people don't think about the day they'll die. They coast through life, blissfully unaware of how their time is ticking away. I wasn't like most people. I welcomed death, wanted her to take me away from the prison I called life, but she refused. I tried twice only to survive. And then, when I thought I had nothing left it came. A reason to live. Rex was a small, unexpected ray of light my world of darkness that blossomed into a beam of sunshine. I thought, maybe this was why Death didn't take me. Maybe she knew that if I held on a little longer things would turn around. But the third time Death came to my door wasn't by choice. Someone else brought her, and I fear this time she might take me.

**Rex**

Being the son of a country star sucks. My parents are never around, I move every year or so, and I have no real friends. Everyone around me has an agenda. Everyone except Piper Lovelace. I can't get that girl to notice me. Trust me I've tried.Thankfully, fate stepped in and gave me the break I needed. I've got her attention, now I need her to give me a chance.

**Fall In love with a
Bailey Black Book Here**

Enemies to Lovers, High School Bully, Athlete Antihero, First Love, Girl Next Door, Completed Duet

## BOOK 2 IN THE BROKEN LOVE SERIES

She's beautiful. Fierce. Nothing at all like the girl I used to know, which is absolutely terrifying because Danika Winters is the only person outside of that room who knows the truth. She could ruin me, and I'm not talking about my reputation. I couldn't give two shits about what the kids at St. A's think. I'm talking major, life-altering, jail time ruined. I'll do whatever it takes to keep her quiet. Even if it means destroying the only person I've ever cared about.

**Fall In love with a
Bailey Black Book Here**

Frienemies to lovers, Fake dating, High school romance, Love triangle

Asher Anderson is a dick.

We aren't friends, so when he seeks me out in the cafeteria on the worst day of my life, I'm suspicious. When he tells Liam Heiter that we're dating, which couldn't be farther from the truth, I want to kill him...Until I see Liam's reaction.

Liam—my best friend, the guy who crushed every hope of us *officially* being together—is jealous. He has never looked at me this way and I love it.

So, I play along. Maybe watching me with someone else will make Liam suffer like I have the past four years. And maybe, just maybe, he'll come to his senses and realize we belong together. It's not like I actually *like* Asher. At best, I tolerate him. What's the worst that can happen?

**Fall In love with a
Bailey Black Book Here**

Small town, Opposites attract, Cowboy, New girl in town,
Unexpected parenthood (+denial)

## Josh

Josh Andrews hadn't expected to meet the girl of his dreams in a
church parking lot—especially not while his best friend was
hooking up in his truck. But there she was, parked two spaces
away, pretending not to notice his predicament. Layla was
gorgeous, sharp-witted, and completely immune to his charm.
He should have walked away. Instead, he couldn't stop thinking
about her. Layla wasn't like the girls who usually fell for his easy
smile and smooth lines. She challenged him, saw right through
him—and he liked it. For the first time, he wanted more than just
a fleeting connection. He wanted her.
Winning her over won't be easy, but Josh has never backed down
from a challenge. And Layla? She might just be the one risk worth
taking.

**Fall In love with a
Bailey Black Book Here**

Second chance, The dare/bet, Insta chemistry, Learning to love,
Shared Pasts

I've sworn off men forever! Okay, not forever, but for a few months. After my last hook-up, my vag needs a reset because the last man to touch me broke it in the worst of ways. Not a problem until my new dance partner comes into the picture. He's turning into my forbidden fruit, tempting me in ways I didn't know possible.

I have three months of celibacy ahead of me and eight weeks to whip my new dance partner into shape.

Someone save me.

**Fall In love with a
Bailey Black Book Here**

Fake dating, Second chance, Friends to lovers, Everybody can see it, Short and Spicy novella

A wedding. A lie. And regret.

I'm in over my head with not one but two ex-boyfriends at the same wedding. Both of which I haven't seen in over a year. When the one who ripped my heart into pieces backs me into a corner, I grab the other and kiss him.

Yup. This is how I ended up fake dating Noah Ruckers, and let me tell you, it's an emotional roller coaster. I thought I'd put my feelings for him behind me. We spent years as friends after our break up, nothing more. But no matter how hard I try I can't forget what his lips feel like. Or the way his arms wrap around me.

In two days, I'm walking away. There is no future for us. But that doesn't mean I can't pretend.

Fake dating, Second chance, Friends to lovers, Everybody can see it, Short and Spicy novella

Holly Flynn is a leprechaun who grants wishes—but with a dangerous twist. Each wish comes at a price: once it's fulfilled, the "victim" forgets everything before their wish—and her.

When a gorgeous stranger asks for one unforgettable night, things take an unexpected twist. The chemistry between them is electric, and soon, Holly's struck by a terrifying thought: She doesn't want him to forget her.

Then, a week later, he knocks on her door. And he remembers everything.

Why does he remember, when no one else does? Is it fate—or is her magic betraying her?

**Fall In love with a
Bailey Black Book Here**

Fake dating, Forced proximity, Office sleepovers, Ex drama, Slow burn tension, He's a little grumpy. She's a little unhinged. And together? Sparks.

Emma Evans had the perfect wedding planned—until her fiancé dumped her a week before the big day. Now she's heartbroken, homeless, and stuck with a non-refundable, high-end wedding package she can't return... or use.

So she does the unthinkable: gives the whole thing away in a viral giveaway.

What she doesn't expect...The winning groom is best friends with her frustratingly attractive landlord, Matthew Anderson. The same man who catches her illegally crashing in her office with a bottle of wine and a Taylor Swift playlist.

Matt has every reason to evict her. Instead, he makes her a deal: fake date him to help sell the love story, and he'll look the other way. It's outrageous. It's risky. But if pretending to be in love for one week keeps her business afloat, Emma's in.

Only, somewhere between staged kisses, scorching chemistry, and one very real wedding, the line between make-believe and something more starts to blur.

And Emma's about to find out that the best love stories never go according to plan.

**Fall In love with a
Bailey Black Book Here**

## How About a Fantasy Adventure?

Dive into the completed Neverland Novels. Characters have been aged up for this darker, grittier version. If you like your fairytale retellings with hot, ruthless, morally gray love interests, you'll enjoy this series. The Lost Darling is the first book in the main storyline. Please read this series in order.

Twisted Fairy Tale, Peter Pan Retelling, Multiple Love Interests, Morally Gray Males, She's Mine, Scorching hot lost boys, Spice, and more!

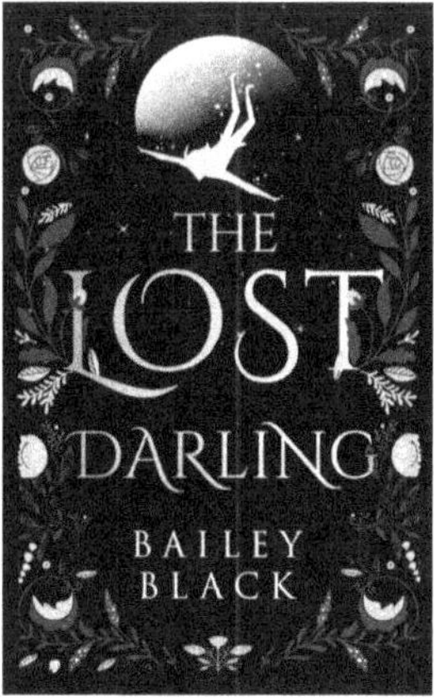

Second star to the left and continue until morning.

I got that line tattooed on my wrist the day I turned twenty-one. So much symbolism in such a simple sentence. At the time, it was a nod to the future and the infinite possibilities to come, while reminding me to remember the past and to look for magic in the world.

Growing up, nothing was ever what it seemed. The shift of leaves on a tree was a faery skipping by. Shooting stars were a chance to make wishes. Shadows were souls stuck between this world and the next, mirroring a life they once had.

My imagination was limitless, the world a wonderful adventure waiting to unfold.

It's easy to lose that sense of wonder with the weight of life on your shoulders and I wanted a reminder to get me through the hard days.

Most importantly, it was an ode to the boy who earned the title of my first crush, even if he was animated. Peter Pan wasn't a *save the damsel* kind of prince. He was daring, and selfless, and took care of the ones he loved. He was a friend to all but never afraid to fight the Pirates when their moral compass broke. Wendy was an idiot for leaving him. She rushed home to a heartless world full of men willing to lie through their teeth to get down her pants.

But that's the beauty of a book, the characters are perfectly flawed. Damaged just enough that we still love them. Whereas reality is nothing but empty promises and baggage the size of mountains.

The day I got my tattoo, I would have given anything to be whisked away into a fairytale. My world was crumbling, and all I wanted was to go back to when life was simpler. I didn't realize I had sealed my fate in ink.

Branded myself as one of the Lost.

Neverland was everything the stories made it out to be. Beautiful. Full of magic. Filled with handsome men and debonair pirates. But the author of my favorite tale left out one crucial detail.

In order to get there, you have to die.

Tinsel Evergreen didn't get a say in her future. As the Grand Elf's daughter, she was signed, sealed, and delivered to the next Santa before she hit kindergarten...destined for sugar cookies, sleigh rides, and a picture-perfect happily-ever-after she never asked for.

But two weeks before the holiday that defines her family, Tinsel steals a little magic and runs. She lands in Winter Key, Florida—a fishing village trying to reinvent itself with twinkle lights and tacky holiday contests—and discovers freedom for the first time. No expectations. No fiancé. Just sunshine, salt air, and the terrifying possibility of figuring out what she actually wants.

Mason Kraus isn't looking for complications. His family's bait shop is shuttered, his father's legacy weighs heavy on his shoulders, and he's barely holding his sister's bar afloat. Letting a runaway stranger crash in his spare room is the last thing he needs, but when a booking mishap leaves Tinsel with nowhere to stay, she ends up in his spare bedroom.

Living under the same roof is supposed to be temporary. Instead, it feels inevitable. One look across the kitchen counter, one brush of his hand, one late-night conversation on the dock—and suddenly, the line between roommates and something more is impossible to hold.

But Tinsel can't hide forever. Her future is waiting at the North Pole. And Mason knows better than to believe in miracles.

Still... when the one person you weren't supposed to fall for becomes the only one you can't walk away from, rules and even Christmas start to feel negotiable.

**Fall In love with a**
**Bailey Black Book Here**

A witch in a world where magic is illegal, A revenge mission, A rescue mission, Death. People die. Sorry, not sorry, 2 love interests (not a RH and not a triangle), A touch of enemies to lovers. He falls first she falls harder

I had a plan. Find the soldier who killed my family and make him pay. It should have been an easy feat. I'd done it over a dozen times, taking out each member of that regiment one by one, but the mission went sideways. It all started with the man in the woods. The one my webs of magic couldn't sense even when he stood before me. Then my partner made a mistake, and now he's lying in one of the Crown's dungeons, fighting for his life. I couldn't leave him to die, but I couldn't just walk into the castle either.

Or maybe I could.

With the help of some unexpected allies, I entered the Culling —a one-in-a-lifetime chance to become queen. I have no interest in winning the prince's heart, or the crown. My only goal is to get into the castle, find my friend, and get out before someone realizes I'm a Cerise.

But when the welcome ball turns from a grand event into a nightmarish dance of death, all eyes are on me. As if that's not bad enough, the soldier, the one who took my family, he's here.

If you loved "The Selection" by Kiera Cass and "From Blood and Ash" by Jennifer L. Armentrout, get ready to fall in love with this enchanting fantasy romance!

**Fall In love with a
Bailey Black Book Here**

# Acknowledgments

Every time I sit down to write this part, I swear I go completely blank. Maybe it's because no amount of words ever feels big enough to thank the people who help me bring these stories to life —or maybe it's just because my brain is, in fact, made of holiday glitter and caffeine. Either way, here we are.

To Sarah, Jessica, and Gina—you three deserve a medal (and probably a vacation). Thank you for helping me survive the final rounds of this book and for bringing some much-needed organization to my chaos. You each made this story stronger, sharper, and far more cohesive than it had any right to be in the beginning. I couldn't have done it without you.

A super special thanks to Michelle, who shows up for every release and is my cheerleader on social media. I see you and I appreciate you!

To my husband—thank you for reading this book (finally!) and for having *very strong feelings* about Mason. In truth, he only read one chapter, but that's more than any other, and he had some bones to pick with Mason. It was fun going back and forth because he couldn't understand how a bait shop could fail in the Keys lol. Thank you for supporting the chaos even when you don't quite get it and for loving me through every draft, deadline, and creative meltdown.

To the bloggers, bookstagrammers, and readers who share, gush, and fall in love with my stories, you're the reason I get to keep doing this. Your support turns each release into something truly special.

And to every reader who picks up *All I Want for Christmas*

—thank you for believing in sunshine, small towns, and the kind of magic that doesn't always come wrapped in a bow. You make my dream come true with every page you turn.

**Xoxo,**
**Bailey**